Praldia

Chaos Star Trilogy

Book 1

Ebony Olson

EBANDMUSE & PUBLICATIONS

Published 2023

Published by EbandMuse Publications Sydney, Australia

Cover by Sarah Paige Designs

Editing by Striding Ibis Editing

http://ebonyolson.com/

Chapter One

Standing on the small bridge crossing the river that ran through the middle of our country estate, my hands trembled as I read my father's foreboding letter. It was written and sent moments before he and my mother Eliora, former Princess of Avalonia, were arrested for high treason and executed.

There was no such thing as a trial in Prince Saboa's court, nor anywhere on this peaceful planet. The prince was fair. No one was arrested and sentenced until the evidence was overwhelming. The letter that I held in my hands confirmed my parent's disloyalty, and I would be condemned because of it.

Folding the last word my parents would ever say to me, I placed it back in the envelope. Walking up the road to the front stairs of our château, I remained deep in thought. There was nowhere to run, no one I could turn to for protection.

As I took the first step to the front doors, I heard the teleportation channels click behind me. Closing my eyes for a moment, I turned to face a small contingent of the Royal Guard. They were Cyrans, just like the prince, and aliens to Praldia as much as I was. While Avalonians had mainly stayed in seclusion, Cyra had conquered and dominated any planet worth something in our system.

Even to the tall and lithe Avalonians like me, Cyrans stood head and shoulders above us. Unlike my frail-looking race, they were built to run through solid walls and were nearly unbeatable in hand-to-hand combat. They were perfect soldiers and fiercely loyal.

"Lady Zira, you are to come with me." Commander Stark stepped forward, giving a curt bow of his head.

"Commander Stark," I returned his greeting, gripping the letter as I took in the elite guard before me. My voice gave away only the slightest unease at their presence. The prince wasn't taking any chances. "I guess I should be flattered that Prince Saboa would send you to collect me. I'll change into something more suitable for court." My free hand ran over the fabric of my country dress, which I found more comfortable than the tight-fitting silks that were the fashion in the city. My eyes, however, were all for the soldiers before me.

The Commander watched how I assessed his men before he stepped forward, his face stern in the standard harsh lines of a Royal Guard. The Cyrans' mouth was not made for smiling.

"Your abilities will not score your freedom here, Lady Zira." Stark gauged what I was thinking. Relieving me of the letter in my hand, he showed me the medallion he wore. A protection amulet. "Best come with us willingly and hear the prince out before you attempt suicide."

"I guess that you're not here to kill me gives me some hope," I returned softly, understanding they came prepared to deal with one of my kind.

"You would be dead already if that was your sentence."

"I'd prefer death to enslavement."

Nodding, Stark gave me his arm. "Hear the Prince out, child. He is not an unfair ruler. Your dress is more than suitable."

Stark wasn't letting me out of his sight for a second. Taking his arm, I appraised the raised scar on the back of the Commander's hand, touching it lightly. Blinking down at my hand, Stark then met my eyes. He was brave; not many would have the balls to meet my liquid blue gaze for fear I would bewitch them. Medallion or no, my eyes could drown a man if I so desired.

"The chaos star," he murmured. "Branded upon me when I proved I could control the inner chaos of myself."

"A rite of passage?"

"Men are subject to their desires. Until we can control such, we are not worthy of being part of the elite guard." This explained his bravery looking into my eyes. Raising his large hand, Stark touched a rough finger to the dark blue star embedded under my left eye. "Even your culture has its rites, Lady."

Wondering just how much he knew of our customs, I flinched. With no more patience for further delay, the Commander took my arm. The teleportation channel closed around us with a large crack, like lightning splitting the air above my head. The earth slipped beneath my feet, the air floating me for a mere moment, then my feet hit the solid stone of a floor, jarring me a little as it always did. It all took as long as it did to blink.

Focusing my eyes, we stood in the royal palace's open court, or palats in the Cyran language.

The room was mostly empty, allowing the beautiful Crystalstar flooring to sparkle with the light filtering in from the many windows. Commander Stark stepped away with a bow to the prince, who waited, his dark eyes watching me intently. Taking a step forward, I curtsied low and stayed there.

Rising from his chair, Prince Saboa walked around me, looking me over before returning to stand before his throne. As far as Cyrans went, Saboa wasn't unattractive. Many Praldian women fawned all over him and fantasized about marrying him. I was not Praldian, and I held no desires concerning the prince.

"She gave you no trouble?"

"None, Prince Saboa," Stark acknowledged. "I believe she was forewarned." Stepping forward with the letter, Stark handed it to the prince.

Opening it, Saboa read it, then gave it to Stark to read. "It must be hard for you, Lady Zira. You've worked hard to be accepted by the Praldians, to live a just existence, only to have it all mean nothing with your parent's treason."

"I have done nothing iniquitous, my Prince. Though, I understand, after reading my father's letter, why you cannot take the chance and let me be," I uttered respectfully. Because I did understand that my parents hoped to seat me on the prince's throne.

Nodding, Saboa sat again before gesturing for me to rise. "So, what are we to do with you, Lady?" Saboa pondered. "You are innocent of your parents' plotting. I was sure of that even before reading that letter. However, you are still a threat. I could send you back to Avalonia, but, as I understand it, because of your royal blood, you would be forced to marry the now-seated King. I would not wish that even on the lowest Praldian."

The usurper of my home planet disgusted me. He was not of royal blood and had taken the throne by force. He held the misguided impression that he could marry me and have a legitimate claim to the throne. He was why my parents had escaped here, to prevent such an abomination.

"So, our choices are limited. You can't be enslaved as a common lemming; the people would hate me for degrading you such. I either put you somewhere I feel secure enough to keep you, or I kill you."

"I agree, my Prince. I will not be enslaved to anyone." Kneeling, I sat back on my ankles, pulled my blue-black hair around to expose my pale neck, and bowed my head waiting for the death blow.

Taking out a small leather pouch, stained in what looked to be the green of Cyran blood, Saboa cast dice from its hold. He watched me as he took the dice in his hands, discarding them gracefully to the table beside his chair. Nodding once at the dice, Saboa sat thinking for a moment longer.

Standing, Saboa moved forward to stand above me so that all I could see was his boots. His finger traced the line of my spine at my neck to the base of my skull lightly; I gasped and shivered.

Saboa dropped to one knee before me suddenly. Taking my hand with his, he urged me to stand before dropping my hand and moving back to his throne. There, he considered the die once more than turned to appraise me. "Do you think the fountains of Praldia would not run with blood if I took your head, Lady Zira? The small, simple natives love you. I would be a fool to kill their goddess. No, better I give her a pedestal they will adore me for, but from whence I can still control you. It is about time I thought about future sons to take over my rule anyway."

Confused, I glanced at the prince before catching on to my fate. My mouth fell agape, and I started shaking my head as I began to argue, to beg for death instead, but the Prince held up his hand.

"I was not giving you a choice, Lady Zira. The melding of our bloodlines will not only secure this planet, but it will give me leverage in Avalonia as well. I suggest you accept it and make the most of your new station. You have petitioned me often in the past to help the natives. You will find I will be more negotiable as a companion than a prince."

"Cyrans control their inner chaos," I argued, half-panicked. "I will have no power over you."

The prince's downward mouth formed a straight line—the Cyran version of a smile—as he sat back upon his throne. Collecting the dice from the side table, Saboa put them into the bloodstained leather pouch, tucking them away. "Commander, show my companion to her new quarters. Once she is secured, send an announcement to the broadcasters. Lady Zira and I will be joined in a private ceremony this evening."

"Yes, Prince Saboa." Stark stepped back to my side. When I didn't move, he took my arm in his and led me from the room as tears fell down my face.

Chapter Two

"Tonight?" I breathed as Stark half-dragged me, with a gentle grip on my arm, out of the throne room. "No courtship?"

"There is no courtship necessary, Lady."

"But he doesn't know me. I don't know him." My voice hitched on my emotions. "He can't possibly love me." Looking over my shoulder to the throne, I blinked more tears. "I don't love him." Despite holding a piece of paper in his hands that his Chief Advisor, Aldous, was now referring to animatedly, Saboa's blue eyes were locked on me.

Stark came to a stop, turning me to face him, gripping both my upper arms with a little more pressure to force me to look at him. His eyes were the darkest blue I'd ever seen. There was no softness to them. I think it was impossible for a Cyran to even feign compassion.

"You are royal heir to a throne, Lady. Surely you never believed joining for love was an option?"

"I did, Commander. My parents told me after we moved here that I should only consider companionship if I truly loved someone." My tears flowed impossibly faster as I thought of everything a royal joining usually entailed. Avalonians were emotion first, but Cyrans were practicality, and I needed to control my emotions if I wanted to be heard. "Tonight is too fast. Even in Avalonia there is a courtship. Time to connect, to grow familiar, to prepare for the formal requirements. I don't even have a dress for the ceremony."

Eyebrows jumping high, Stark considered me as his mouth thinned into that flat-line smile. "Lady, in a Cyran joining, a dress is not required."

My thin brows furrowed in confusion yet again while Stark dropped his chin to stare at me intently. When his meaning hit home, I forgot myself and spoke loudly. "I have to have sex with him?"

The room went deathly quiet around us. I hadn't meant to sound so disgusted about it. I wasn't. Sex was fantastic with the right person. Not that I'd done it in some years now. Not since... My heart ached just thinking about that.

A sound of material drew all our gazes to the throne where Saboa stood, a look of pure amusement across his face as he readied to leave. The rest of the room, near-empty as it was, stood wary. "You seem surprised, Lady Zira? I didn't realize you were foreign to the concept of reproduction. For you to get with child, we need to have sex, possibly on multiple occasions."

Those in the room tried to muffle their humor. The guards did nothing more than press their lips tighter together.

"Do not worry, I am quite adept and well-practiced. I will talk you through it!" Saboa teased sarcastically.

Embarrassed beyond the possibility of my chalk-white skin displaying, I'm sure I still flushed a color that was unnatural to my species. "I'm sorry, my Prince, I didn't mean that how it sounded. I just didn't realize that merely the act of fornication with a Cyran could see you joined to him." *If so, I might be coupled several times over by now already.*

"I wish it was that easy," Saboa mourned. "There are contracts of companionship to be signed in front of witnesses to make it official." Saboa was nearly at our side now. The councilmen and guard continued past us when he stopped to address me further.

An idea entered my head and came out of my mouth without thinking. "And if I refuse to sign?"

Cupping my cheeks in his hands, Saboa used his thumbs to wipe away the tears that cascaded over them with a gentleness I thought the Cyrans devoid of. "It has been an emotional week for you, Zira. Go and rest, or grieve. Tonight after dinner, we will sign our contract, and tomorrow, we will make our first appearance together as companions." Bending forward, he pressed his lips to the blue star beneath my eye. There was no doubt in my mind that he understood just what an intimate gesture that was.

"Let me go home?" I murmured, my eyes pressed closed. "Let me live at my family's chateau. I will come to you whenever you require, but it's too soon for joining our lives."

The room stayed silent. Daring to open my eyes, I found Saboa looking over my head at Stark. Flicking his gaze back to meet mine, Saboa stepped away with a sigh. "I'll let you choose where you would like to make your first appearance as my princess. Let Aldous know at the signing tonight, and he will have it organized by morning." Without another word, Saboa strode out of the throne room, six of his personal elite guard waiting at the door, falling in behind him.

"Come, Lady Zira." Stark placed his hand to the center of my upper back to guide me forward. "Let me show you your rooms, so we can get you settled before dinner." Stark guided me out of the throne room and turned left into the ring corridor connecting to all the palats living areas.

The palats consisted of two concentric circles of buildings joined by a large corridor that formed a continuous ring. The buildings on the inner side were all small single-story structures. They surrounded a sizeable circular garden where the public teleportation channels were situated. Only Prince Saboa and the royal guard could freely teleport from within the castle itself. Every other occupant, staff member, councilman, or visiting diplomat was required to use the public channels. It was the only way in or out of the palats.

The outer ring of buildings was longer, more comprehensive two-story structures that looked out over either the ocean or the forest and city from atop the cliff. They were segmented from each other by large courtyards of gardens or pools. The Prince's residence was isolated from the rest of the palats, and was the only building taller than two floors. He also had his own kitchen staff and housekeeping. No one who worked within the Prince's residence worked anywhere else in the palats. It also housed fifty elite guards—the Prince's personal guard.

Prince Saboa's residence was flanked by the two royal guards' wings on each side. These buildings housed the two thousand strong army of Cyrans he'd brought with him only fifteen years ago. Saboa was only a year past coming of age when he'd claimed Praldia as his with nearly no resistance.

To either side of the guard's wings stood the throne room and ballroom respectfully. It was well designed to set the Prince apart from the rest of the palats while still being connected. It also ensured no one could approach the Prince's residence without first passing by several royal guards. All the other habitation areas were on the opposite side of the palats.

On my visits, I'd only ever been to the ballroom for celebrations or the throne room to petition the prince, and waited in the courtyards outside. Both of those structures permitted direct access via walkways between the inner buildings to the public teleportation channels, so this was my first time walking the ring.

The flooring in both the throne room and the ballroom was Crystalstar. This near-translucent shimmering white crystal was mined here in Praldia, and was one of its top export minerals. The central ring was a dark grey metal-looking floor, but beneath the Commander's boots, it sounded like he was walking on thin, fragile glass.

Stopping, I stared at the flooring and the sound of its cracking beneath our feet. "I've never heard that before. I've always crossed the ring when there were lots of people around. I've never walked on it alone."

"We call it Is," Stark advised. Pressing lightly on my back to start me walking again, he watched me roll the new word around my mouth. "I believe in Avalonian it would be ice, Lady. It is from Cyra and prevents any form of sneaking around. It is throughout the King's castle in Cyra."

The king of Cyra was Saboa's father, which is why Saboa never assumed that title. When his father died, and Saboa became king, even if his eldest son were to take the throne in Cyra, Saboa's heir would not hold that title until Saboa died and it passed to him.

"Why was the throne room so empty today? Wouldn't it have been better for Prince Saboa to have a few neutral ears in place in case he chose to execute me? That way, the Praldians would know it was justified?"

Stark didn't answer, just kept moving us forward into the alcove of the first royal guard wing. There were a few guards on duty here. They watched us walk by with barely-disguised interest.

"Commander?" I pressed when we were in the confines of the connecting corridor again.

"The prince was never going to kill you, child. Did you not wonder why he waited so long after your parents' execution to bring you to him?"

I had expected them the first day, though I didn't know what my parents planned, only that they were taken from their city residence. Then the broadcasters announced their conviction of treason, and every sound for the next thirty hours bore the royal guard coming to take my head. But they didn't.

By the second day, I'd concluded that Saboa realized I was ignorant of whatever treason my parents committed. Days later, the letter came, and I'd found out just what my parents intended. That's when I realized my innocence wouldn't matter.

"We were waiting. Watching to see if you fled, and, if you had, we would have caught you in minutes and brought you to him. The outcome would have been the same, but he would not have trusted you. The prince would have ensured there were witnesses to see your guilt then. But you did not run, did not contact anyone to try and safeguard yourself. You kept a low profile, like always, and answered the calls of the natives for assistance. It proved your innocence better than this letter ever could have."

Removing my father's letter from his pocket, Stark held it for me to take. Doing so hesitantly, I slipped it into the pocket of my dress.

"Prince Saboa was not scheduled to hold court today. No one but his personal advisors that he trusts and the guards I trust were present because he understood this would be hard for you, Lady Zira. You have lost your parents, and, for the time being, you have lost your freedom. The Prince, however, has lost nothing. In fact, it's quite the opposite for him. He is not cruel, Lady. He will not gloat while you grieve."

"Gloat? What could he possibly have gained from my parent's treason?" I stopped walking. We approached the prince's wing, and I wanted to hear what Stark meant.

Grumbling under his breath, Stark turned to face me impatiently. After a moment, his stern face cleared to a look of concern. "Your parents never told you?"

"About their plans?" I shook my head sadly. "No, they truly didn't."

"Before that? Your parents never told you about the offer of companionship?"

"What offer? No one has ever asked for my hand. No one has even courted me. Unless you mean that abomination who sits on my brother's throne, but that was hardly an offer."

Stark just stared, then rose his face to the ceiling and swore quietly before meeting my gaze again. "Lady Zira, since you came of age, the prince has petitioned your parents for you to be his companion on nearly a yearly basis. They always refused, stating that you weren't ready to take a companion as yet. By law, Prince Saboa was unable to force the issue, since our laws give the parents control until you reach adulthood at age thirty."

Staring at Stark, disbelieving, I had to force my mouth to work. "If what you say is true, why would they say no? They wanted me on the throne. It would have been the most peaceful way to get what they wanted."

"Because they did not want you joined to a Cyran. They wanted you on the throne so they could join you with a man of your own kind. They didn't want half-breed heirs."

Anger shot through me. "My parents were not like that. They weren't purists. They helped the Praldians as much as I did, and they loved it here. They admired Prince Saboa for the world he created and how he ruled. They were always singing his praises and discussing his rule over dinner in front of me. So don't you dare taint their memory with such ignoble notions!" I stormed forward toward the Prince's wing, but Stark blocked my way suddenly.

"You are a child." When I opened my mouth to argue, Stark cut me off. "You may have come of age five years ago, but you are not classified as an adult in society for seven more years. There is no way that your parents would risk speaking their treason in front of you for the reason that should be obvious. If they succeeded, you would take the throne innocent. If they failed, you would be untainted by their treachery.

"When your parents were executed, you, having not reached wisdom yet, instantly became the property of the throne along with the rest of your family's land and belongings. I was there, Lady. I watched the Prince tell them exactly what power they gave him with their treachery, and I saw the horror on your parents' faces."

My hands were shaking, my legs ready to crumble, and my heart was racing in my chest. My voice came out weak as I struggled to control my breathing. My last thread of hope just snapped. "Prince Saboa is my guardian. I have absolutely no rights. Even if I refuse to sign the contracts, he can do so on my behalf with guardianship authority. He can use it to overrule me for the next seven years. I'll have no voice. I'm at his mercy."

Chapter Three

As my vision focused, I realized the room was full of windows down one whole length of the wall and then again above the bed on which I was lying. There were no blinds, so it let in the bright white daylight of Praldia's summer, shimmering off the Crystalstar floor and walls.

Sitting up, I found myself on one of the standard low-lying beds of Praldia. Most natives made their beds on the floor, but the city folk, including my family, used slightly raised platforms to put the mattresses on.

The bedroom was decorated for a man, but it was sparsely furnished. The décor held a certain elegance. Getting up, I moved to the sliding doors in the far wall. Pushing them open, I stepped into the sitting room.

"Lady Zira."

My heart pounded in my chest at the sound of that voice. Hartwin was a Cyran guard I knew well, just barely an adult, and one of the youngest to ever make elite. He was one of the Prince's personal guards, and he was also Commander Stark's only son.

Setting aside a book, he stood from one of the white sofas. "Do you remember what happened?"

"I hyperventilated and passed out."

Hartwin nodded. "The Commander carried you in and directed me to stay until the prince comes back." Moving to a small side table, Hartwin lifted the lid from a steaming plate of food. "He also instructed that you eat something. Apparently, you have not eaten since breakfast. We all know that Avalonians must eat regularly, that your metabolisms burn through everything too quickly."

Swallowing hard, I nodded and sat at the table. Of all the people to leave in a room with me, this was the worst. Thankfully, Hartwin stepped away once I started eating, moving to the window, and watching the sky outside.

"This will be a beautiful view to wake up to every day," he offered.

Pausing, I considered that I couldn't see much beyond the sky from where I sat. Placing my fork down, I went to see what Hartwin meant. The window looked out over the ocean. From how high up we were, I concluded this was the upper level of the prince's residence.

"The view from the other side is of the city," Hartwin informed me, watching me take in the beauty of it. "Saboa designed his palats to give views of the city and the ocean from every window, but only his residence gets to see it all."

Going back into the bedroom, I could see the south side of the city in the distance from here. I was sure other rooms would offer views of every part of the city or ocean, but the south end was the beautiful part of the town. Full of parks, its skyline was the glinting glass of the buildings and the green and mauve canopy of trees.

The palats was built on an inaccessible cliff over eighteen hundred meters above sea level. The only way in or out of the palats was through the teleportation channels. There was nothing but forest from the cliff's base to the city fringes—several hundred kilometers from the palats - where the city sprawled in a large arc from coast to coast. The view was mind-blowing.

A large, strong hand cupped my elbow. When I looked up at Hartwin's dark blue gaze, he dropped his focus to my lips. "You need to eat, Zira."

Growing up, he'd been my friend. His father's property was not far from our own. When I was only fourteen, I caught him trespassing, just a youth out for an adventure. I'd attacked him. He'd thrown me from him, and I'd landed in the river. Guilt-ridden, he waded in to pull me to safety, not realizing that water gave me the advantage.

By the end, we were laughing as we fought, and we soon dragged our cold, exhausted bodies up the riverbank and collapsed. It was the start of a good friendship. Even when Hartwin was accepted to the royal guard a year later, we stayed friends. But we hadn't spoken in two years now, not since he became elite and took the man I loved from me.

"Did the Commander tell you what's to come of me?" I asked as he guided me back to the table. Picking up the fork, I started eating.

"Yes. Even if he didn't, that you are here in the prince's private quarters would have told me anyway."

Stopping with the fork half-way to my mouth, my eyes focused on the bed on which I woke. "That's Saboa's bed?"

Hartwin took the seat opposite me. "Your bed as well now, Princess."

Hartwin was the only person who could get away using my birth title, possibly because when it slipped through his lips, it was anything but official. However, tomorrow, I would again be known by that title for good.

He took my hand, pulling my gaze to his. "He will be a good companion and a good father to your offspring, Zira. I can vouch for him. He will treat you well."

"He's forcing me to join with him—"

"I know." Hartwin cut me off, dropping my hand and standing. "I know everything that has taken place since your parents' treacherous intentions first came to the Prince's attention, Zira. My father practically raised the prince. When his father sent him here to seize control, my father volunteered to command his army. Prince Saboa has been like an older brother to me my whole life, and we confide in each other about everything."

My head snapped up. "You didn't tell me. You could have at least warned me."

"I am one of the Prince's personal guard and am honor-bound." Hartwin shook his head. "Despite that, Luther is family in my heart. I would never betray him."

A tear escaped down my cheek. "I've lost everything, haven't I?"

Dropping the fork, I rose to go back to the bedroom to be by myself, but Hartwin caught me and hugged me to him. "You have your life," he whispered in my ear. "You have a good man as your companion. I will always be your friend, Zira, but do not ask me to forego my honor."

Stepping away from me so quickly that I stumbled, Hartwin went back to the window, keeping his back to me. "Your life as you have known it may be over, Zira, but you have the opportunity now to forge a new life. How much easier will it be to serve your cause as Princess of Praldia rather than a runaway Princess of Avalonia?"

"You prey on my empathy and ignore that I am a woman being forced to marry a man she doesn't love. You expect me to be willing because it comes with a title?" Hartwin didn't answer.

The door at the end of the sitting room opened. A Praldian woman, her blonde hair wrapped tightly in a bun, wearing the Prince's stone-grey livery, entered carrying several garment bags. Assessing her, Hartwin nodded. Walking around the sunken lounge, the woman went into the bedroom, where she laid the garment bags on the bed.

"Lady Zira, I'm Padget, Prince Saboa's personal attendant, and as such, yours. If you need anything, please just ask. I'm number eight on the comms." She gestured to the communications system next to the sitting-room door.

"Water," I barely voiced, my emotions still strangling me. Padget stopped, looked at me as if I had insulted her, then moved to the table to collect a glass of water. "No, not to drink. A body of water in which I can swim."

Padget looked to Hartwin then back to me. "I'm sorry, Lady Zira, but we were directed you were not to leave quarters for the rest of the day. The most I can do is pour you a bath."

Eyes on the floor, I nodded. "Then make it deep, please."

Hesitating a moment, worry clearly etched in her tanned face, she looked to Hartwin for direction again. "Go ahead, Padg, an Avalonian can't drown themselves." Bobbing her head, Padget went back into the bedroom before opening a door disguised as a wall and moved through it.

"She thinks I'm suicidal?"

"She overheard the Commander cursing how your parents left you completely in the dark about everything when he bought you in. She knows you are grieving, and grief makes people do stupid things."

"You're my guard, aren't you?"

"I am one of them. Luther is still to complete your personal guard, but I was the first to be reassigned."

"When?"

"The day after your parent's execution."

I couldn't meet his eyes. He'd known for nearly a week what my fate would be. "I thought you abandoned me as a traitor."

"No one on this planet believed you were involved for even a second, Lady Zira." His eyes flicked over my shoulder. For Hartwin to be using my title meant Padget was standing there listening. "Prince Saboa made sure at your parent's execution that everyone knew you to be innocent."

"Why didn't you come?" Padget suddenly blurted from behind me. "We all expected you to come running into the chamber begging mercy for your parents, but you didn't."

Bowing my head with the pain in my heart, this time, my eyes stayed dry as I lifted them to meet hers before looking out the window to the ocean.

"I learned that lesson long ago. When word the Barbarian was moving to attack our king reached us, my brother and I rushed to the castle to help protect it. The barbarian was already there. He'd murdered the king and killed the royal envoy originally sent to collect us. The one who carried word to us was one of his men. When we arrived, he spilled my brother's blood at my feet."

Setting my eyes on Padget, I filled my eyes and voice with the anger I still harbored. "I possessed no desire to be left standing alone in a throne room full of the enemy, with my family's blood soaking through my shoes, while the king told me of his plans for me again. I barely survived the first time."

Behind me, Hartwin cursed and activated his comms.

"Yes?" Commander Stark's voice came through as clear as if he were in the room.

"Send up Jervaise. I need to talk to you privately." There were no farewells. Hartwin simply disconnected and turned to look at me with anger burning in his eyes. "You never told me."

I'd never told anyone. Turning my attention back to Padget, I ignored him. "Is the bath ready?"

Padget curtsied. Following Padget into the bathroom, she showed me where a small pool was set into the floor. I almost sighed with relief. I'd imagined the bath would barely fit me like most Praldian bathrooms, but this could fit multiple Cyrans and still allow me to float on the surface. The bathroom window was floor to ceiling and provided an uninterrupted view of the city.

"I added lavender and geranium, Lady Zira. I thought you might want something relaxing."

Keeping my back to her, I nodded. I didn't want her to see the tears threatening to overcome me.

"I brought a selection of dresses in earlier that the prince ordered for you." A door clicked open behind me. "I'll hang them up in the wardrobe, and you can select one after your bath. Prince Saboa gave me permission to purchase any other clothing items or personal products that you'd prefer. If you'd like to make me a list, I'll make the purchases when I take your dress for cleaning."

"Thank you. Master Fabrice knows my sizing and preference for clothing and personal wear. I have my shopping delivered to the estate from Chalvey's. They will have a record of my most recent order, which will cover personal items and food preferences."

"Of course, Lady, that will make things a lot easier."

"Padget, I can undress myself. If you could close the bathroom door on your way out and the bedroom doors. Let Elite Hartwin know when you leave that no one is to come through the bedroom door until I open it."

"Of course, Lady Zira, but your dress?"

"I'll leave the dress by the door for you. You can collect it after a few minutes."

"Yes, Lady." Padget backed out of the room, shutting the door.

Once I heard the click, I touched the fabric release at my shoulder. The dress sideseam unwove itself to fall away from me. Removing the silk underslip from my body, I let it fall on top of the dress. Sweeping my leg outwards, the dress skidded across the Crystalstar floor to hit the wall next to the door.

Folding myself down, I stepped into the heated water of the tub. It was a little too hot, but I didn't have time to wait for it to cool. Only one person other than my parents had seen me naked since I left Avalonia. A mature Avalonians body is not seen away from home, and I didn't wish to have to explain it to anyone today.

Slipping beneath the water entirely, I breathed the water into my lungs. Tranquillity descended upon me. Concentrating, I felt the burning flash of one of the symbols imprinted up my spine and dispersed myself into the water. It was a forgotten ability even among my people, but I was born with it. If anyone came into the bathroom and looked in the tub now, all they would see was a bath full of water.

Walking into the throne room, I held my brother's hand. The king hated me and was always cruel, but I wouldn't let Zimri come to fight alone. We were stronger together. Only our uncle, the king, wasn't there, and the Barbarian sat on the throne. The king and queen's bodies were decapitated on the floor below. Zimri stepped in front of me protectively, as if he could shield me from their deaths. The messenger who rode with us moved like lightning, slitting Zimri's throat before me. Falling over his body, screaming and crying, my eyes went from him to the other dead bodies in the room. My family was killed. The floor was flooded in their black blood.

Grabbing my arm, the assassin dragged me through all that blood before dropping me at the Barbarian's feet. Fisting my hair, the Barbarian hauled me to my feet. "Don't cry, Princess. You get to be the youngest queen in history."

Chapter Four

Screaming as my body converged against my will, I sat up in the bath, purging the water from my lungs. I shouldn't have done it. I was too emotional to hold myself apart.

The door flew open. Sinking down until only my head was out of the water, I readied in case I needed to protect myself. A strange Cyran checked over the room carefully before gazing back at me. "Are you safe, Lady?" his deep voice boomed.

"Just... grief escaping me. I'm sorry for startling you..."

"Jervaise. Elite Guard Jervaise, Lady Zira. Elite Guard Hartwin needed to duck out." Giving the room one more check, Jervaise moved backward out of the room. "I'll leave you to finish... bathing, Lady." He shut the door.

Waiting to hear the bedroom doors close, I wondered how long I'd been dispersed before my memories dragged me from that peace. My dress was gone from the floor, so Padget must have collected it while I was dissolved.

Pressing the button to empty the bath, I climbed the steps out and dried myself looking out the window towards the city. Our family city house was in the south, but not one so big that I could see it from here.

Closing my eyes, I turned away and made my way to the still open wardrobe. Most of the dresses Padget delivered were in the latest city fashions, which was to say, not to my taste. There were only two country dresses, a pale pink and a pretty blue one, both a lot fancier in design than I would typically have worn at home.

Choosing the blue dress, I hung it on the hook in the dressing area while I retrieved a pale blue silk undergarment and slipped into it. Stepping into the blue country-style dress, I pulled it into place, pressing the shoulder connectors together, and felt the seam weave closed.

Using the reflective glass wall, I admired how the blue made my eyes and the star below my left eye stand out. Going out into the bedroom, I finger-combed my long blue-black hair over my shoulder since I didn't have a brush.

The light was starting to fade from the windows, a sign of evening being upon us. I considered lying down for a while, but I couldn't bring myself to relax on the prince's bed, so I stood staring out the window until a knock on the bedroom door made me jump.

Realizing the sun was nearly set, the sky strewn with greens and purples of the coming night, I blinked. The room was dark when the door slid open behind me, letting light from the sitting room illuminate where I stood by the darkened window. The silhouette of the prince was unmistakable.

"Zira, are you feeling any better?" he asked, stepping into the room and shutting the door behind him. It left us both standing there in the near darkness.

The rustle of material let me know he was moving towards me. I could just envisage him in his military dress uniform, hands clasped behind his back as he deftly moved around his room towards his target. "Jervaise told me you were quite shaken earlier."

I nodded, though I wasn't sure if he saw it or not. Cyrans possessed fantastic night vision, but I wasn't sure to what extent. "I need to know, Zira. When you were captured by the Barbarian King, were you joined?"

"No," I whispered, tears stinging my eyes again.

Saboa's hand brushed down my arm until he took my hand in his. The size of his hand almost swallowed mine. "Are you sure? There were no words of ceremony spoken by an elder, no... physical indication of a ceremonial joining?"

"No," I sobbed. "He tried. They started the procedure, but my uncle's army attacked before it happened. My mother dragged me out of there, bundled me up, and shipped me off here. I... I'm bound to no one. My mother had it officially documented just in case the Barbarian tried to convince the people otherwise. The documents are hidden among other important papers at the estate."

Saboa squeezed my hand gently. "I'll have it found and brought to the palats, so the Barbarian can't challenge our legitimacy."

When I didn't reply, Saboa gave my hand a slight squeeze again. Stepping back, Saboa forced me to move after him. Sliding the doors open, he still held my hand as we entered the sitting area. Blinking rapidly into the sudden light, my eyes took a moment to clear to take in the room.

Hartwin stood talking to his father in the sunken lounge. Jervaise stood by the door chatting with two of the prince's elite guards. Aldous was sitting on the sofa reading over what I could only gather was our joining contracts.

Everyone stopped when we entered and watched us. Leading me to the sofa opposite his chief advisor, Saboa sat, still holding my hand, forcing me to sit.

"Well?" Aldous addressed the prince.

"Apparently, there is official documentation at the estate which proves she has never been joined," Prince Saboa declared loudly, then looked at the Commander pointedly.

"I'll send some men to collect it immediately." Bowing his head before stepping into the bedroom, Stark activated his comms unit, sliding the door closed as he started talking.

"Well, that makes things less complicated." Aldous breathed a sigh of relief.

"Complicated?" I asked skeptically. "If I was already joined, I guess my life would be forfeit, wouldn't it?"

"Not at all." Saboa squeezed my hand again. "Zira, you hadn't come of age, and he didn't have your parent's approval. Any joining would have been void immediately."

"My King and Queen were dead. He'd just added my brother's body to the pile, effectively erasing all line of kin. Just like now, I was at the king's mercy."

"If your parents are dead, who were the two we killed last week?" Aldous asked suspiciously.

"The King and Queen were her aunt and uncle. Her biological parents rescued her," Saboa answered quietly. "In Avalonia, the king must be born from the womb of royalty. So, it is the king's sister who usually gives birth to the next king. The throne is passed from King to nephew, unlike in Cyra, where it goes to the eldest son. It's why Zira is important to the Avalonian people. As the prince's sister, her womb was always going to produce the next king. From birth, her parents weren't recognized as kin any longer. The eldest son and daughter of the King's sister immediately become the heir to the thrones, and thus, are under the care of the throne.

"The heirs live with the King and Queen, are raised by them. Because Zira's world was at war, their King insisted they stay away that last year. The elders frowned upon it, but apparently, now, they are relieved, as it probably saved her."

"How?" Hartwin asked curiously as his father came back out of the bedroom.

Swallowing at how much Saboa knew already, I found my voice. "Had I been living at the castle, the Barbarian king wouldn't have been delayed by having to wait for us to be fetched and brought to him. That delay allowed my parents to gather the royal army's last vestiges and lead an attack to get me free. If I'd been there when he took the castle, he would have... won."

Lowering my face, I shivered at the idea. Squeezing my hand, Saboa indicated the contracts. "Are they ready, Aldous?"

Nodding, Aldous turned them so that we could read them. Flipping his open, Saboa started reading. I stared at the cover page.

'CONTRACTUAL JOINING of Prince Luther Saboa and Princess Zira Sallee.'

GRUNTING, Saboa flipped my first page to show many bulleted paragraphs. "You will want to read this, Zira, so that you know what is expected of you and what is expected of me."

"Please don't do this." I barely breathed; my eyes locked on my knees. "How are you any better than that barbarian if you do this?" Suddenly my hand was empty.

Saboa stood above me angry, Hartwin stepped forward, mouth open ready, but his father beat him to it. "Lady Zira, you are not looking at the whole picture." Movement caught Stark's attention. He turned to face the elite guardsmen. "Out! You can serve your shifts from the rest of the residence."

Waiting for the three by the door to leave, Stark looked over his shoulder at his son and gave a gesture he should follow. Moving to the table to pour himself a drink, Saboa now stood watching Stark and me.

"Child, this isn't about a throne to the prince. He already has the responsibility to produce heirs; by marrying you, he takes on another. If he really wanted Avalonia, he has the men and the technology to go in there and destroy Abaddon. But your planet's only resource is water, and we have both that and Crystalstar here in Praldia. Luther doesn't want you for your womb and the crown that gives his son."

"Then why me?"

"Because I've wanted you since the first time you came into my throne room calling me a sack of shit for not caring enough about the natives," Saboa answered from across the room. Glancing up at his prince, Stark bowed his head and stepped away from me.

"I didn't know who you were, your title, or anything other than your species. You stormed into my throne room, flung a report at me, and proceeded to call me several names no one else on this or my home planet would call me, even behind my back.

"I was just shy of reaching wisdom, and I think you were barely sixteen. You hadn't even come of age yet. It was probably the only thing stopping me from getting up and kissing you until you didn't have the breath to call me any more names."

That had been the first time I'd attended an open court session. The report I'd thrown at the prince detailed the abominable ways the natives were being treated in Simpia. I gripped the sofa beside my thighs. "Why... why didn't you court me?"

Saboa chuckled. "I tried. Your parents forbade it. So, I did everything within my power to force you into my presence. Do you know how much research was involved in finding causes for you to fight for, getting them brought to your attention just so you would be forced to come and petition me for help? Aldous here earned his position as a chief advisor after discovering and sending you the information about Claymar. Those miners' mistreatment brought you to my palats ten times in one week. That included two long walks around the cliff-top that we spent negotiating. Though, trust me, I tried several times to get you off subject, to attempt to seduce you, but you were so passionate about the welfare of the natives, it never worked."

Mouth falling open, I stared at the prince. "You were my anonymous informant?"

The prince gave a noncommittal shrug. Closing my eyes against the onslaught of emotions, I cursed beneath my breath. All this time, I'd thought those envelopes full of reports and photographs came from another Cyran man I befriended. The last person I would have ever suspected was the prince himself. "You made me your bleeding heart."

"No. You made you my bleeding heart. You never had to take

action. You could have been like many of the wealthier Praldians and ignored those in need." Saboa sat back down next to me. "You made them your cause, your way of avoiding who you were and where you came from. You did what I couldn't do without looking weak, but in letting you fight for them, I got to look merciful, and it endeared you to the people. For that reason, we will make the best companions, Zira. You will never let me lose sight of the little people because you were raised not to rule but to give of yourself and let others rule."

"You promise not to block me in helping the less fortunate?"

"So far as it doesn't cause conflict in my interests, you will have my full support. That's how it has always been between us, Zira. Though, I won't make you work so hard to gain that support any longer." The quirk of a smile was upon his lips, and it suddenly made them so very appealing.

All these years, he'd been courting me through my cause, supporting it secretly, wanting me for who I was, not the title I was born with. Or so he claimed. How could I trust that? Words were easy and as a prince, he would know how to use his words to manipulate others to his will.

There was too much in my head. Things were changing too quickly and revelations I never expected had me doubting my instinct of Saboa's goodness. Good instincts were something Avalonians were renowned for.

All those years of petitioning him. The long walks to negotiate his support for whatever my cause was. It never occurred to me he always arranged for privacy while we discussed what brought me to him. I'd admired Saboa. No, I didn't love him, but he was a good man as far as rulers went.

Could my admiration grow to be more? Especially after he revealed his part in helping the Praldian natives all these years. My instinct around Saboa always told me I could trust his word. That he did care about the people. Did I believe his feelings for me were true?

Sighing, I realised it wasn't as if I had any choice. Still, knowing he was behind those anonymous tips just to have a reason to spend time with me endeared him to me for more than just the respect I'd always had for him. There was also the benefit that joining with Saboa protected me from the Barbarian. If he ever found me, he wouldn't dare try to abduct the wife of the most powerful ruling family in our system.

"Okay." Turning to the contract, I flipped through to the last page, ready to sign.

Grabbing the pen from my hand Saboa stopped me. "You need to read that first."

"Why? Have you got a clause that says I have to tie you up and spank you every third moon?"

Saboa, Stark, and Aldous actually laughed, but Aldous finally answered. "Lady Zira. This is a contract—a binding agreement. Once you sign it, you will be obligated to abide by it for the rest of your life. It states what is expected of you within a set time frame of your joining. There is a promise from the Prince to yourself regarding things you have requested, but with restraints. You must understand every aspect of what is being demanded of you."

Tired, I sighed. "Fine, but I'm starving. I need to eat, or concentrating is going to be impossible."

Stark walked to the comms. "Padget, bring dinner in, please... enough for four."

"Yes, Commander."

Taking a deep breath, I started reading.

Chapter Five

"Three children?" I balked. "No one ever has more than two in Avalonia. No wonder Cyra is overpopulated."

While Stark and Aldous sat at the table chatting quietly, Saboa and I ate dinner on the sofa while I read our contracts. Saboa already finished reading and signing, having only read to make sure the changes he'd requested were correct. I, on the other hand, was still only halfway through.

Saboa chuckled. "We need a son for each throne, Zira, and since the continuation of the throne in Avalonia comes from the King's sister, we will need a daughter as well. In fact, three is the minimum. We will need to keep having children until we have at least two sons and one daughter. So, if we have five daughters to start with, we will need to keep trying until we get our bare minimum heirs."

Staring at Saboa, I waited for him to say he was joking, but the other shoe never dropped. "Surely there have been occasions in your own history which have required the King's sister to bear more than two children to gain a male and a female heir?"

"No, why would it? The females select to get with child, and the males select what sex they will have."

Saboa dropped his fork to his plate. "The male selects the sex at any given conception?"

Surprised he didn't already know this, I nodded. "Isn't that the case with every species?"

"No, Zira, it's not," Saboa huffed. Now it was my turn to look dazed. "Most other species play a game of first in first served with male and female sperm competing to fertilize the female's womb. You say you can elect when to conceive?" Intrigued by his explanation, I nodded.

"That's also unusual. Most females go through cycles where there is a conception window. For Cyrans, that window is only six hours long on average and can happen anytime, day or night. For Praldians, it is over several days each month," he educated. "So, in Cyra, a couple trying to conceive will be given leave from work to ensure they are introducing fresh sperm to the womb regularly to ensure the opportunity isn't missed."

"So, you're a bunch of sex fiends, and you just use reproduction as an excuse to have it more often?"

Saboa laughed. "Well, none of the males ever complain about the extra practice." Considering me for a moment, his face grew more serious again. "Explain how it is for your people?"

Shrugging, I chewed another bite of meat, swallowing before talking. "I'm not entirely clued in on it. My mother gave me a book to put away for later on how it is done... how to force my body to reproduce, not the sex part. I'm pretty sure I've got that part nailed. Pardon the pun."

Choking on a piece of his dinner, Saboa looked at me with a raised brow.

"Anyway, from what I understand, when a woman is ready to conceive, she can meditate and bring her body into that phase of being. Then, during copulation, the male will only release the sperm with the sex chromosome they wish to have. I grew up with that as a common understanding. I didn't realize that wasn't the case for every other species."

"So, if you chose to get with child tonight, you could?" Saboa asked. He tried to hide an annoyance, but it was still slightly evident in his voice.

Shaking my head, I avoided his eyes. "As I said, I was never told the exact '*how*' to do it. I'd need to go home and find that book and learn first. But..." I looked up and met the Saboa's curious gaze. "I don't think it's a good idea."

Holding up my hand, I indicated he should let me finish as he went to argue. He held his tongue. "Prince Saboa, when my mother gave me that book, she instructed me not to read it until I was safe. She basically told me that while the Barbarian lived, I should put all thought of children out of my head. Eliora believed ruling men would seek out my womb for the same reason the Barbarian wants it. And once they had the heirs, my life would be worthless and expendable. She even paid a Praldian medic to examine me and sign official documentation that I was barren to deter possible suitors."

"I know; she showed it to me two years ago," Saboa responded spitefully. "I summoned the physician, and my medic questioned him in front of me. The outcome was that you may be a late bloomer, that your womb was healthy, but you apparently were yet to cycle. I decided to take the chance that my medic was right and that your mother may have led the Praldian medic to believe what she wanted him to." Saboa watched me closely. "Why were you honest with me if your mother told you to hide it?"

"I have only ever been honest with you, Prince Saboa. You have given me a reason to believe that your intentions here are not what my parents feared, and I've always been a good judge in character. I'm hoping you won't give me a reason to regret it."

Dipping his head suddenly, Saboa kissed me. I wasn't expecting it. When I went to pull back, he held my neck to keep me there. Our eyes were open, watching each other as our lips moved gently against one another. He wasn't drowning in my eyes like most men would. He was entirely in control of his senses and his desire while he kissed me. Something about that stirred my own passions.

Closing my eyes, I turned my head slightly and opened my mouth a little. A cough from the table drew the prince back. He still held me as he turned to consider the two men in the room.

"I believe there will be plenty of time for that after the contracts are signed, Prince Saboa," Aldous objected, then returned to his meal.

Chuckling, Saboa released me, indicating the item I'd questioned him about. "So, now that we've cleared up the quantity issue, are there any other questions on that point?"

Licking my lips, I glanced to where he was pointing. "The first two to be born within the first five years of our joining? As I was trying to say, I'm—"

"Scared of what Abaddon will do?" Saboa interrupted. Shivering at the Barbarian's name, I nodded. "He tried to abduct you. Did you know that?"

Eyes wide and fearful, I shook my head. How much had my parents hidden from me?

"He sent an assassin and a team of men to kill your parents and bring you back to him when you were seventeen," Saboa informed me. "Apparently, it took him three years to find out where you were hiding. Your parents chose your country estate because it was surrounded by Commander Stark's and Councilman Burchard's estates. Both estates have armed guards present year-round."

The Commander allowed guards on leave to stay on his land, so there was always a rotation of around twenty men there, and Burchard kept a personal guard of ten men.

"The team the Barbarian sent made the mistake of trying to approach your estate via the Commander's," Saboa continued. "In fact, it was that event and the resulting interrogation of the one man who survived that exposed who you were to us. Until that moment, you were just another Avalonian refugee, high born, obviously. Still, when I first desired you, I had no idea you were the missing princess."

Saboa placed his hand over my trembling and cold hand tenderly. "What I'm saying is that we've been protecting you ever since then.

We've had soldiers stationed at both residences keeping an eye on who comes and goes from your property. And yes, he has made a few more attempts, but by the third one, he accepted that unless he were willing to declare war, you were out of his grasp."

Whenever I didn't think I could get more surprised tonight, something else would just come along.

"Zira, you are now surrounded by over two thousand highly trained soldiers. Cyran soldiers at that. Until Hartwin informed us just how close Abaddon came to having you, we honestly didn't know why your family was so terrified of the Barbarian. I understand now that he must be the stuff of nightmares for you, but Zira, Abaddon will never touch you again. I promise you that."

Swallowing at the certainty in his voice, I tried to put the image of the Barbarian from my mind. "So, two kids in five years, two boys and one girl minimum?" I checked, and Saboa smiled. "I wonder if that book tells me how to conceive triplets?"

Saboa laughed, touching my cheek affectionately. "Sadly, my Princess, I am not Avalonian, and therefore cannot pick the sex of the child. Knowing our luck, we'd end up with three daughters instead."

"Now you are scaring me," I grumbled.

Saboa laughed again. I was starting to like that shy laugh of his. It was as if he rarely ever laughed and wasn't sure how to do it. Turning back to the contract, I kept reading, returning to my meal. Saboa relaxed, watching me for a few minutes before getting up to go and talk to Aldous and Stark about some other issues. Several pages later, I found myself on the brink of tears. "You're giving it back to me? Why?"

Turning from the men to face me, Saboa set his hands behind his back as he leaned over to see what part of the contract I was referring to. "I have no need of your parent's money or their properties, Zira. You were innocent, so they will be transferred to your name once you confirm you carry our first child. Until then, the money will be held in trust, and the staff you already have will be paid their usual wages to keep the properties in good condition."

I studied him for a moment. "But I can't return home to live?"

"Not yet." Saboa took a step closer. "Right now, you are safer here and more so when you conceive the first time. It's written in the contract that after the first child is born, we will reassess your safety. If you are no longer under threat, we can discuss your moving home. Though, I'm hoping that by then, the idea of being away from me for that long will be unbearable for you."

"It's not about you," I consoled. "I'm not cut out for being around a lot of people. I like the peace the country holds."

Leaning forward, Saboa smirked. "Give living here a chance, Zira. My side of the palats is quieter than you think." He sobered, resuming his serious voice. "No matter where you live, from now on, you will always have a minimum of two elite with you at all times. The only time they will not be in the same room is when you are in bed or in the bathroom. Even in residence, there will be one inside our quarters with you day or night; the second will stay in the outer rooms. This is not negotiable."

Since I didn't object to this, I swallowed, returning to reading the contract. "Saboa?" I said his name without his title tentatively.

"Luther. My name is Luther. When we are here in our room, that's what I'd like you to call me."

Biting my lip for a second, I took a deep breath. "Luther, sell the city residence and donate the money to the native schools. We can make it my first act as your companion to have negotiated that as part of our joining."

Bowing his head slightly, Luther nodded to Aldous, who scribbled something down before they returned to their conversation, and I continued reading.

Chapter Six

Taking a deep breath, I scribbled my name on the last page of the contract where Saboa already signed. Then I started autographing each page in the Prince's copy. My hand was trembling terribly. Even to me, my signature was barely recognizable.

I was just signing the last page when Aldous looked over. "You're finished?" he asked, bringing everyone's attention to me and the pen in my shaking hand.

"I am." Dropping the pen, I clasped my hands together to try and still them before looking up. "What time is it? I need food."

"Again?" Aldous asked, coming to look at the contracts.

"I eat a lot."

"Apparently, so. I've met Avalonians before and have never seen one eat as much as you. You eat like a soldier in training," Aldous responded quite seriously.

Suddenly shy, I drew away. "It's a genetic thing. Some of us need more energy than others."

"I'll have one of the guards run down the kitchen," Stark advised and moved to the door. Sticking his head out, he spoke quietly to someone outside. When Stark came back, Aldous called him over to witness our signatures.

"It looks like you didn't need to sign on her behalf after all," Aldous quipped under his breath to the prince. Saboa glared at him but moved around the table to me. Running his hand down the outside of my covered arm, he took my hand in his again.

"Would you have done that to me?"

"Yes," he answered honestly.

Stark finished signing his signature and then went to the door calling Hartwin to sign as a witness. Once they finished, Aldous signed, then gathered up the contracts filing them away. "Congratulations, Prince Saboa. You have your companion. Did the Princess decide where she would like your first public appearance to be?"

"Tomorrow is Fredag. I usually go to Fastlandet and visit one of the schools. I haven't got my schedule, but I think I was due at Mymark in the morning."

Aldous looked to the prince, who only nodded once. "Fine, I'll let the Broadcasters know where you will be. I'll see you both in the morning."

"Good night, Aldous." Saboa waited until he got to the door. "And Aldous?" Aldous turned to look at him. "Let's keep the finer details of the joining and how it came about in-house. I'd prefer the Praldians celebrate this union."

Aldous nodded but stepped through the door without another word.

"Are your councilmen unhappy about your choice in a companion?"

"No, but Aldous wouldn't hesitate in revealing Saboa's power over you in this joining," Hartwin answered, taking a seat on the opposite sofa with his father. He looked at me studiously. "You need to eat, Princess. You're running on empty again."

Stark gave his son the slightest nudge with his thigh. Saboa looked at Hartwin, interested. "How could you tell?"

"Her eyes," Hartwin answered matter-of-factly. "They become

more congealed when she's deprived herself. They were like that this afternoon. Soon as she'd eaten, they were liquid pools again."

Taking my chin in his hand, Saboa studied my eyes. "Huh, you're right."

Jervaise entered with a tray of food. "I found Ost, Kex, and cabanossi." As soon as he put the tray on the table, I started eating.

Rising, Stark grabbed a bite, then walked Jervaise to the door. "I think I'll also retire for the night. Hartwin, I think just for tonight, the elite can stay in the outer quarters."

Hartwin nodded. "Shift change should be up in a minute. I'll let them know not to disturb unless it's an emergency." His father bowed to the prince, Jervaise doing the same before leaving. Hartwin sat forward, elbows on his knees, running his hands over his face.

"Something on your mind, Hart?" Saboa asked cautiously.

"I need to be honest with you," Hartwin started. "Zira and I have been friends for years. We haven't been in regular contact, but we've remained friends. I know her well enough to spot things like when she needs to eat or sleep or when she is angry enough that going swimming with her probably isn't a safe option."

"How close?" Saboa asked, his hand growing a little too tight around mine.

Hartwin smirked. "She knows about the girls you don't, but I've never discussed your business with her. Our conversations are only about us and our lives."

Saboa's hand relaxed. "Why would you tell her about certain lovers and not me?"

"Because you'd kick my ass, and she just laughs at me." Remembering some of the stories he'd told me, I smiled shook my head.

"And do you tell him about your lovers?" Saboa asked casually.

I raised a brow. "Worried I'll be making comparisons between past lovers and my new companion while I'm on house arrest?"

Saboa balked, but Hartwin snickered. "She has never even revealed a lover's name to me, let alone discussed one's technique." Saboa visibly relaxed.

"That's not true. Hart was my only male friend until I came of age. When it came to that time, I interrogated him about what it's like, and about what men enjoy the most."

"Oh, stars, I'd forgotten about that," Hartwin chuckled. "She just wouldn't relent and kept asking until I was blushing like a morning sunrise."

"Do you care for her?" Saboa watched us both intently.

"Yes, though I never carried any designs on courting her. She's always been out of my league. Still, I couldn't bear to watch her get hurt. I admit I was worried about how tonight would go after this afternoon. I didn't realize how today was like a repeat in history for you, Zira. I understand now why you were so freaked out."

Picking up some more food, I ate quietly. Hartwin returned to Saboa. "I understand if you're upset that I hid this friendship from everyone, including you, but you know how this life is, the lack of privacy. My friendship with Zira was the only thing that was mine. The laughs we shared helped me learn to control my temper. It's why I was able to rise so quickly through the ranks, because I'd use a joke she'd shared with me to help control my emotions during testing. If you need to reassign me, I'll understand."

"Who was your first lover?" Saboa suddenly asked. For a moment, I thought he was talking to Hartwin, but then they both looked at me.

Swallowing what I was eating, I looked at Saboa, confused by the sudden line of questioning. "A Praldian named Shipton from the Skogar region. Why?"

"Why a Praldian? Why not a Cyran? A friend who you felt safe with?"

"I..."

"She was scared of us," Hartwin answered. "Our size, strength, and violent natures. She didn't feel safe with even me in that regard."

Looking from Hartwin to me, Saboa waited for confirmation. "It took me two years to have the guts to take a Cyran as a lover. He was a trader in the city, a friend, but someone who was not immune to my glance, so I knew I could control him if needed."

Saboa breathed a sigh of relief before glancing up to Hartwin. "You care for her, and you know her moods and can recognize if she isn't well. She confides in you and trusts you. I'd be a fool to reassign you, Hart. Right now, you're my alarm system until I get to know her better than you do."

Jervaise stuck his head in. "Shift change."

Hartwin put out his hand to his prince, and they clasped elbows. "Congrats on your joining, Luth. I couldn't have picked a better princess for you." Hartwin turned to the door but stopped just before leaving. "Keep an eye on her eyes tonight. If they congeal, she needs food. If they turn dark, she needs sleep. If they go bright blue, she's about to attack and try and drown you in some body of water nearby," Hartwin laughed, stepping outside and shutting the door behind him.

Raising an eyebrow, Saboa gazed at me. "You tried to drown him?"

Not amused by Hartwin's joke, I shrugged. "Once or twice." Getting up, I walked into the bedroom and stood looking out the window towards the city. I knew what was expected of me. I'd taken casual lovers once or twice before, though none in a while now. Saboa wasn't the man I loved, but now he was my life companion and would eventually be the father of my children.

Following me into the room, Saboa moved to turn on the light. "Don't," I begged. He stilled his hand above the switch. "It will ruin the view."

Gazing out to the city lights in the distance, I watched him close the doors in the reflection of the window, plunging us into complete darkness. The advantage now was his due to his night vision.

Brushing my hands over the front of my dress, I sighed. Cyran soldiers repressed their desires so strongly that anything between them and their desired object was collateral damage when they finally relented to them. I didn't want this dress ruined, it was too lovely. Touching the release clasp, the dress loosened as it unwove at the seam. Letting it fall to the floor, I continued to watch the city lights.

I couldn't even hear the prince breathing in the room now. He was somewhere behind me, standing in the dark watching his prey, fighting his instinct to pounce.

Another minute passed. Then Luther's hands fell on my upper arms with an almost hesitation as he pressed his body to my back. My eyes went wide as I realized he'd already disrobed. I hadn't heard him at all. This suggested that each time I'd listened to his movements today, the noise he made was deliberate, to either gain my attention or put me at ease.

"Zira, I need to know your limitations. Your kind is not built like mine. I don't wish to hurt you out of ignorance of what your body can endure."

I'd heard those words voiced before, and the desire for the memory of the one who uttered them rose within me. Turning in Luther's arms, my face level with his chest, I didn't look up at his face. I didn't want to ruin the memory.

"I'm sturdier than I look. Trust your instincts, and they won't lead you astray," I advised. Lifting to tiptoes, I put my mouth to Luther's ear. "Don't use my hair to hold me. You can touch it, but I react badly to someone fisting it."

His grip on my arms tightened as I went to drop back to my flat feet, keeping me on my toes. "Say my name?" he whispered into my ear.

Closing my eyes, I licked my lips. "Luther," I whispered.

Turning his face, he kissed my neck. I shuddered. My desires were raging within me from the memories I was calling forth. Encircling me in his arms. Luther hugged me tight against him as his lips traced across my collarbone. My hands found the back of his broad shoulders and were holding fast, my feet dangling above the ground where he had me.

When his teeth found the silk undergarment's strap, he used them to peel it from my shoulder slowly. The way his muscles strained against me, without adding more force, suggested Luther was trying to act in the way a Praldian might. Slow and gentle was not the way Cyrans copulated.

"It's okay, Luther. I'm finally yours. You can give in to your desire."

Tensing against me, he inhaled a deep, shaking breath. Then, with a fierce growl, he threw me to the bed, ripping the front of the silk undergarment open in almost the same movement.

Pressing his body over mine, his mouth found mine, and the slow, tentative kiss from earlier was long gone as he gave in to his wants. The force of Luther's need hit me like a wave of hot water and started churning inside of me like a waterspout. There was a split-second of automatic reaction where I nearly crashed that wave over him, drowning him in his desires and putting him at my mercy. But I remembered who it was above me and could only hazard at the fallout of doing that to a ruling body.

The problem was that I could barely draw breath under the onslaught of his passion. I'd been here before, unable to destroy the man above me. I'd chosen to drown myself, and it left me heartbroken. Maybe this time, it would save me.

Letting it go, I cried out. Luther's desire washed over me, through me, and swept me away to be lost in the physical joining of two beings. Pleasure, passion, and lust.

When I drew breath again, I was panting, hot within but cold without. Shivering, my skin was covered with beads of water. Opening my eyes, two large hands nearly encompassed my waist within their grasp. Running my hands around Luther's wrists then along his arms as far as I could reach from where I straddled him, I finally met his eyes.

Luther's face was a mix of emotions. Shock, joy, fulfillment, possession. What he'd revealed in the other room had been truth; his desire had whispered his long-held craving to me. Why couldn't he have disobeyed my parents and courted me? He could have saved me from so much pain.

A sob escaped my throat. Sitting up quickly, Saboa hugged me to his chest, holding me tight. "It's okay, Zira, let it out."

Thumping his back with my fists, I yelled and ranted against his hold, against what happened. "You killed my parents, you stole my freedom, and I still couldn't bring myself to harm you. I should hate you. Despise you for what you've taken from me!"

He didn't refute it, just held me so tight that I couldn't move in his arms. I wanted to hate him, but I knew my parents were at fault for their own downfall. Saboa was just opportunistic, taking what was denied him for years.

Hugging him tightly, I cried, my tears drenching his flesh in blue rivulets until my eyes ran dry. Exhausted from the outpouring of my emotions, I fell asleep, still cradled in his arms.

WAKING to a heavyweight sitting over my thighs and hips, I opened my eyes to the grey of first morning light. When I tried to roll from where I lay on my tummy, a hand pressed my shoulder back to the bed. "Stay."

"Luther?" I felt fear course through me.

"These markings, some look ancient, and others look fresh as if they were only inked yesterday. What are they?"

Breathing a sigh of relief, I relaxed back onto the bed, closing my eyes. "They are my natal scale. Every Avalonian is born with one. Some will only bear a few symbols; others will run half the length of their spine." I squirmed uncomfortably under his weight. "Luther, you're sort of a bit heavy."

He smacked my bum. "Stay still; I'm trying to read this."

Gazing over my shoulder, aghast by the smack, but Luther paid no attention, so I buried my head back in the pillow.

"I recognize a few of these. This one" –Luther touched the symbol that allowed me to dissipate in water— "it's your people's symbol for water. This one is your symbol for a knife, or blade, or sharp, something like that, and this one is love..."

"Desires," I corrected, cringing over the memory of nearly losing control of my own talent last night.

Brushing his fingers over several more symbols, Luther muttered to himself as he tried to puzzle out those he recognized. "You say you were born with these? So, why do some look freshly done?"

"Get off me, and I'll explain it as best I can."

Collapsing to the side of me, Saboa waited patiently for my explanation. His hand played along my spine while the other was propped to support his head as he watched me.

"When we are born, all the symbols are faded and can be barely legible. As we learn to utilize our abilities, the symbols come to life. Each time we activate a specific talent, it gives... what Cyran word would describe it? A blossa—a flare. So, those talents that you use the most will look fresher than those you never used or never learned to use."

"Genetic markers of what you'll be good at?"

"Basically. There are only two marks ever inked on true Avalonian skin." Rolling to face him, I took his hand from where it caressed my hip and placed his index finger to the star beneath my eye. "The pentagram is marked under our eye when we utilize our first ability. I was marked at six, my brother at five. The youngest age for activation before us was eleven."

Saboa's brows rose with interest.

"How many symbols did you see?" I asked.

"Eighteen."

"My brother bore seventeen. Our uncle, the King, wore fifteen and was known as the most powerful king in centuries."

Saboa concentrated. "Wait, you're saying it's abnormal to have this many symbols?" I nodded. "So, your brother would have been one of the most powerful men to ever rule your planet?" I nodded again. "And if you carry all this power, your offspring would be expected to..."

"Possibly, it's not guaranteed. Since my children will not be full-blooded, I'm not sure if they will have any power at all," I mourned. Taking a breath, I dragged his hand to cup my left breast. "My brother was marked as king. Tradition demanded his chest tattooed at six weeks old to indicate a royal heart."

Eyes intent on the mound of flesh he held, Saboa licked his lips. Dragging his hand downwards, I pressed it to the mark a couple of inches below my navel. Saboa blinked, then bent to get a better look, but I waited until his eyes flicked back up to me questioningly.

"I was marked at six weeks of age to indicate I carried the royal womb."

"How barbaric," Saboa murmured, astonished.

I laughed. "Funny, we think that of some of your customs."

Lowering his mouth, Saboa kissed the mark on my abdomen. "So, there is no mistaking your identity, and your people know how powerful you are—"

"No!" Looking up suddenly, Saboa blinked wide eyes at my outburst. "We are kept covered from birth. Only the throne and our parents ever see us bare. None would have known until my brother was crowned. Only then would he bare his back to his people to show his power to protect them. However, none would have seen mine until I took a companion, and then only he would know."

"But your previous lovers?" When I shook my head, Saboa sat back onto his calves, his eyes and mouth forming perfect circles. "Not one of your lovers has seen you naked? How the blackness have you managed that?"

The disbelief on his face was hilarious. "Luther, have you always undressed every woman you've enjoyed sex with?" His eyes sparkled. "The majority of my experiences in the past have not been leisurely paced."

Saboa crawled forward over me. "Well, that's something we can definitely remedy."

Kissing me slow and deep, he pulled back to slip between my thighs. Cupping his face in my hands, I forced his eyes to meet mine. "Luther, never tell anyone what you've seen? No one can know I have any more than ten abilities, and they should never know what they are. It's for you only."

Smiling wickedly, Saboa hovered above me, shifting the tip of his cock to rub between my folds. "I appreciate that." Lowering his face,

Saboa kissed me passionately just as the door slid open. Groaning loudly, Luther dropped his head to my shoulder. "What?"

Eyes wide, I was glad Luther was big enough to hide me. While I didn't recognize the Elite guard who entered, I was grateful that he turned to face the window looking over the ocean when he saw our intimate position. "Prince Saboa, you asked to be informed when the Broadcasters released the news."

Chapter Seven

Our first days as companions went better than I expected. We made our debut at the Mymark school in Fastlandet. The Broadcasters waited for us, along with a larger-than-expected crowd to cheer us in and out of the school. Master Fabrice worked all night to ensure I had a dress worthy of a Princess for my first public appearance.

When we returned to the palats, a reception was held in the ballroom, which the Praldian-based diplomats, councilmen, and other people of note attended to congratulate us. A few councilmen expressed their disappointment at finding out from the Broadcasters and not being invited to the private ceremony. Still, all showed support for our union.

The next morning, Saboa refused to tell me where he was taking me. Our guards surrounded us, and we teleported. It took me a moment of looking out the window of the new building we were in to realize we were in Simpia. It was the opening of the new mining facilities, the one that brought me to Luther that very first time. The following six months, I'd visited the palats weekly to negotiate for funding to improve the living and working conditions of the natives here.

Overwhelmed by seeing the first project I'd ever put my heart into completed, I threw my arms around Saboa's neck and hugged him fiercely. When Saboa cleared his throat, I stepped away shyly, then stood passively beside him for the opening. Ambassador Twyford, president of the Native Rights Committee that Saboa formed as a result of another of my petitions, then gave a speech to the Natives of Simpia in praise of Prince Saboa and his continued support.

Today, our third day joined, Saboa had meetings all day to deal with Praldian affairs, so I was left to my own devices, albeit on a very short leash. In the morning, I walked the ring and wandered in the Roseraie, accepting this was the closest I would get to time by myself for a while. By lunchtime, all I wanted was a swim, but I settled for the bath instead.

Raised voices drew me back from my dispersed meditation. Surfacing, I purged the water from my lungs, gasping from the pain of pulling together too quickly. Turning from where he was yelling at someone at the door, Luther looked furious.

Stepping toward me hesitantly, he visually inspected the water. "You weren't there a moment ago."

"Yes," I panted, "I was. You just couldn't see me because I was... meditating." Coughing, I clung to the side of the deep bath.

"Are you okay?" His voice was concerned despite the fierceness of his features. Coughing again, I nodded. "Good, get dressed and get down the throne room now. An Avalonian diplomatic craft has just entered our system." Luther stormed back out to the sitting room. "Get her downstairs immediately. I want her beside me when the ambassador enters the throne room."

Dragging myself from the bath, I shivered despite the heat of the day. Over the last two days, I'd received gifts from most of the high society families of Praldia, including a gift of a black opal pendant from Luther's father, King Saboa, in Cyra. However, I doubted that the Avalonian Ambassador was here to wish us a happy union, many offspring, and give us a gift.

When I stepped into the sitting room, Padget was dancing from foot to foot anxiously, and Jervaise was pacing the length of the window. "Princess" –Padget rushed forward— "you haven't done up your dress." She pressed the closure on the city-style fitted dress that Master Fabrice sent over along with several others yesterday.

While they were fitted through the bodice, he folded more material into the flowing floor-length skirt, allowing me to walk at my normal stride. It was a departure from the current fashion, which wrapped women in fabric from neck to knee, restraining their every movement.

Padget ushered me to the lounge to sit while she promptly braided my hair into one thick rope down my back to the base of my spine. She'd tried to do my hair on the first morning in the city ladies' fancy up styles, but my hair was too fine to stay in place. Frankly, I found it too flamboyant. So, we'd compromised on letting her bind my hair with ribbons or braid it to make me look less... 'wild' was her word.

"She's trembling like its winter, Jervaise."

Watching me intently, Jervaise nodded. "She's terrified, Padg. These people killed her family and have tried to abduct her on numerous occasions. She knows why they are here."

Dropped to her knees in front of me, Padget took my hands in hers. "Princess, look at me." When I did, she instantly dropped her eyes to my mouth, avoiding direct eye contact. "The Prince will not let them harm you or take you. You are safe here. You must stand beside your prince and show that you have every faith he can protect you. Don't let them see weakness. Trust in your prince. If you show them you do not fear them while at his side, they will fear him."

"Who are you, Padget? A simple Praldian attendant would never offer such wisdom."

Lowering her eyes, Padget rose and stepped away. When I looked to Jervaise, still shaking, he shrugged. "She is the prince's half-sister.

His father enjoyed some fun here before we settled. Padget was the outcome. Prince Saboa brought her to the palats when it was finished, and she has grown up here. Still, due to her illegitimacy, she will never be recognized and is forbidden to claim her bloodline."

"Oh." I looked at Padget, taking her hand. "Well met, Sister."

Smiling, Padget pushed me towards Jervaise. "Get going. Your prince is waiting."

Taking my elbow in his hand, Jervaise forced me to keep up with his stride. Another elite guard named Clovis fell in on my other side. He was the first Cyran I'd met with light eyes. He looked over my head to Jervaise. "Are we expecting trouble?"

"I suspect so. Luther has half the Elite waiting in the throne room and encircled the public channels with the royal guards."

"They don't really expect to just walk in here, demand her, and for us to hand her over after all this time, surely?" Clovis's tone was full of sarcasm, another unnatural characteristic for a Cyran.

"Yes," I answered for them, "that's exactly what they expect."

We passed through the luxuriously furnished private entertaining area, primarily used by guards on watch duty since Saboa rarely brought anyone into his quarters. All of his friends were elite since Luther was still an elite guard for his father, so they were who he hung out with.

Marching through the apartment door, we stepped onto the lift pad and, in under a second, we dropped the four levels to the ground floor. Grasped my stomach, I looked up, trying not to vomit. I felt like I'd left my innards on the top floor. Usually, the guards smirked at my discomfort, telling me I'd get used to it, but today they were on high alert. There would be no jesting until the Avalonian Ambassador left our system.

On the ground floor, four more elite joined the escort. Two in front, two beside me, and two behind because I wasn't allowed out of the residence without six guards minimum. Hartwin took Clovis's place beside me, taking up my other elbow and giving it a reassuring squeeze.

"You will never for a minute be in danger, Princess," he assured me quietly. I didn't trust my voice not to give away just how terrified I was, so I kept my mouth shut. The ice floor cracking loudly with so many feet sounded ominous enough.

As we were in the last section of the corridor before the throne room, I heard the buzz of the public channels come to life. Stepping to the window anxiously, I noted five of the public access points lit up announcing incoming teleports.

"Princess," Hartwin squeezed my elbow.

Turning towards the throne room, I started running, my guard catching quickly, flanking me again. I ran until I entered the throne room, then kept a fast pace until I reached the three steps to the throne. At the bottom, I stopped and curtsied low out of habit, which made the watching council chuckle, whispering about me knowing my place.

Rising, Luther took my hand, drawing me up the steps to stand before him. Kissing my forehead, he put his mouth to my ear. "Stay to my left and slightly behind the throne. If anything looks out of place, you let me know by touching my shoulder. If they are stupid enough to attack, then you get behind the throne. The elite will protect you."

Over Luther's shoulder, twenty elite guards stood on alert. Hartwin and the others who escorted me were joining their ranks directly behind where I would be. Standing where I was directed, I tried to calm my nerves while Saboa retook his seat. Once Luther scanned the room, he signaled Stark to come closer and report.

"The ship landed in the diplomatic airfield. Five Avalonian men disembarked, approaching the public channels. The ship is refueling, so it appears they have no intention of staying here any longer than it takes to deliver their message."

Saboa nodded. "Stand by the Princess."

"Yes, Prince Saboa." Stark moved to stand at my left-hand side.

Most days that I'd been in the courtroom, it was during open court where any one of the citizens could step into the petitioner's circle, and the Prince would hear them. On those days, the throne room was so packed you couldn't breathe without touching someone. Today Saboa was meeting with councilmen and other elected representatives of Praldia to discuss infrastructure. They didn't even fill a third of the room. Still, they were obviously annoyed at having to put their discussions on hold for an uninvited diplomatic envoy.

On the few times I had turned up at the palace demanding to see the prince outside of open court, I'd been forced to wait. Sometimes it took hours before Saboa would meet me in whatever courtyard one of the royal guards escorted me to. I never considered before now that I was never turned away. The guard that greeted me would simply mention my presence in his comms, receive an answer and escort me, informing me the prince would see me when he could. Saboa was just a caring prince who made time for his people. How utterly naïve was I?

"Ambassador Tudal of Avalonia and his envoy," a Praldian voice announced. Saboa hired Praldians throughout his palats. The only Cyrans he'd brought with him were his soldiers. Every other Cyran on Praldia immigrated after settlement. Still, I'd never seen one on staff in the palats except for the three who sat on his council.

Four Avalonian men all wearing the official robes of Avalonia marched into the throne room, sure and intent. All were of the powerless barbarian race. Instead of the star of power beneath their eyes, they bore dark blue tattoos over half their faces to indicate their tribe. Putting a hand out to steady myself using the back of Saboa's chair, I didn't even realize I'd half-stepped behind it until Stark touched my elbow. It was a subtle connection to remind me he was there, and I was safe.

The ambassador's envoy stopped in the petitioner's circle, fanning out. They bowed politely, but the ambassador's eyes were scanning the room. When they found me, he beamed with self-congratulations. "Princess Zira, you've grown up beautifully. Your Companion, the King, will be overjoyed with your beauty."

Grumbles of disgust broke out amongst the councilmen. It was blatant rudeness not to have addressed the Prince first. Avalonians were known for politeness and formality. This ambassador just disgraced my entire race within two sentences.

Cocking a brow, Saboa assessed the ambassador. "Have Avalonians lost all their civility under the Barbarian's rule? You come here claiming ambassadorship, then immediately insult the throne by not even addressing me. I suppose, if I were to visit the throne of Avalonia, I would find you all eating dead carcasses with your hands and raping children on the throne room floor?"

The last was a personal stab for what they tried to do to me, and if the scowl on his face was any indication, the Ambassador recognized it. Tudal balked at Saboa's words, looking from me to the Prince. "Prince Saboa," Tudal recovered, bowing low, "forgive my rudeness. I was just taken with how much our Princess has grown."

Saboa didn't reply, a clear announcement that the rudeness was not forgiven.

"Prince Saboa, I'm sorry to announce I bring sad tidings. It would seem that you have joined with a woman who already has a companion. Therefore, by law, your joining is void. The King wishes his companion to return with us and resume her duties as his queen."

"You have proof of this joining taking place?" Saboa asked casually.

"Sadly, the joining took place during a time of war. The Princess was joined with King Abaddon by the Elder Othniel shortly before the Princess was abducted by rebels."

"The Elder Othniel completed the joining, you say?" Saboa inquired, holding his hand out to Aldous, who stepped forward with a scroll that bore the Avalonian Royal seal at its ends.

"Yes, that is correct," Tudal frowned as Saboa unrolled the scroll and read what was written upon it.

Over Luther's shoulder, I recognized the official document stamped by the four elders to decree the joining never took place. Happy Luther's men were able to find this document, I turned my attention back to the Avalonians.

Tudal was absorbing everyone's attention, but the three beside him were watching the room nervously. Their eyes shifting from side to side, distracted as if waiting for something. It bothered me. This wasn't the behavior of ambassadors come to make a petition. These men acted like mercenaries on a job.

Stepping forward without thinking, I placed my hand on Saboa's shoulder. Tapping each of my fingers from little finger to index once on his shoulder, I then swiped my thumb three times. Stark said five men left the ship. I'd seen five public channels light up in the garden. Someone was missing from this party, and in Avalonia, that only meant danger.

Casually patting my hand four times, Saboa then gave it a firm squeeze. He'd noticed. "Would that be Elder Othniel Sampson Nekoda who performed the joining?"

Mouth falling open, the Ambassador nodded. "That would be right, yes."

"And you say this joining took place before the Princess's escape?"

"Before her abduction, Prince Saboa," the Ambassador corrected politely.

"That's interesting, because this" –he held up the scroll— "is a declaration by Elder Othniel and the three other Elders present at the time. They free Princess Zira of any accusation of companionship with King Abaddon. That is who you claim she is joined with, correct?" Luther waited for the Ambassador's gawping face to nod. "Well, this states that Princess Zira was a child. That none of her Kin gave permission for a joining. And that the Princess was" –Saboa smirked as he eyed the Ambassador— "let's go with 'abducted' before any joining could be completed and formalized."

Rolling the scroll, Luther handed it to Aldous, who stepped down and held it for the ambassador to read. "Do you claim falsehood of that document, Ambassador?"

Shaking his head, Tudal scowled. "No, Prince Saboa. The document bears the official seal of all the elders and is on the official letterhead of the throne."

Restraining a smile of satisfaction, Aldous stepped away. Licking his lips nervously, the ambassador surveyed the room and murmured something to the mercenary on his left. Inhaling deeply, Tudal forced a smile. "Prince Saboa, I wish to address the Princess, if you'll allow it?"

Looking bored, Luther nodded. Tudal leveled me with his most authoritative stare. "Princess, you have a responsibility to your people to provide them with the next King."

"I'm well aware of my responsibilities, Ambassador."

"Good!" The ambassador held out his hand, and the mercenary handed Tudal some papers. "Then you will happily sign this contract agreeing to produce an heir of pure Avalonian blood and a daughter of the same to carry on the line. Once you have done so, you will be absolved of all responsibility to your people, and you can whore yourself to this monarch all you wish."

The council broke into an uproar. Luther merely held up his hand, and they quietened. "And who do you suggest be the stud to procure the future king, Ambassador?"

The Ambassador looked unsettled by Saboa's calm. "Why, the King, of course."

"So, you stand here spouting the values of tradition and purity, and yet what you are offering flies in the face of your tradition entirely?"

"You know nothing of our ways!"

Ignoring the ambassador's aggression, Luther continued. "As I understand it, the currently seated king does not procure the next heir. The male who studs the royal womb is not blood-related to either the throne or the Princess. Traditionally, a call goes out for a companion. Any male of power may present himself to the throne to be considered. The men are interviewed, and their natal scale is noted. A shortlist of candidates is presented to the Princess. She courts those men before choosing who will be her companion for life and the stud to her womb. Did I get any of that wrong?"

Absolutely livid at having our traditions thrown back in his face,

Tudal clenched his fists around the contract. His face was the peach color of our people's rage. "That is correct."

"Good." Saboa stood, taking my hand in his. "Consider the Princess courted all the warriors presented before her, and she has chosen her companion and stud as your tradition dictates."

The ambassador stepped forward angrily. "We will not allow you to sully our throne with some half-breed bastard!"

When I took a step toward Tudal, enraged, Luther grabbed my arm, pulling me back. "Half-breed bastard? What do you think sits upon the throne of Avalonia already? Don't think I am ignorant to why you barbarians are shorter than the average Avalonian. Why you rely on brute strength instead of power you don't possess. Why you hire assassins to deal with us who hold true power."

"You are a disgrace to your people, Princess. You will open your legs for the one who killed your parents to gain your womb, but give your people not even a true heir!"

My anger was quickly boiling into something physical. "As opposed to letting the Barbarian who murdered two true blood kings rape me? I will choose eternity floating in the blackness of a starless system before I will ever willingly let that murderous thug touch a finger to my flesh again!"

"Stark!" Luther called, trying to pull me back while the Ambassador glanced around.

"I see it, my Prince." Coming forward, Stark took my arm, dragging me back beside the throne. It wouldn't be seemly for the Prince to shove his wife in public, I guess. "They are baiting you, child, trying to get you away from your protection," Stark whispered in my ear while Luther took back control.

"... said your bit. Your claims are lies, and you fall to cheap insults to try and offend. It will not work. The Princess has made her choice; there is naught you can do about it. Your time here has expired. You have twenty minutes to be out of our system, or I will take your presence as a declaration of war..."

Feeling the presence without seeing it, I struck out at Stark with a ball of air. Not waiting to see him hit the ground or turn to see the surprise on his face, I threw myself at Luther. Turning just in time to see me, Luther put his arms out to catch me, his eyes wide open. Slamming into the prince with all my force and speed, I took him off-center enough that I could pivot to put my body between his and the assassin's.

Fire burst to life in my right shoulder as the assassin's blade thrust where Saboa's heart was only seconds earlier. Ribbons of air snapped from my wrists as I twisted free of Luther.

Swinging my left arm out, the pale blue sheer ribbon whipped out behind me, catching the assassin around the legs. Yanking it back hard, I turned again before the invisible killer hit the floor with a loud grunt of pain.

That grunt gave the assassin an auditory shadow, giving me a silhouette to work with. Flicking my wrist, I wrapped my right ribbon around the invisible man's throat, pulling it tight.

Tugging at the air ribbon, the assassin gasped for breath. Reaching behind my shoulder, I reefed the blade from my back, grimacing at the pain as I dropped to the man's chest and put the knife to his throat. "Show yourself or die unknown." Our assassins were proud. There was no chance any would allow themselves to go to their death without their identity for the attempt at which they died being known.

The elite guard was already beside me, their weapons drawn and aimed at the body I knelt on, even though they couldn't see it.

"I won't ask again," I warned as I pressed the blade deeper at his chin.

The black blood of an Avalonian burst free as the assassin materialized with a grim smile. A face that haunted my nightmares stared back at me. Returning to that throne room in Avalonia for a moment, my left arm pulled back, then jabbed forth faster than the Cyrans could react.

The assassin gurgled beneath me, black blood spurting from around the blade I'd driven hilt deep through his throat and possibly having pierced his spine behind. "By the stars! I've never seen one of them move as quickly as she just did," one of the elite exclaimed as I tore the blade free.

Rising, I pushed through the guards toward the ambassador. An arm grabbed mine. "Zira." Luther caught me.

"Let me go!"

Luther pressed something soft to my bleeding shoulder. "They are subdued, and you are injured."

"I'm fine." I glowered at him. He met my gaze with his own authoritative glare. "It will take but a minute," I returned politely, getting my rage under control... somewhat.

Studying me, Luther released my arm but put his hand out for the dagger. Refusing to give it up, I shook my head. "I won't kill him. I give you my word."

Bowing his head, Luther stepped back then followed me. The guards cleared a path before me where they surrounded the ambassador and his mercenaries. My ribbons danced around my feet as I strode forward. Glaring down on the Avalonians kneeling, already on the floor and bound, I flicked my wrist, and the ribbon wrapped around the ambassador's throat.

"You can ribbon?" His eyes bulged. "No one has ribboned in even the elders' lifetimes."

Yanking the ribbon tighter, I smiled menacingly. "You backed the wrong player, Barbarian. Today you made a fatal mistake. You brought an assassin to a diplomatic petition; strike one. That assassin tried to attack the throne; strike two. That throne is the companion of the royal womb. What is the penalty in Avalonia for raising a hand against the royal womb's companion?"

The ambassador paled, gasping. Raising an eyebrow, I loosened the ribbon enough for him to collect air. "Impalement," he choked.

"Death by impalement. Strike three." Releasing the ribbon, I stood to my full height. "Councilman Aldous."

"Princess?" Aldous acknowledged from not far away.

"Send a message to the elders of Avalonia. Inform them of the

Ambassador's side mission and all three of the charges I just mentioned. Then add that during the attack, the royal womb was stabbed by the ambassador's assassin."

The ambassador's face was completely drained of color as he started shaking his head energetically. "No, Princess, please, show mercy?" he begged.

Spinning, I drove the blade of the assassin into his shoulder then twisted it, enjoying his strangled scream. "This is mercy. I've granted you a warning of what will be awaiting your return. Do with it what you will."

Luther's hand was at my elbow again, but he wasn't dragging me away. Instead, he supported me as I stepped back from the bleeding ambassador. My shoulder was throbbing, but I needed to finish this.

"I believe the throne of Praldia gave you twenty minutes to leave our system before he took your presence as a declaration of war, Ambassador. You've wasted ten minutes already."

The ambassador looked around at the guards desperately. The elite deferred to Saboa, who nodded. One of the elite unbound the ambassador. Springing to his feet, cradling his shoulder, he dashed through the opening the guards made to the door.

"The others?" Stark asked from my other side.

"Kill them," I breathed, pain burning through my shoulder. Leaning into Luther, I was glad when he held me tighter.

"Where's the medic?" Luther yelled as the world swam around me. Then, lowering his voice, he swept a strand of hair from my face. "What's the penalty for harming the royal womb?"

"Impalement and left for the carrion to eat... alive." My voice seemed to carry no weight to it. Luther lifted me into his arms just as everything went black.

Chapter Eight

"You were lucky, Princess. Just one centimeter higher, and he would have got an artery," Medic Ellery stated frankly as he tended my wound. Slumped over the arm of the lounge chair while the medic cleaned the area, I gritted my teeth as ice-cold gel forced its way into my injured shoulder.

"This synthetic healing gel will seal and hasten the healing process. It'll take a full day—thirty hours—before that wound will have knitted enough to take this bandage off. Nothing strenuous until then." Ellery's fingers brushed over a bruise of Luther's hand on my upper arm to make a point.

"By all means, you tell your newly joined Prince he has to sleep on the lounge tonight," I mumbled.

"Does he hurt you?"

Sitting up, I slipped my arm back through my right sleeve. When the medic came, I didn't allow him to remove the dress entirely, just unfastened it. Then I slid it from my right shoulder, so he could tend the wound. Grimacing with pain moving my right arm, I pushed through it and pressed the closure.

"I'm not prying for personal reasons, Princess. It's my job to ensure a healthy throne, but your species is quite frail compared to ours, and it would be easy for him to forget his strength with you."

"The princess pushed the prince out of the way to save him from an assassin. Then she proceeded to take that assassin out, Ellery," Hartwin announced his presence, having come through the door without us hearing him.

I'd demanded privacy while being tended to, not wanting everyone to see me cringe. "I think it's safe to say the princess is nowhere near as fragile as she looks." Hartwin held up a big steaming bowl of delicious smelling stew. "You need to eat, Princess."

Placing the bowl down on the table, Hartwin started ladling some into the dishes already set. Ellery grumbled under his breath. He couldn't ask me about Luther's treatment of me in front of the elite; he knew I wouldn't be honest if I was being mistreated in front of them.

"The Prince wants you to report to him when you finish up here." Hartwin didn't look up, but I caught the tightness in his cheeks that indicated fighting a smile. "You can tell him he needs to sleep on the lounge tonight while you're there."

Ellery packed up his supplies while Hartwin sat at his bowl without waiting and started eating. "I'll come back and check on you in the morning, Princess." He helped me stand before leaving the room.

"Thank you, Medic Ellery." Once the door closed behind him, Hartwin came to my side, guiding me to the table to eat. Since I still felt relatively weak, I didn't argue. For once, I felt as frail as I looked.

"I think Luther is even more in awe of you now than he's ever been." When I didn't look up, Hartwin reached across the table and put his hand over mine. "You saved his life, Zira. We are all in awe of you."

Meeting his eyes, there was too much floating in them. Withdrawing my hand from his, I placed it in my lap. "If he dies, the Barbarian gets me. I was telling the truth in there. I'll take death over letting that savage lay a finger on me ever again."

Picking up my spoon, I started eating. Hartwin watched me for a few minutes quietly. When the door opened, he returned to eating his lunch.

Padget entered with more garment bags over her arm and another bag from Chalvey's over her other.

"Princess, Master Fabrice has sent over some more dresses in the style you prefer, and I collected the personal items on your usual order for you." Walking through the room, Padget didn't even spare us a sideways glance. "I'll just put everything away for you."

Following Padget, Jervaise brought småfranska and a carafe of apelsinjuice. "Sorry about the delay; I got held up," he excused himself way too enthusiastically.

"The Princess should come first."

"Well, I'm sure Prince Saboa does his best to achieve that, but even the best of us lose control, Hartwin," Jervaise replied, full of mirth.

Body heating before I could help it, I stopped eating and watched Jervaise with curiosity as he poured us all drinks. Glancing at Hartwin, I watched how he smirked and shook his head. Nudging Hartwin's leg under the table, when his eyes flicked up, I tilted my head towards Jervaise questioningly. Raised his eyebrows, Hartwin simply returned to eating his stew.

Breaking off a piece of bread to hide my amusement, I was glad everyone didn't feel the need to be formal around me. My staff at the estate was always relaxed and open around me. It made it feel more like a family that way. Thinking about my home caused me to miss it desperately, and I dropped my spoon with instant heartache.

Jervaise and Hartwin both stopped to watch me.

"I'm sorry. I was just thinking of home."

Hartwin nodded. He knew how much I'd loved the estate. I'd chosen to live there full time while my parents only came out on weekends.

Coming back into the room, Padget stopped to assess my sudden change in mood. She went to leave without saying anything, but

Hartwin saw her. "Padg?" She stopped, blushing before he said anything. "I get it, but the princess isn't like us. Going without food for extended periods weakens her. If I find out you put him before her again, the Prince will hear of it. Understood?"

Padget bit her lip, looked at Jervaise before back to Hartwin, and bowed her head. "Of course, Elite Hartwin." Hartwin returned to his food. Padget left embarrassed. Jervaise said nothing, but the look Hartwin gave him indicated they would discuss it later.

"I wasn't about to die of emaciation, Hartwin. What harm was there in waiting a few more minutes for bread if they are in love?"

Jervaise nearly spat his food across the table. Hartwin glared at me. Surprisingly, it was Jervaise that chastised me. "Princess, Elite Hartwin is right. I was on duty, and so was Padget. What if someone attacked while I was off having a bit of fun?"

"Fun? That girl doesn't look at you as if you're a bit of fun, Jervaise."

"I'm an elite guard, Princess. She knows what we're about." He didn't need to say anymore. I'd already heard that speech.

'Elite guards don't fall in love, they don't take companions, and they don't have kids. We live to protect and serve.'

"The prince is an elite guard," I argued with more hostility than I intended.

"The prince is the prince. Even so, he sought permission from the King before taking his companion," Hartwin responded dryly. When I went to argue more, Hartwin cut me off. "End it, Princess! We are honor-bound. There is not a girl who comes to our bed naive of the fact that she will never be more than a way to let off steam."

Standing abruptly, I glared at him. "I doubt the validity of that statement greatly!" Storming into the bedroom, I slammed the doors shut behind me. Leaning back on the doors, I tried to bring my emotions under control.

"Is this still about Padg and me, or did she change the subject somewhere in the middle?" Jervaise asked Hartwin.

"She's not having the best of the times recently, Jervaise. Avalonians are highly emotional. She's just looking for someone to fight with."

At that moment, I hated Hartwin. Not only because he'd just dismissed my feelings as a temper tantrum, but because he was right. I wanted to yell, scream, and physically beat the crap out of something.

"What? Getting stabbed and killing a man wasn't enough of a fight for her?" Jervaise joked. "Maybe those Avalonians are just as badass as she looked today."

"Avalonian assassins are the most highly paid and sought after for a reason, Jervaise. Look how close that one got to the prince this morning."

"Which begs another question? How the blackness did she know he was there, and we didn't?"

"That's an excellent question, Jervaise," Luther's voice was clear with annoyance in the other room.

Groaning, I slipped down the door to the floor. When the door flew open behind me, I fell back to lie on the floor. Grimacing at the pain when my shoulder hit, I absorbed it and opened my eyes to see Luther peering down at me with frustration.

"What the blackness were you doing leaning against the door?"

Lifting my arm wearily, I pointed to the bed. "Those last few meters seemed more like light-years."

Shaking his head, Luther lifted me into his arms and set me down on the sofa gently before moving to the table to help himself to food. "Tell me."

"There are some who can bend light around them and thus seem invisible. When I realized one was missing, I started feeling around for disturbances in the air currents. I should have sensed him before he got that close, but Tudal distracted me." Annoyed with myself, I hung my head in shame.

"He was baiting your anger to try and draw you nearer to him, so they could snatch you when the assassin struck." Luther took out a syringe and held it up for me to see. "One of the mercenaries carried this tranquilizer." He placed it on the table. "I knew they were drawing you out, but I couldn't see how they expected to snatch you. I had no idea your people could turn invisible."

"It's a rare talent," I shrugged. "Only one percent of the population is born with the glyph."

"And you have what? A counter-glyph?" Jervaise asked, his eyebrows drawing close together.

Slouching on the sofa, I cuddled in against the armrest. "If royalty is going to be assassinated, it will be by an assassin who can bend light. We're trained from the time we can walk to feel air currents for movement and to look for shadows."

"Shadows?" Hartwin asked.

"Yes, outside in the sun, they still cast a shadow. A well-trained assassin will avoid the path that would leave one, hence the need to feel the air currents. I almost do it as second nature now. The problem today was that I was distracted, and everyone was moving. It wasn't until everyone stopped that I could feel what was out of place. I barely made it in time."

"You could have just yelled instead of taking the hit," Luther chastised, but there was admiration in his tone.

"By the time the message sunk in, you'd have been dead. I knew I had speed on my side."

"The element of surprise helped too," Luther growled. I had the decency to look bashful. "Commander Stark didn't know what hit him. I turned to his response only to see you blurring at me. I truly didn't expect you to come barrelling into me with such force behind you that you put me on my ass in my own throne. You were gone again so quickly that by the time I'd realized what had happened, you were stabbing a man in the throat."

"You could have at least let us question him," Jervaise grumbled.

"She knew him," Hartwin scowled. "I got to her side just as she dropped on him. She recognized him."

All three men sat watching me, waiting for an explanation. Clearing my throat, I blinked away tears. "He was the royal envoy that slit my brother's throat in front of me then dragged me to the feet of the Barbarian. His name was Zodack. I don't think I could ever forget his face."

Luther considered the food in the bowl before him for a moment before speaking just loud enough for me to hear across the room. "I'd never understood why your parents sought my throne for you. I assumed they figured you possessed the peoples' support, and if you held your own throne, then rulers would leave you be. But, today... today I saw the queen they knew was in you." Luther didn't look at me, just spooned a mouthful of lunch into his mouth.

"She was pretty scary in there," Jervaise agreed. "I mean that speed thing was scary enough, but the way she smiled at the ambassador as she stabbed the bastard." Jervaise shivered. "It was a blackness of a turn-on."

Surprised to hear that said out loud, let alone about me, I looked at Jervaise wide-eyed. Luther smacked him across the back of his head. "Put my companion and your erection in the same sentence again, and I will demote you faster than she can kill an invisible assassin."

"Yes, Prince Saboa." Jervaise was suddenly deadly serious. "I apologize for my response." I don't think he meant the verbal one. "But, if you even try to deny you were straining your pants in there, I will call foul."

Luther actually laughed, smacking Jervaise on the shoulder hard enough to make him rock in his chair. Apparently, putting the prince's erection and his companion in the same sentence was not a faux pas.

"How the blackness did you ever survive the five-year celibacy to become a royal guard, let alone the testing for elite?" Hartwin grumbled.

Jervaise feigned a wretched appearance. "Those five years were torture. After that, I was able to survive anything."

Chapter Nine

Three days of companionship, and we'd already managed the routine of dinner, bath, and within a short time of me climbing into bed, Saboa joining me. Tonight I stood by the bed looking at the city lights for over an hour. He still didn't come to say goodnight.

Sighing, I frowned at the empty bed. Of all the nights Luther could have left me alone, he chose the night I was feeling the most vulnerable. Right now, I welcomed his arms wrapping around me. Of course, I knew there would be fallout from today and that he was probably dealing with it. Sending an assassin into the throne room under the guise of an ambassador's visit couldn't be ignored. Still, I couldn't crawl into that bed alone.

Sealing my robe around me, I opened the bedroom doors. Elite Erhaird was sitting lazily on the sofa with a book in hand. "Something wrong, Princess?"

"Is the Prince nearby?"

"In his office, Princess."

Nodding, I moved to the door to the outer quarters. Erhaird kicked off the lounge, following me out. Of all the elite on my watch so far, he was the most relaxed and formal. He didn't try to engage me in conversation or speak inappropriately. He didn't discourage me from moving freely either; he would just follow wordlessly.

I'd worked out he was one of the elite's newest members within a short time by the way the senior elite mumbled about his not questioning my wandering the palats. Hence, why he'd been given the night shift.

In the main room, the other three elite on duty lazed around playing a game of Kort. They all looked up at my entry, raising their eyebrows to Erhaird. He shrugged and went to join them.

Making my way across to the Prince's office, I stopped hesitantly at the door. No one ever knocked entering our rooms, but what if he was on a call with a diplomat? By the stars, what if he had a woman in there with him? Our joining contract didn't say a word about fidelity. I'd just assumed it because that was the way of things in Avalonia. But Padget's existence hinted that may not be the Cyran way.

Anberon, the captain of Saboa's personal guard, read my hesitation. "He's alone, Princess, and currently not talking to anybody." When I looked over my shoulder, unsure if he meant I should walk away, Anberon pointed to a comms unit. "He has us filtering comms tonight. No line is lit up."

Nodding, I raised my hand to knock. Anberon coughed, drawing my attention. He wasn't looking at me any longer but shook his head slightly. His eyes flicked to me as I lowered my hand. Giving him a smile of thanks, I slid one side of the office door open.

Saboa sat in his office chair, reading a document in front of him. Glancing up at my entrance, he watched me slide the door shut behind me. "You should be asleep. It's been a long day." Putting down his stylus, he pushed back slightly from the desk, waiting to hear why I was interrupting him.

"I... I don't want to be alone."

Luther's eyebrows rose with surprise. "Medic Ellery told me you need to rest for a full day."

Spying the book on the corner of his desk, I put my hand on it. "Your men found the book?"

"Yes." He watched me pick it up and start flicking through it. "The part for female conception is rather short. The majority of it revolves around the man learning to control his input."

I smiled through my lashes at him. "You think you can learn to control what sex you produce?"

"It is worth a try, is it not?"

Moving to the window, I flicked through the pages on female conception. I recognized the symbol located at the very base of my natal chart, possibly the case for every female of my species. Half an hour later, I closed the book with a sigh, placing it back on the corner of Saboa's desk.

Looking up from the markup device where he'd returned his focus, Luther considered me. "Have you read it yet?" I asked, tapping the cover. He nodded, sitting back in the chair again. "Have you tried it? While we've been...?"

"Last night. I'm not sure if it worked, obviously. But it felt different. As if by trying to control the release, it takes some of the... intensity out of it."

"Shall we try it now?" I asked beneath my breath, looking sidelong at him.

Standing, Luther shook his head. "Ellery said..."

"He said not to get rough, Luther. Do Cyrans honestly not know how to be with a woman without ripping her clothes off and slamming her against the wall?"

Shrugging, Luther shook his head. Placing a hand on his chest, I pressed him back to rest on his desk. Leaning into him, I kissed his lips gently. "Then let me teach you how an Avalonian woman can love a man. Sit on the desk."

He did as I asked, watching with growing intensity as I touched the release on my robe, and it fell open in front. When Luther reached out to grab me, I caught his wrist. Taking his hand to my breast, I moved my hand over his to show how he should touch me slow and tenderly. Pressing my hand over his hardness, I stroked it slowly through the cloth. Luther moaned, his head lolling back slightly.

Touching the release on his uniform so that it gaped open, I exposed his heavily muscled chest to me. Lowering my mouth, I dropped tender kisses over his sun-hued flesh. My hand released the weave on his pants as I lifted my mouth to his, kissing him slow and deep.

When I climbed up onto the desk to straddle him, Luther slipped back further to make more room for me. His hand gripped behind my neck as I slid over him, kissing me so deeply it left me breathless.

When Luther released me, he rested back on his elbows, smiling up at me wondrously as I started to move over him. "Show me how to touch you," he instructed.

Running my hands up my thighs, over my abdomen to my breasts, I showed him how he should hold my breasts while he teased my nipples. Placing his hand to mine, I showed him all the places on my body that would delight me.

Luther wasn't lying that day in the throne room; he was an adept lover. With only the slightest guidance, he took over competently. His restraint was visible in his bunched muscles and the set of his jaw as he held back from taking control and taking what he wanted from me.

As things progressed to a higher intensity, his hands took small sojourns to increase my pleasure as we reached the crescendo together.

Swelling inside me, Luther gripped my hips hard. His eyes closed, breathing controlled as he staved off that last indulgence a little longer. Wondering what it would be like to bring a new life to being within me, my eyes drifted to the book on the desk. After all, it's what I was raised to do.

Warmth spread through my core as I reached the pinnacle of pleasure. Yanking my neck forward, Luther kissed me passionately.

The way he held my face to his as I moved over him unsteadily only made the fire of our desire burn hotter.

"Give me a son, Zira," he whispered to my lips. My eyes sprang open. The depth in Luther's eyes was hypnotizing. "Give us a son," he demanded more forcefully.

His pleasure exploded within me, taking mine with it. It was the most intense sensation I'd ever experienced. Lying on his desk, almost curled over Luther with my head on his chest, I focused on regaining my breath.

Anberon's voice made me jump when the comms buzzed to life. Luther cuddled me tighter. "Prince Saboa, King Saboa is in the queue for you." Realizing that Anberon kept the King on hold until they could hear that we were finished, I gasped.

Smiling as I pulled away from him, Luther righted his pants but didn't bother to close his shirt. "I'll talk to the king, then I'll come to bed, Zira." Sealing my robe, I smiled as he kissed me before putting his mouth to my ear. "The best part just now is that from the word-go, it was me you were with."

"You knew?"

"I knew it would take you time to warm to me, Zira. I didn't mind. You were doing what you needed to do to get things started. But even that first night, it was my face you were focused on by the end. That was enough."

"I wish you'd disobeyed my parents and courted me when I came of age, Luther. You would have been a fantastic first lover."

Kissing my forehead, Luther smiled. "I would have been your only lover." Smacking my bum playfully, he pushed me towards the door. "Go to bed and rest. When I get in there, we'll be doing this again."

Activating the comms before I could respond, an older version of Luther burst to life in front of the window. The king looked over his son's half-dressed state and scowled. "Have you been fighting?"

Luther laughed. "Quite the opposite, Father. I'm newly joined and have been practicing the method of procuring you a grandson."

"So, your companion has warmed to you despite the circumstances of your joining?"

Shifting his eyes to me, some of Luther's joy dropped away. "I wouldn't force..."

The king's digitalized three-dimensional image turned, observing me as I opened the office door. "I was referring to her saving your life today, Luther. She was raised a princess. I had no doubt she would perform her companion duties willingly, even if she wasn't enthusiastic about the joining. I can't say I blame you for partaking several times daily with a beauty like that to sate yourself with."

Dropping my face to hide my anger at his words, I curtsied. The king bowed his head. Sliding the door closed, all the elite eyes stayed intent on their game. I was under no illusion they hadn't heard at least half of what just took place. They were doing me the honor of not trying to make me self-conscious about it.

Relieved at their consideration, I moved lightly to the inner quarter's door. I doubted the king meant to be offensive. He was right about my upbringing, and while I understood what was expected of me, it didn't make it any easier to hear.

"Guess I'm out," Erhaird laughed, standing to resume his post.

The outer door opened. "Kvällsmat," one of the Praldian kitchen staff called.

The elite all stood to move to the large meals table while the staff set out the late-night banquet for the night shift. Making my way to the table, I pulled out a chair, causing everyone to stop and watch me.

"Princess?" Erhaird cleared his throat.

"I'm starving," I whined.

"I can bring some food in for us."

"Or, I can eat here with everyone like I would at home and not feel so alone." Erhaird looked to Anberon, so I looked between them. "Look, I need to eat. I'm perfectly safe here with you, and it stops me staring at the ceiling pining for my old bed and home. The Prince can collect me on his way to bed for round two."

Smirking, Anberon nodded. All the men returned to filling their plates. They gossiped quietly about councilmen or the high society ladies. I didn't want to be alone feeling vulnerable as I did. The elite were the perfect distraction.

By the time Saboa emerged from his office, I was curled up on the lounge watching the elite play Kort. I was trying to understand the game, but without seeing their hands, I was only getting a general gist.

Tilting his head in curiosity about my presence among the men, Luther said nothing as he took the empty seat next to me. Without asking, he was dealt in on the next hand. Snuggling into his side, I watched him play. By the second hand, he was tapping select panels in his hand as relevant tickets were tabled, so I could understand what the best to play was.

"How did the King react?" Anberon finally asked as he dealt the third hand.

"He is declaring war. I'm to return to Cyra tomorrow to discuss strategies and make plans. I'll be gone three days at least. Let my guard know at shift change. We'll disembark from the airfield after breakfast."

"And the Princess?"

"Will be remaining on Praldia, Erhaird. It's safer than putting her in unfamiliar territory. The barbarian knew we were joined before the word even reached the Metasystem. I'm sure we have a spy in our midst. Taking her somewhere there is a higher population of Avalonians would be like dropping her at the door to the Avalonian throne room."

Cyra was one of the central planets. Therefore, it was subjected to high populations of mercenaries and traders from the surrounding systems. Automatically, I shivered.

Pulling me into his lap, Luther cupped my face in his large hands. "You will be safe here, Zira. Even if they are suicidal enough to attack, you will have your elite and two thousand royal guards here to protect you." When his lips touched mine, I closed my eyes. "I think it's time for bed." Rising, Luther dropped my feet to the ground, and we walked hand in hand.

Erhaird and Anberon stood simultaneously, following us into the inner quarters. Once we were closed away in the bedroom, Saboa practiced touching me how I'd taught him. When we reached climax, we both concentrated on the method of conception.

Chapter Ten

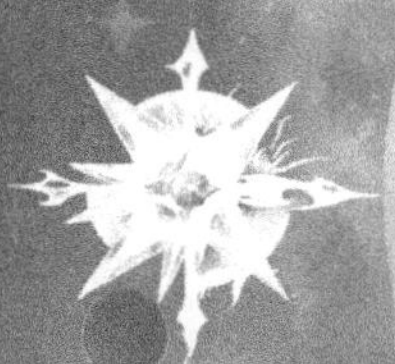

Luther woke me by nuzzling my neck. "Wake up, Zira. We only have a short time until I have to leave."

When I mumbled something unintelligible, he chuckled. "This morning, let's forget about heirs and just enjoy each other."

Moaning agreement into the pillow, I didn't move from my tummy. A moment later, I was wide awake, moaning in a different key. It ended all too soon. Eating breakfast in the sitting room, our two in quarter elites for the morning, Hartwin and Kylar, sat with us. "Hartwin, I want you to swap shifts with Erhaird during my absence."

Hartwin looked from me to Luther. "Did he step out of line last night? I wouldn't think you would have an issue with the Princess having a bite to eat with the elite while she waited for you?"

Luther shook his head. "No, but he's not a close friend, and I want someone I can trust with the Princess in my absence." When Hartwin tilted his head and furrowed his forehead, Luther sighed. "Kylar, go get me a progress report on our departure. Make sure everyone understands what we are doing."

Leaving his food without a word, Kylar closed the door behind him, aware that the Prince wanted privacy. "Hart, I trust you with her. I want you here of a night in case she needs someone to hold her while she sleeps."

"No," Hartwin answered without even considering. "If anyone found me in your bed with her, it would start some pretty nasty rumors, Luth. I don't want that. You don't need that. With her parents recently executed for treason, Zira doesn't deserve that."

"So, don't use the bed," Luther replied calmly. "Let her cuddle up to you on the couch. Once she's asleep, put her to bed. Blackness! Sit out and play Kort with the elite all night and let her fall asleep next to you, so there isn't any hint of secrecy about it. Just make sure she sleeps and that she feels safe."

Kylar returned to the table. "Twenty minutes, Prince Saboa. Everyone is ready."

"In that case, Elite Hartwin, Elite Kylar. I'd like that twenty minutes privately with my companion."

Both the elite rose and left the room. Laughing, Luther dragged me to the sofa with him. It was a torrid encounter that left me breathless beneath him. "Luther, what if they still attack you? You have to coast past Avalonia to reach Cyra."

"They won't."

"Don't get arrogant, Luther. Arrogance is the first fatal step to the downfall of power."

"Zira, the ship is a decoy. Once on board, we will teleport to my father's palats before it even takes off. I will never be in any danger, but it's nice you care."

"Luther, you're all I have standing between me and being used as an incubator by that barbarian. Of course, I'm going to care what happens to you."

Leaning down, Luther kissed me. "I'll be home in three days. Don't leave the palats while I'm gone." Kissing me again, Luther straightened his dress uniform and left.

We walked hand in hand until we met with Luther's entire contingent of personal guards in the ground-level entryway. Kissing my forehead, Luther moved away from me to step in amongst his guard. My guard closed around me; I blinked, and the lobby was empty.

"I want to watch them leave," I informed Jervaise.

Bowing his head, Jervaise led me to the viewing deck that overlooked the airfield. While the sun had not yet breached the horizon, Luther and his elite guard moved from the airfield teleport channels to the waiting ship, too far away to see detail.

"They will do a long-range teleport," Jervaise explained. "Then the ship will take off. It is going to Cyra, but the ship will return with supplies for us Cyrans from home."

"Why do the decoy at all?" I asked quietly as the last of the guard disappeared from view in the morning's greyness.

"No one is aware we have long-range teleport technology. Everyone thinks we are restrained within planets, and we like them to believe that. It gives us a certain edge when it comes to warfare, Princess." The ship powered up. "They should be en route by now."

"How long does a long-range teleport take?" I asked, curious since we could teleport across the planet in less than a minute.

"Several minutes."

The ship sprung into the air, ready to depart. A loud rumbling reached our ears. Never having heard that noise before, I frowned. "Is that normal?"

As a loud explosion roared through the sky, Jervaise threw his body at me. We were too far away to be in danger from the blast, but Jervaise protected me on instinct. Turning my head to suck in the air that was forced from my lungs, I could just see the enormous bright blue fireball in the distance.

"Jervaise?" I screeched in panic. What if they hadn't teleported yet? What if my companion was just murdered? A loud crash sounded as the burning ship crashed back to the tarmac.

"Get her inside and in quarters now," Jervaise instructed as he rolled away from me. Hands were pulling me to my feet as Jervaise regained his.

There was a momentary pause amongst the guard. "The channels are shut down!" The guard holding me bellowed angrily.

Cursing, Jervaise pulled his comms unit free. "I want the full squad to intersect the Princess on her way back from the viewing deck. There was another attempt on the Prince's life, and the palats has gone into lockdown."

"On our way," another voice responded with a burst of activity in the background.

A hand grabbed my elbow, moving me off the viewing deck to the inner sanctum of the palats. Over my shoulder, I caught a glimpse of emergency ships zipping towards the burning inferno. Jervaise was at my side, and I was being rushed towards the inner ring corridor.

There was a beep in Jervaise's comms unit, and he pulled it out to see what came through. "They've arrived safely, Princess," he whispered in my ear. Relieved, I relaxed in his grip. "Not yet, Princess. We need you safe in quarters before we relax."

"But I'm safe in the palats..." But then it occurred to me. "No one knew he was leaving. It was decided late last night. No one else was told until this morning, and even then, it was only the elite who were informed." Stopping in my tracks, I stared at Jervaise wide-eyed.

"No, Princess, don't even think it. None of the elite would ever betray the prince. It has to have been a staff member who overheard." Giving my elbow a slight tug, Jervaise took one step and stopped.

"Jervaise?" Erhaird inquired as Jervaise cursed.

"We have a traitor in the prince's staff, in his residence. We need to cease all staff activity 'til we find our leak."

"Jervaise!" his comms burst to life with Hartwin's voice.

"Here."

"There's been some commotion in the ring, and the corridor is blocked. We can't get through, so we have to come around the ring the long way." With the palats in lockdown, the central courtyard was inaccessible.

"Should we move to meet you?" Jervaise looked back the way we'd come.

"No, it's a trap for sure. Move to the area in front of the throne room and stay put. We'll come to you. You know what to do if someone else gets there first."

"Got it." Shoving his comms unit away, Jervaise escorted me forward the last few meters to the throne room alcove. The other elite were putting earpieces in their ears and releasing the locks on their weapons. Inserting an earpiece as he tugged me towards the wall, Jervaise put my back to it. "How much attention did you pay to the layout of the throne room, Princess?"

Closing my eyes, I imagined the room. "There are fifty windows, and the fire exits are two windows located halfway down each side and the main window at the far end. The room is..."

"That is great," Jervaise cut in. "If anything happens and we get separated, you run for that back exit and get out of the palats. Cross through the courtyard behind the royal guard's compound and find their fire exit. The entry code is the year of settlement. Do you know it?" I nodded. "Good. Get inside, find a hide, and stay there 'til we come to find you." Turning his back on me, Jervaise and the other five elite formed a semi-circle around me.

"A merc ship is lapping the palats. They're making a grab for her again," Elite Utz growled.

"This is too well-organized for this short notice. They'd already planned this and were just waiting for an opportunity to present itself," Jervaise grumbled.

The ice floor was crackling to the right with the sound of several footsteps at a run. "Hartwin," I near sighed in relief.

Turning his ear to the sound, Jervaise shook his head. "Wrong direction." He touched his earpiece. "We've got incoming from the compound direction, sounds to be ten bipedal." Not all mercs walked on two legs. "Have any of the guard got through?"

Because they'd switched to earpieces, I didn't get to hear the response. But by Jervaise's reaction, it wasn't positive. "Blackness.

The others have hit the trap. Whoever this is isn't our backup. Assume hostile."

The five men before me fanned out across the corridor facing the oncoming footsteps. Their heights and build formed a high wall which stopped me from seeing what was coming. "By the darkness of a black hole," Jervaise cursed. He turned to me quickly. "Go, now. Do what I told you."

In the gap he'd created, I saw what was coming at us. There were four Avalonian mercenaries, two of the short, burly Meta mercenaries well known for their brutality, and two quigs. Quigs were a tripedal race that was barely civilized, but enough to take paid work that involved violence of any sort. My eyes bulged. Hesitating, I started shaking my head; they weren't who you'd hire for a kidnap.

"Run, Princess!" Jervaise ordered. Shoving me into the throne room, Jervaise pulled the door shut.

Turning to assess the empty throne room, fear roared through me. Cyrans were the best soldiers in our galaxy. They couldn't protect me and fight, so they were doing the smart thing and getting me away from the action.

Locating the fire exit on the far wall, I ran like darkness for it. Considering my speed, I crossed the length of the throne room before the first roars of the fighting broke out in the ring. Reaching the main window quickly, I pushed on the emergency exit. An alarm pealed through the palats as I threw the window open and flung myself out into the summer heat of Praldia.

Halfway across the courtyard to the royal guard's compound, the merc ship flew down low above me. Looking over my shoulder, I spied three Avalonians landing only a few meters behind me. While I was still running toward the compound, I knew I wouldn't have time to key in the code to get in with the men not far behind me.

Changing direction, I kept running for the prince's residence. There was a pool between the first guard compound and Luther's building. If I got there, I could disperse in the water, and no one would be able to find me or take me. As I rounded the guard compound's furthest wall, two Meta's dropped from the merc ship in front of me. There was nowhere to run but away from the palats.

Angling for the ocean, I bolted for the edge of the cliff. Both guard compounds' back door burst open, and royal guards sprung out at a chase to get to the men who were chasing me. Slowing when I neared the edge of the bluff, I looked overhead as the merc ship swung low behind me. A hand grabbed my shoulder, and I reacted instinctively.

The symbol for air flash-burned on my spine at the same time the one for sharpness came alive. My air ribbons whipped out from wrists, but this time they were sharp razor-wire. They flicked up, the Avalonian screamed as his hand separated from his arm.

Reaching the cliff edge, I looked back just as another Avalonian sprung from the merc ship a few meters from me. Flicking out my ribbons, I seized him around the throat. He countered using a fire sash to repel my ribbon before it grabbed his neck, turning himself into a living fireball. The ship settled just above me. Turning back to the cliff edge, I ran the last few meters and dove, plummeting to the raging ocean below.

A mechanical roar sounded as the ship dived after me. Blocking out everything, I focused on speeding towards the surface of the ocean. Concentrating, I activated the water symbol on my natal chart. Just as I was about to hit, I released my physical hold so that I was on the edge of dissipation to prevent injury.

Diving beneath the waves, I sank to the bottom before completing the liquefaction. Two bodies disturbed the water around me. Avalonians who followed me over the cliff or who dropped from the ship. They wouldn't find me. There was no physical body to find.

Chapter Eleven

The sun was setting, and everything was quiet again when I reached the beach several kilometers north of the castle. The current dragged my molecules north past the cliff, but I resisted being pulled out to sea. Only when things were peaceful did I rematerialize and swim to the beach. Naked, having lost my clothes when I dissipated, I popped my eyes above water and assessed the forest opposite the beach.

After going the day without food and staying out of my body for so long, I was exhausted. The longest I'd ever dissipated before was thirty minutes. With the sunset, I guessed it had been nearly six to seven hours this time. Avalonians were only built for short bursts of energy output because they needed to refuel often.

There was a Cyran royal guard stationed a few hundred meters up the beach. As I listened, I could make out a few more in the forest not far away. There were always patrols through the woods, but I'd never seen one standing openly on the beach.

Standing up, I started stumbling towards dry land, the waves helping to propel me forward. The guard spotted me and was running towards me in an instant. His hand pressed his comms unit in his ear as he ran. "I've got the princess."

Tapping his uniform clasp as he neared, allowing his shirt to swing open, he pulled it off and wrapped it around me. Slipping my arms through the sleeves, he pressed the clasp to close it. Cyrans were so tall that the shirt was huge on me, almost like a loose short dress, reaching my knees.

"Thank you," I rasped. Barely able to stay upright, I leaned into the guard, and he supported part of my weight with his arm around my back. Once we were entirely on dry land, he closed his eyes in concentration, and the teleportation channels closed around us.

A breath later, we were in the entryway to the Prince's residence. Hartwin was in front of me, scooping me into his arms before I could take a step. Cuddling into his shoulder, I whimpered a little as he carried me to the inner quarters. Medic Ellery was there waiting.

Taking me straight into the bedroom, Hartwin laid me down on the bed. "Make it quick, Ellery. When I contact the Prince to let him know we have found her alive, I want to be able to tell him she is safe and healthy."

"I'm fine," I moaned. "Just exhausted. I need food and sleep. Though, not necessarily in that order."

Ellery placed a monitor over my eyes as they started to close before he started checking my limbs. "The princess seems intact. The monitor shows fairly normal vitals, just a few abnormalities that could be related to exhaustion and shock. I think she is a bit traumatized and is fatigued like she said, Hartwin. You can tell Prince Saboa the princess is safe and healthy."

Releasing a sigh of relief, Hartwin left the room, shutting the bedroom door. "I need to do a full check-up on you tomorrow, Princess. The past two days have put you in danger twice. While I'm not an expert in Avalonian health, I know enough to know some of these observations are not within the norm."

The comms came to life in the other room. "Well?"

"We've found her. Zira emerged from the water onto Norr beach only twenty minutes ago. Exhausted but unharmed. Royal guard Sampson found her, covered her, and brought her straight to the residence."

"Did Zira say anything about what happened?"

"All she has said is that she is hungry and tired."

"Get her fed, then find out what happened before she sleeps. I want a report within the hour." The comms buzz switched off.

Hartwin slid the door open. "Food is on the way, Princess. I need you to stay awake long enough to eat."

Removing his monitor, Ellery rose to leave. "I'll come back in an hour to check on her, but I think Princess Zira will be fine."

Waiting until the medic left to sit beside me on the bed, Hartwin took my hand in his. "By the stars, Zira, you scared the skit out of us. We were not sure if you were dead or if they had gotten you. What the blackness happened out there? Start from where Jervaise locked you in the throne room."

Half asleep, I told Hartwin everything. Where I ran, the merc ship, the Avalonian's, the royal guards, and why I jumped from the cliff.

"I saw you go over. I must have been maybe one hundred meters away when you took that merc's handoff. Then you ran and jumped off the cliff. By the time I got to the edge, the Merc ship was hovering above the water. A few minutes later, it was gone, and there was no sign of you. One of the guards found your dress on the rocks about an hour later, and we were hoping you slipped out of it to swim faster." Watching me, Hartwin touched my cheek tenderly.

"Luther told me you vanished in the bath yesterday. He said I could not tell anyone, but you may have pulled the same trick on them. We searched for hours on foot, guards swimming down to find any trace of you, ships searching until after lunchtime. At that point, I figured you may have found a hidey-hole and were not coming out while you could hear ships or anything in case it was not us. So, I pulled the search team back to the coastline and doubled the forest patrol just in case you already made it to shore. I was just about to admit to myself they got you when Sampson announced that he found you."

"What happened, Hart? How'd they get in the palats?"

Shoulder's tensing, Hartwin growled. "Someone left a courtyard door blocked open. It was probably the same person who set the fire in the alcove outside the Royal guard compound to prevent us from reaching you. The Merc ship must have dropped their first team off when the explosion happened at the airfield. There were probably fifty in the palats fighting the royal guard, plus the eight that attacked your guard.

"When the prince's ship exploded, we automatically locked down the public channels. That meant we were locked into the ring, and we couldn't cut across the center of the palats to reach you in time. It was a well-planned attack, Zira. They nearly got you. They obviously had not heard about you being able to do that ribbon thing. But you can bet your life they will all know about it now."

"There is a traitor in the residence, Hart."

Bowing his head, Hartwin blew out a long breath. "I know." He met my eyes. "Jervaise told me what you said. I can promise you the traitor is not an elite, Zira. You are safe with us if no one else. All staff is forbidden to come to the fourth floor for the time being, and we have the royal guard re-vetting every single employee."

Elite Chas stuck his head in. "Hartwin, the food is here. Did you want me to bring it in so the princess doesn't have to walk?" Elite Chas's dialect intrigued me. It was a mish-mash of Cyran and Avalonian like he was exposed to both as a young child.

Giving Chas a quick nod, Hartwin stood and put his hands under my shoulders, dragging me up to sitting. When I hissed at him, Hartwin leaned me forward slightly to peer down the back of the shirt and check my wound from yesterday. "I will get Ellery to recheck that when he comes back. You may have reopened it during the fighting."

Placing a tray of food next to me on the bed, Chas left again.

Hartwin tucked my hair back from my face. "Eat, then rest. I will be right outside that door all night if you need me."

"Luther?"

"He is safe but furious. The King is enraged by such a brazen attack. We are going to war. Luther will stay in Cyra 'til they have their strategy set. The Barbarian is going to wish he just forgot your existence."

"I don't want this, Hartwin. I don't want my people to die protecting a king they don't even want."

Hartwin cocked his head to the side. "Zira, this war will be over before your people even know their country has been invaded. Eat, rest. When you are back to health, we will talk more."

As Hartwin left, I picked up one of the sandwiches on the plate and started chewing. Managing five bites, I slumped down beneath the covers and fell asleep.

Chapter Twelve

When my eyes opened next, the room was full of light. Lifting my head, I was a little dazed when I saw the bedroom doors wide open. "Hartwin," I murmured.

Erhaird jumped up from the couch and was at the door quickly. "Princess. Hartwin is sleeping. Let me just call the medic; he has been waiting for you to wake. Already been back three times to check on you." Erhaird pulled his comms from his pocket and hit a button. "Ellery, the princess is awake."

Dropping my head to the pillow, I groaned. "I slept too long. Someone should have woken me." I felt lousy and absolutely devoid of even enough energy to sit up in bed.

"We tried to wake you for breakfast, Princess, but you barely made semi-consciousness. You woke enough for a few sips of whatever concoction the medic gave you, then you were gone again."

Ellery came into the room with a frown. He looked back at Erhaird. "Get me a glass, Erhaird." Erhaird walked to the table and came forward to hand the medic the glass. I watched as he took a cooling flask from his bag, pouring a thumb of white liquid into the glass. Kneeling beside the bed, Ellery helped lift my head and put the glass to my lips. "It will help give you your energy back faster than a mouthful of food will. What is in this glass is the equivalent of a meal."

Drinking the liquid down, I smacked my lips and sighed. "Hälsodryck, I recognize it. We always keep some on hand in our houses in case we need a boost."

"I know; it is where we got it from," Ellery revealed. "When the men went to your house to seize the papers they needed for your joining, your senior attendant, Nyla, insisted they take this flask. She said you would need it if you got with child because there is no way you could ever eat enough to sustain you both."

Ellery poured another measure and put it to my lips. "I contacted Nyla after the single dose at breakfast was not enough to rouse you. She informed me that without the addition of food, it would be near useless. She suggests I double up doses for the rest of the day."

Drinking the second glass, I already started to feel a little less limp. "When women are pregnant in my world, they drink a serving of hälsodryck after every meal. It contains all the nutrients and minerals a woman with a child needs and gives the mother enough energy for them both. Nyla started producing it for the native women to drink while with child. It's seen a massive drop in missfall and dödfödda just in the five years of circulation."

Ellery's eyes lit up. "I know. I have been watching the administration and outcomes of it closely over the years. I also know that you supplemented the production cost and paid Attendant Nyla double her wage to continue the production. I believe you hired a second attendant to complete the mundane household duties so that Nyla could concentrate solely on the production of hälsodryck." He watched me for a second. "Feeling any better?"

"A little. Give me a third hit, and I might be able to manage a bath in the next hour and try some real food."

Ellery nodded, pouring a third glass and helping me drink it. This time I could lift my own head, so I was sure the third drink would give me enough energy to actually bathe and eat something solid.

When I'd finished, Ellery put the flask on the ledge beside the bed and pulled out his sats monitor. Lying back, I let him place it over my eyes.

"There is not much of an improvement, but I think you are over the shock. Your body temp is back to normal at least." He removed the monitor. "After you have your bath, I will look at your shoulder again and make sure it is healing correctly. Then I think we should have a talk."

"Talk?"

"I have never cared for an Avalonian, Princess. What I am taking as norms right now I am getting from a cyberbase of statistics for Medics. I need to know more of your history to establish your norms."

"Oh." I considered for a moment. "Have Nyla come to talk to you. She can bring my records from birth."

Ellery looked surprised. "She has your medical records?"

"Yes, Medic Ellery. Before we fled Avalonia, Nyla was the throne medic appointed to the heir and the royal womb. That is why she received double the normal wage of an attendant."

"You trust her?" Ellery asked, suddenly cautious.

"Medic Ellery, Nyla's position is to keep me alive, get me with child, and see that child become the next ruler of Avalonia. I trust her with my life. At least until I've produced another heir and royal womb. After that, my life is worthless, and my existence is forgotten."

"That is what happened to your mother?"

"That's what happens to all of our mothers, Medic Ellery. The royal womb is treated as an incubator. My brother was always Heir Zimri while I was always the royal womb. We are never referred to by name. We are valuable only until the heirs are born, and then our people couldn't care less about us. We hold no rank, and the title of Princess only lasts until the next is born. We become commoners who receive a good supplementary income from the throne for services rendered."

The last came out with such spite that Ellery actually sat back away from me. "You hate who you are?"

"No, I loathe what my people make me. If the royal succession so heavily relies on the royal womb, why does our throne not pass from mother to daughter? Why do the males still get to rule, and the females get treated as incubators for the next generation? I actually have the Barbarian to thank for that clarity. I was raised to believe that's all I was suitable for.

"It wasn't until I escaped here and experienced the value the Praldians and Cyrans give their royalty that I realized just how messed up the Avalonian line of succession is. My parents' mistake wasn't in seeking to seat me as the queen. It was that they vied for the wrong throne."

Ellery sat quietly for several minutes after I'd scowled the last of my annoyance. Eventually, he eyed the metal flask. "Out of curiosity, Princess, is there some ingredient in hälsodryck that may lower a person's inhibitions if ingested in large quantities?" I raised a brow at the medic. "It is just, I would never have picked you to be so fiery, Princess. You have always seemed so passive."

At this, I laughed. "You've obviously never been in the throne room during one of my showdowns with the prince about funding?"

Ellery smiled. "No, Princess, I have not. Though, now that I have seen this more passionate side of you, I dare say I have missed some quality entertainment."

"Apparently. All these years, it turns out the prince was just as entertained by my passionate petitions." Closing my eyes, I smiled at the memory of some of my less ladylike phrases. When I opened them again, Ellery was gone, and the sun was setting.

"I HOPE you can understand how hard it was for us to make this decision, Princess Zira. It is in no way a negative reflection on you, but we don't believe we can rely on your impartiality with the way things currently stand."

Standing in Luther's office, I faced the Ambassador's digital image for the Praldian Natives as he tried very hard not to offend me. "Of course, Ambassador Twyford. How can I represent an impartial view when my companion and legal guardian is the very man you need me to stand against? I hold no grudge and will still endeavor to do the work I was doing before my new status. If you need anything, please just ask. I no longer have to make an appointment to gain the Prince's ear."

Twyford smiled, but I didn't join in. It had been four days since Luther left for Cyra and the most recent assassination-abduction attempt took place. I'd spoken to Luther once in that time. It wasn't an intimate conversation between lovers. It was a Prince and a guardian putting a child in its place. He hadn't been happy to learn of Nyla's role. The suggestion she be allowed to visit me at the palace only infuriated him.

Twyford bowed his head. "I am sorry, Princess. The vote was not unanimous, and I personally feel you have done so much for my people that there is no way you would give up fighting for us so easily. It was you who initiated the Praldian Native's Council in the first place." Twyford pursed his lips, contemplating saying more, and decided to risk it. "I have heard the rumors of how your joining came to be, Princess. That, coupled with your homeland's attacks, must be very... distressing for you. Please know, if there were aught we could do, we would."

"Thank you, Ambassador. I do hope things settle down again soon, and I can return to helping the people of this world."

Twyford bowed his head even deeper in a sign of great respect. "As do I, Princess. May the stars keep you and the Prince safe for many eons to come."

Bowing my head, I disconnected the call and collapsed into Luther's office chair with a sigh. It was the final nail in the coffin of my charity work. Now anything I took part in or worked towards would be classed as the throne's interest. I would be seen as Luther's pawn, at least, until I became a legal adult. That was clearly indicated by the Ambassador—that when the Prince was only my companion and no longer my guardian, he'd like to readdress my involvement in the Native community.

"Princess?" Erhaird prompted gently from the office door. He'd heard it all.

"I need to go for a walk."

Erhaird opened the office door as he pulled out his comms to alert my guards that we would be leaving quarters. Jervaise joined us in the lounge room, following with just a raised brow at Erhaird, who merely frowned and shook his head. It wasn't the first call I'd taken this week that politely dumped me as a spokesperson.

"Usually, people would be clamoring to have their princess as a spokesperson, not the other way around," Jervaise grumbled.

We took the lift to the ground floor, both guards catching my elbows to steady me after the drop - it was still unnerving. The rest of my guard on shift joined us quietly as we exited the Prince's residence to start walking the ring.

Since the last attack, I wasn't allowed outside, so walking the ring became my daily exercise. It was a fair walk due to the size of the palats, over nine kilometers, and it allowed me some semblance of freedom.

"Good day, Princess," Councilman Berchard greeted. He was waiting by the front of the compound that he lived in during the week.

"Councilman." Giving a short curtsey as polite behavior dictated, I continued walking to indicate I wasn't in the mood to converse today. We spoke for over an hour yesterday about the state of living conditions on Gruvdrift, one of the central mining continents. When it became clear that our opinions differed on acceptable habitation for those who effectively made Praldia wealthy, we talked about his estate instead. Which was located next door to mine.

Berchard recognized my anti-social mood today and merely stepped aside to let us pass. "I swear he has started lurking in the alcove of his compound just to engage you each day, Princess," Jervaise murmured quietly once out of earshot.

"Great," I sighed, "because we have so much in common."

Jervaise chuckled beside me. "Well, you do share the prince's bed and, therefore, his ear. I'm sure Councilman Berchard is just trying to gain yours, and through you, the prince's."

"Maybe I should invite him to join us in bed when the prince returns then, so he understands how little talking occurs between the prince and me in the bedroom." The guards smirked.

As we approached the next compound's alcove, I noticed a shadow pacing. I restrained a laugh. "Berchard may not be the only lurker these days, but this one only pretends to be interested in talking to me."

All the guards focused ahead, giving sly smiles to each other as they took in the highly fashionable form of Councilman Nilson's eldest daughter, Ancelin. She was a pretty Praldian with the usual short height, blonde hair, and tanned skin appearance. She carried a curvaceous and heavy physique which the tight city clothes showed quite clearly. Ancelin was beautiful and strong. I admired that.

So did many of my Cyran guards. Back home, Cyran women were tall and built solid. The only real difference between Praldian women and Cyran was that the Praldians were half the height and predominantly some blonde shade.

To most Cyrans, I was not attractive due to my frail-looking physique. The prince fell for my fiery passion and willingness to stand up to him for what I believe. Years of personal admiration led to a physical one. To my guard, I looked breakable. Ancelin, however, looked like a fun time to be had.

"Princess Zira." Ancelin feigned surprise with a high soprano voice that made me hesitate in my next step.

"Ancelin, how lovely to see you... again."

It took me a moment to take in the slight change in her attire. The dress she wore was no longer the leg-binding fashion. Instead, Ancelin now wore a dress in the same style as my city clothes. Firm from bust to hip with a more flowing floor-length skirt. The only difference was that hers sported a split up each side that reached nearly to mid-thigh.

"That's a beautiful dress, Ancelin. Has there been a change in fashion?"

"Of course, Princess. Your style choice has affected designers planet-wide. Of course, Praldians are less conservative in our clothing, and as such" –she grabbed her skirt at the split, flashing us a heavy thigh— "we have made some adjustments to define our own styles."

I was grateful in that moment that the royal guard was trained to restrain their desires, or I think I would have been surrounded by a pack of panting dogs. "I like it." I smiled. Ancelin beamed and blushed so profusely I thought her head would explode, it turned so red. Her presence lightened my sour mood. "Would you care to walk with me to the throne room, Ancelin?"

You could have pushed my guard over with a feather. In the four days that I'd been walking the ring, I'd barely tolerated anyone's company and definitely did not invite anyone to walk with me. Ancelin's smile grew impossibly bigger. "I would love to, Princess."

Falling in beside me, Ancelin chatted animatedly about her upcoming adulthood. She told me her ideas for a party to surpass that of any other Praldian socialite's wisdom party. That's what reaching adulthood was called: gaining wisdom. I'd met enough adults to dispute the accurateness of that title, Ancelin being a little too giggly to convince me otherwise, either.

The public Channels in the courtyard activated, but I paid no heed. There were now twenty royal guards posted around the channels and intermittently throughout the ring to watch courtyard doors, all in pairs. The palats was still in lockdown, but staff still needed to come and go. It was basically from throne room to ballroom that was off-limits to anyone, not royal guard, elite, or me.

The first traitor was caught using the security feed. Luther was near incensed when Hartwin sent him the video of his half-sister Padget chocking open the courtyard door. She was locked away in her room, awaiting Luther's return to hear her reasoning for her betrayal. I was so lost in my sorrow over Padget's treason that I'd stopped listening to everything around me.

Jervaise grabbed my elbow, bringing me to a halt, returning me to my current surroundings. "... possibly use the ballroom here if everything has settled by then," Ancelin was saying.

Following Jervaise's gaze to the alcove of the throne room, there seemed to be some commotion.

"I tell you we come in peace to offer an alliance with your prince," an Avalonian accent rumbled ahead. My heart rate picked up as I watched two Avalonian men escorted into the alcove by royal guards with their weapons drawn.

My heart skipped a beat when I recognized my father as one of the men. Except, it wasn't my father, and the younger version of him standing next to him wasn't my brother. I didn't even realize I'd taken off at a run until Jervaise yelled behind me.

"Princess, stop!"

The Royal guard surrounding the Avalonian's tensed, bunching together to form a barrier between the intruders and me. "Move, now!" I directed tersely. They were trained to follow orders from their superiors. While the older ones hesitated, two new guards created an opening. With my speed, that's all I needed.

"No, stop!" Jervaise bellowed.

I was in the arms of both men before anyone could stop me. More yelling exploded through the room as the rest of my elite guard burst from the other side of the ring corridor.

"Princess, please!" Erhaird exclaimed

"Unhand her this instant or die," Hartwin's tired voice carried above the rest of the commotion. He was on night shift, so a call must have gone out when the Avalonians arrived.

The men removed themselves from me, stepping back with arms raised. Turning, I put myself between Hartwin and my family. "Elite Hartwin, this is my uncle Ravid and my cousin Vered. They are the last of my family, and you will not spill a drop of their blood, or I will spill yours!"

Hartwin almost took a step back with the venom in my tone. Gritting his jaw, he bowed his head shortly. "Princess, I am sorry, but we cannot be sure of their purpose here. If they want to stay alive and unharmed, they should leave immediately."

"No." My uncle stepped forward, touching my shoulder. "I came here to speak with Prince Saboa. I will not leave here until I have."

"The prince is not here, so your purpose is lost," Hartwin returned politely.

"My intelligence informs me the prince is preparing his return as we speak. It should be no longer than by lunch tomorrow. I will wait in the prison if need be." It was my turn to look shocked. Did my guard know Luther was returning and kept it from me?

"We have no prison," Jervaise answered this time.

My uncle looked stumped. "The Cyrans take no prisoners, Uncle. They kill traitors and murders, banish the rest. They believe it is a waste of resources to shelter and feed the uncivilized," I informed him quietly.

"But that is not the Praldian way," my uncle returned, sure. "They sentence their people to prison."

"That would be enslavement within the mines or as a lemming for whatever term is judged to be fair," I answered quietly again.

"Well, whatever. I won't leave until the prince has seen me."

"That is not your choice to make." Hartwin stepped forward, towering over us. "You will leave, and after the prince has returned, you can petition to be seen."

Hating this, I turned, touching my uncle's arm. "Go to my place. *She* would love to see you. Elite Hartwin can let you know when the prince returns."

"That is not your property to grant access to any longer," Hartwin reminded me. He was angry, possibly thinking I'd put myself at risk again.

Folding my shoulders back, I leveled him with my gaze. "Elite

Hartwin, my uncle has come here in peace and to offer aid. We will not treat him like an assassin nor banish him to the mines. If he cannot be a guest here, then he will be a guest of my house whether it belongs to me or not. I don't think what I propose is that unreasonable."

"You trust them?" Hartwin asked warily.

"More than I trust any person in this alcove."

The silence was thick as the crystal star walls. Everyone was watching Hartwin and me face-off, neither of us backing down. Eventually, Hartwin nodded then pointed to ten royal guards. "You will escort these men to the princess's *former* estate. Place them under house arrest there until the prince calls them forth."

The guards bowed their heads and went to escort my uncle and cousin out. My uncle took my arm, and the guards became more rigid, if that were possible.

"You've grown up even more beautiful than your mother, Zira. You are the rightful heir, and you have our allegiance." He bowed over my hand, kissing it the way he would have our king's. When he stepped back, Vered imitated his father then allowed the guard to lead them from the palace.

The royal guard filed back out to surround the public channels. Left standing in the alcove with twenty Elite and a terrified Ancelin, I struggled to speak. "Forgive me, Ancelin. I believe I'll return to residence now." My uncle and cousin just recognized me as their queen.

Ancelin curtsied, but I'd already turned, heading off towards the residence before she could offer any courteous farewell.

Chapter Thirteen

No one said a word to me. Jervaise and Erhaird took my elbow to accompany me up the lift to the top floor. Hartwin stood at my back. Once we reached quarters, he split from us to use Luther's office. No doubt calling Luther to tell him what just occurred.

Jervaise and Erhaird both followed me into the inner quarters but stopped in the sitting room when I entered the bedroom, slamming the doors in their faces. Stepping backward in an arc, my back hit the wall beside the door. That's when the panic washed over me.

"I should have told them to leave, to run. Luther will kill them just because they are Avalonian. I'll lose the last relatives I have." Slipping to the floor, my emotions broiled to the surface.

Hartwin threw the door open before slamming it shut again. "What the hell were you thinking? They could have killed you!"

The tears flowed faster as I shook my head. If there was one person in all the systems who would never harm me, it was Ravid. Hartwin was ready to yell some more but held his tongue. Dropping down in front of me, he gripped my upper arms, speaking quietly,

"Zira, we can't protect you if you keep putting yourself in harm's way."

"What do I have to live for, Hart?" I asked between sobs. "I've lost it all. My family, my freedom, my cause. If Luther kills Ravid and Vered, that will be everything gone." My voice croaked. "By the stars, I don't even have love anymore."

Hartwin's face fell as he shook his head. "You will learn to love Luther, Zira. You are already warming to him. I can see it in the way you say his name, the way you move closer to him when he touches you."

"But I will never love him like I loved you."

Closing his eyes, Hartwin sighed. "That was a long time ago, Zira."

"It was only last week for me, Hart. Did you expect me to just stop loving you because you didn't love me?"

"Yes." His grip grew harder on my arms. "That's exactly what you should have done. You knew, Zira, knew I was training to be elite, that it could never be that way between us."

"I know you loved me!" I spat. "You can deny it until the blackness swallows my soul, but I know what you desired, how you felt with me. You will never convince me that it was all a lie."

"I never said it was a lie, Zira. I wanted you, and, for that short time I had you, I never felt so alive. That's all it was, all it could ever be. What you wanted, companionship, children..." Hartwin shook his head. "By the exploding stars! I already knew that Luther wanted you. There was never any chance it was ever going to be more than two people taking pleasure from each other, Zira."

When I shook with my emotions, Hartwin grabbed my chin in his fingers. "Don't give up, Zira. You can find love with Luther. You can still fight for the people; fight for your people. You can create a new family."

"That last, I have no choice over, do I?" Hartwin stood stepping away from me, his face shut down and unreadable. "I hate you, Hart. I hate you because I can't stop loving you. Every day you walk through that door and remind me of the one thing I've ever wanted for myself, and I will never be allowed to have it."

"Zira..."

"I want you off my guard," I sobbed loudly. "It's too much to have you this close to me. I've lost everything, and your presence is like salt in the deepest wound of my soul."

"Luther won't do that. Especially after today."

"He will when I tell him about us," I murmured.

Hartwin's grip was a fire in my arms as he dragged me up the wall to stand before him. "Don't do that, Zira. It will hurt us all. He's just lost his sister to treason, and now you want to tell him I stole his companion's heart before he even got a shot at it? You aren't that cruel and vindictive."

Part of me wanted to spit in his face, to claim I could be that heartless. Instead, I stared into his eyes, and I knew he was right. Squeezing my eyes closed over the tears that suddenly flooded down my cheeks, I sobbed.

"We will just keep on like we have this past week." Hartwin's grip on my arms softened. Touching a hand to my cheek, he slid it down my jawline beneath my chin, and his palm cupped one side of my neck. I softened into the warmth of his large hand. "I will guard you. We will be friends. You will learn to love your companion, and one day, you will wake up, and all I will be to you is a friend in your soul. What happened between us was years ago. It's time to let it go."

"It was you that first night," I whispered

"What?"

"Those first nights with Luther. It was you I felt touching me, your mouth, and hands. It was you I imagined being with to allow him to touch me." Hartwin stood staring at me, his face only inches from mine. Falling against the wall hard, I felt crushed and humiliated. "I never meant anything to you?"

"You are my friend, Zira. I care for you as my friend." His touch was gentle at my waist as he supported me to stop me from crumbling to a weeping mess on the floor.

"Do you rip all your friend's clothes off and fuck them until they can't breathe from your desire?" I stepped into him angrily. "Do you tell all of your friends how beautiful they are, how they drive you crazy, and test your resolve?" I looked up and met his eyes with my final plea. "Do you make love to all your friends then tell them they are too intoxicating and leave them confused and crying by a river? Or was I just a special case?"

"Zira, don't do this," his voice a quiet plea of its own. My hands were clenched with his shirt in my fists, his clamped down over mine.

Lifting my eyes to his, I saw the purest lust I'd ever seen floating in those dark blue eyes. "You still desire me?"

Hartwin almost laughed. "I said I didn't love you. I didn't say I'd forgotten what it felt like to be with you."

On impulse, I kissed him, and Hartwin responded. His hand supported the back of my neck as his mouth crushed mine with suppressed need. My back hit the wall. Hartwin lifted my thighs to his hips. I was lost in our kiss, in his touching my bare skin beneath my skirt. For years I had wanted nothing more than to have Hartwin touch and kiss me just one more time. Finally, I was getting exactly what I'd always wanted, but I wasn't free to anymore.

Hartwin withdrew from me with forced control. Without meeting my eyes, he tidied himself up and moved towards the door. "Hart?" I breathed, suffocating under such intense emotions. "You're all I've ever wanted."

Hartwin looked at me then. The anger in his eyes tore me apart like his abandonment did over two years ago. He'd begged me when I first came to the palats not to take his honor. My selfishness nearly did just that. Sliding the door open, Hartwin stepped through and shut it behind him. Just like that, I'd lost the man I loved all over again.

Stumbling to the bed, I fell upon it and stayed that way until the door slid open just on sunset. Hartwin stood watching me. Eventually, he sat next to me on the bed. "Was there a fidelity clause in your joining contract?"

"We don't have them. Fidelity is just assumed in Avalonia."

Hartwin touched my shoulder tenderly. "Not in Cyra. Luther probably did not insist on it because he could not be sure you would be willing to be with him. You may have refused him except for when you needed to provide a child. He allowed himself the freedom to find release elsewhere in case, but in doing so, he has allowed you that same freedom."

Sitting up, I frowned at Hartwin. "You're saying I'm free to take lovers?"

"Maybe. As long as the children you bear are Luther's... he has no legal rights to object to you doing so." Hartwin looked out the window. "Though, I would suggest you not publicly advertise doing so. Cyrans do not judge someone for partaking in a natural occurrence. It is why to become a royal guard, we stay celibate for five years. To our people, that shows great restraint and patience. Avalonians believe in taking multiple lovers until you join. But the Praldians are not like either of us."

Lying back on the bed, I stared at the wall opposite me. "I didn't advertise my lovers previously for a good reason."

"Yes, I know. No one knew if you had one or not. Come on, you need to eat."

When Hartwin stood, I sat up, observing him. "You don't hate me?"

"I did." He shrugged. "I feel like I betrayed my prince, Zira. Once I tell him what happened, it should... soothe things."

"Tell him?"

Hartwin nodded. "He gave me permission to comfort you, remember?"

My eyes bulged. "I don't think that's what he had in mind, Hart!"

Taking my outstretched arm, pointing to the wall that I could still feel pressing hard into my back from earlier, Hartwin laughed.

Pulling me to stand, he walked me out to the empty sitting room to eat.

"Do you know how many of her personal guard Luther's mother, the Queen, has taken as lovers?" I shook my head as he placed me in a seat in front of a large serving of food. "All of them. And, half of the King's personal guard, plus several officials, laborers, staff..."

"I get the gist," I breathed, holding up my hands in resignation. I watched Hartwin smile, taking the seat opposite me. "Are you suggesting we be lovers again, Hart?"

He picked up his fork. "Let us just see what Luther says about today first. He has been with you now; he may have no inclination of sharing."

Chapter Fourteen

The door opened, and the footsteps of someone approached the bed, but I was too tired to open my eyes. When I tried, I could just discern that it was still pre-dawn by the grey light in the room, but that's as far as I got. A heavy body slid into the bed with me. For a heartbeat, I worried it was Hartwin taking advantage of his post as my night watch. But as soon as the hard body pressed against me, his arm encircling my waist, I knew who it was.

"You're home," I sighed.

Luther kissed my shoulder. "We came back in the night, so no one would think anything of not seeing us alight from a ship."

"Okay." When I snuggled up against the warmth of his body, Luther mistook it as an invitation. His hand slid down my thigh and guided it forward. "Luther?" I whispered. He paused, ready. I could tell by the sudden tightness in his grip he was concerned. "I don't like this bed without you in it. I feel safer sleeping in your arms."

It was as close as I was going to get to admitting that I missed him. We'd been joined just over a week, and while I wasn't in love with him, the days before he went away encouraged a compassion for him.

Turning my face towards my shoulder, Luther kissed me tenderly. When the kiss ended, so did the tenderness, but I had grown used to the Cyran way many years ago. I'd learned to love their roughness as I loved Hartwin. I would always still desire to be touched the Avalonian way, but I would crave the Cyran way just as much if I must go without. Afterward, I slept in Luther's arms—the deepest sleep I'd had in four days.

"Zira, it is breakfast time," Luther's voice called to me from somewhere else in the room.

Opening my eyes groggily, I found Luther just closing a clean uniform shirt. "I'm so tired of late," I groaned, sitting up and collecting my robe from the end of the bed. I'd learned that the elite would just walk in unannounced at any time and started keeping it within arm's reach. I also never got out of bed without having covered myself just in case.

"I'll call Medic Ellery to check you over. He should have your records from Medic Nyla by now." There was only the faintest touch of displeasure in his voice.

"Could you call him now? And can I eat my breakfast in here?" With my robe was secured, I slumped back down under the covers.

Luther frowned at me. "You really feel that drained?" I nodded. "Could your time in the ocean have made you ill?"

"It would be a first for an Avalonian, but I'd never spent so long dissipated either. Maybe it stuffed something up being gone that long."

Luther pulled out his comms, typing something into it as he sat on the bed beside me. "Dissipated... is that what you were doing in the bath that day I could not find you?" Eyes drifting closed, I nodded again. Luther shook my shoulder gently. "You need to eat."

Opening my eyes, Jervaise stood beside the bed with a plate of toast. He placed it on the platform that supported the bed. Picking up a slice, I took a bite, eating it slowly.

"Has she been like this since the attack?"

Jervaise shook his head, the worry clearly evident on his features. "She had recovered by the second day, but has been a lot more sluggish since and fluctuating."

Ellery came in concerned as soon as he saw me. He put his bag on the other side of the bed, took out his monitor, and placed it over my eyes. "According to her records, she is not running at her prime. I would say she is quite sick, but I am not sure with what. I know you are not going to like this, Prince Saboa, but I think we need Medic Nyla."

"No!"

"My Prince, your companion is ill, and I have no idea why. If this is related to her species, then we need a Medic of her species."

Luther stood fiercely. "Until Medic Nyla is cleared as having no contact with her previous employer, she will not be setting foot in this palats."

"Medic Ellery" –I pushed myself to sit— "do you have any more hälsodryck? It may help."

Ellery nodded. "Jervaise, could you run to my office and grab the silver bottle from my medical supply fridge, please?"

Luther's comms buzzed. He took it out, looking at the screen. "I need to go tend to something. I will be back in an hour to check on you, and then, if you are up to it, we need to talk."

My companion left, shooting a final look of warning to the medic before he shut the doors. Ellery took his place on the bed next to me. "Do you have any idea what this could be, Princess?" I shook my head. "None at all?" Shaking my head again, I leaned back on the wall behind me. Ellery placed his hand over mine. "Nyla advised that when an Avalonian woman is with child, food alone will not sustain her. You improved vastly the day you were drinking the hälsodryck."

"No, it's too soon. I don't even know how to. I mean, I read the book and understand the theory, but I haven't even really tried yet."

"Yes, Luther and I discussed the book and the implications of you actually having the control over conceiving."

Understanding what Ellery was saying without actually saying it, I huffed. "I'll do my duty, Medic Ellery. I signed a contract saying he'd have his heir in five years. I will abide by it."

Jervaise entered carrying the hälsodryck and a glass. He handed it to Ellery, who poured a dose and gave me the glass to drink. "He is stubborn, Ellery, and he will lose her if he does not risk letting Nyla examine her."

Ellery sighed heavily. "If she is not up and walking within the hour, send a new elite to fetch Medic Nyla personally under my instruction. I will take the fallout."

Jervaise nodded. Ellery left, but Jervaise lingered. "Princess, may I ask a question?" I nodded, slipping back down to lying. "Did Hartwin hurt you?"

I frowned in confusion. "What? No. Why would you think that?"

Jervaise shrugged. "He was angry after what happened with your uncle. He came in here yelling at you and left even angrier. When the Prince arrived last night, he requested a private audience and was relieved of night duty an hour later. Today, you are weaker than the past two days. It is just conjecture."

Shaking my head, I sighed. "My current lack of energy and his anger are not connected. I dare say the shift change is unrelated also." A feeling of dread buried itself in my core. Hartwin must have told Luther about us when he returned, which meant Luther knew coming to bed this morning. Not daring to speculate, I closed my eyes. I was only partially aware of the glass slipping from my hand as I was swept into the darkness before my next heartbeat.

Opening my eyes to bright daylight pouring through the window and a soft hand touching my face. "There you are, child," Nyla's singsong voice soothed as she disposed of a hypodermic.

"Nyla? You shouldn't be here."

"Shh. The men fight in the other room, unaware you are awake. Let's focus on you, child. Drink." She handed me a glass of hälsodryck, but it was enough for three doses. "Drink and don't question me." By the time the last drop passed coolly over my tongue, I felt ten times better. "Good. It seems you need a stronger dose."

Realizing my robe was open beneath the sheet, I shuffled it closed. "You examined me while I slept?"

"I did." Nyla touched my cheek. "Does he take care of you, child? He seems protective of you." When I nodded, she smiled. "Better a Cyran prince than a barbarian murderer."

"What's happening, Nyla?"

"Well, your companion is considering banishing me. Your uncle and cousin are on house arrest at your direction, and you were nearly comatose. I gave you a shot to bring you back." She smiled shyly. "Thank you for sending them, Princess. It's been too long that they have stayed away for your safety."

I imagined the reunion yesterday would have been emotional. "It was good to see them alive, but it's not what I meant, Nyla."

Pulling the sheet down, Nyla placed her hand over my womb. "You learn quickly, child."

"You DISOBEYED A DIRECT ORDER!" Luther yelled at Ellery as I opened the door to the outer quarters. I'd bathed, dressed, and eaten lunch, but the fight was still going. Everyone stopped when I stepped into the room.

"Medic Ellery, thank you for sending Medic Nyla. She needs to return home to brew some specific medicine for my condition. If you could accompany her out of residence, she will advise you on what care I'll require until I'm well again." Turning my gaze on Luther, I sighed. "Prince Saboa, I believe you wanted to talk? I think we have much to discuss."

Luther was angry; that much was perfectly clear from the way his shoulders were rolled forward to the clench of his fist. When he stepped forward aggressively, I raised a hand to stop his words. "Luther, I'm not well."

It was the first time I'd addressed my companion informally in front of others. Everyone acknowledged my slip with either shock, raised brows of curiosity, or amusement.

"If Ellery didn't call Nyla when he did, I may not have been well enough for Nyla to help by the time you relented. Be grateful for his sense, fine him for his disobedience, and let it go. Nyla is not the enemy. Once she has seen me through this illness and shown Medic Ellery how to care for my kind, I have released Nyla to return to her companion's side, should she wish to."

"You are joined?" Ellery asked, surprised.

"To my Uncle Ravid," I answered while Nyla nodded. "They have stayed apart to protect me. Luther, I will explain, but in private."

Taking a deep, steadying breath, Luther stepped back, sweeping his arm out towards his office. "I will hear you out, Zira. Medic Ellery, attend to Medic Nyla, then return here. Medic Nyla, thank you for your care to the princess."

Nyla curtsied and followed Ellery out of the quarters. Walking into Luther's office, I took the seat at his desk without asking. Luther closed the door. When he observed my occupancy of his chair, he moved to stand by the window overlooking the city proper. "How sick are you?"

"I won't die and should return to full health in a matter of months if I get the care I need."

"Which Nyla can provide?"

"Yes. She will teach Ellery simultaneously for the future."

"So, you will not make a full recovery if she expects you to need future care for the same ailment?"

"With any luck, I shouldn't get this sick again. It was my ignorance that led to me being this ill this time."

Luther looked over his shoulder at me with a raised brow. "Ignorance of what?"

"My people's abilities."

He looked back out the window as if considering. "But you will be healthy and able to bear healthy children when the time comes?"

I smiled. "Yes, Luther. I..."

"Good," he cut me off, turning to face me. "Let us talk. Hartwin was enraged when he contacted me yesterday and informed me of you putting yourself between your guard and two Avalonian men who arrived unannounced."

"I know Ravid, Luther. I know they would not betray me, and for their safety, they could not give you pre-warning to their arrival."

"Why their safety?"

"Luther, Ravid is the leader of the rebellion. If the Barbarian knows where Ravid will be, he will do everything he can to have him assassinated. Here, he could get two for the price of one. As for Nyla, she was never based in the palats because we weren't. She was still at my parent's estate when we were taken. She raised the alarm, and it was my uncle's men and my parents who rescued me. He sent Nyla with us to keep her safe and make sure I recovered from my... capture.

"Luther, Ravid is the reason the people will let my heir retake the throne. He has effectively kept the Barbarian from taking full control. If you are going to war with Avalonia, you are going to need Ravid on your side. Everyone who isn't a barbarian in Avalonia follows my uncle. He came to offer an alliance. He knows that after the assassination attempts, you'll have no choice but to declare war."

Listening quietly, Luther considered me for several moments after I finished talking. Taking the blood-stained pouch from his pocket as he moved towards me, Luther upended the die into his hands, casting them over the desk in front of me. Studying them for a moment, Luther finally bobbed his head. "I will give your uncle audience this afternoon."

Moving to him quickly, I wrapped my arms around him. "Thank

you, Luther. I can't bear to see another member of my family killed senselessly."

Removing my arms from him, Luther moved me back a step. "Hartwin told me as much. He said you threatened to harm him if he spilled their blood."

Swallowing, I looked away, ashamed. "He told you what happened?"

"Between the two of you? Yes." Unsure where his temper was, I stepped away from Luther. "Anberon told me you thought I had a woman with me the other night. I guess I should have realized that if you suspected I might have a lover in residence, then I certainly would in Cyra. I am not sure if one of the elite has let it slip in front of you; I guess that is not important. Hartwin assures me that he was comforting you. Your acceptance of my return confirmed it was not out of spite or of anything that could be harmful to our joining."

It hurt for Luther to acknowledge he had another lover at home. "I love him," I blurted. "I have since before I even came of age. He was my first crush, my first kiss; I would have had him as my first lover if he would have had me." Taking a breath, I lowered my voice. "I would have joined with him if he'd loved me." Jaw clenched, Luther just stood there watching me. Sighing, I fell back into the chair, tears stinging my eyes. "But he didn't."

For a long moment, the silence stretched out. Luther collected his die from the desk, weighing them in his hand. "I knew that day in the throne room that your heart belonged to someone else. When Hartwin admitted your friendship, I suspected there was something more behind it." He put the die back in their pouch, pinching it shut.

"Zira, I asked Hartwin to be there for you because I trust him. If you were to turn your affections or desire to any other man here, I would prefer it be him. He will always be honest with me. However, the children are to be mine, and your affair is not to take place while I am in residence."

I must have looked as shocked as I felt because Luther touched my chin gently to bring my focus back to him. "Cyrans do not have an issue with someone finding pleasure where it exists, Zira. I should not feel jealous about you desiring another man. Still, I admit to feeling slighted that your heart belongs to him, despite it being his first."

"I... Avalonians don't do this, Luther. I was upset last night. I'd never thought it possible or even considered it. It just happened, but I'm not sure that means it would happen again."

Luther gave a half-smile. "I never for a second believed it was your intention to seduce him, Zira." He moved towards the door. "You should rest."

"Luther." He stopped from opening the door, turning to face me. "My illness..." I reached forward, taking the book of conception from the corner of his desk, and looked at it with disbelief. "I tried to tell you earlier."

Taking a step back towards me, Luther looked from me to the book, his mouth falling open. "You are with child? That is what made you ill?" When I nodded, Luther looked at the book in my hands. "The night before I left?" This time when I nodded, he rounded the table, sweeping me up into an embrace. "By the stars, I thought it would be a few years yet."

"Me too. I didn't even realize I'd called to that ability. But Nyla is sure of it. Apparently, all of my symptoms indicate a double up."

Luther released me back enough to frown at me. "A double up?"

"You asked me to give you a son twice that night. The first time here" –I ran a hand over the edge of his desk– "and then again in bed."

Luther's eyebrows shot up to his hairline as his eyes fell to my belly. "She is sure it is two?"

"No." I gripped my hands together in front of me, letting my eyes drop to his chest, my natural eye level. "She says that my energy expenditure indicates two, but it could just be a conflict between our species. You're quite a bit bigger than me."

Concern radiated across Luther's face. Taking his hand quickly, I shook my head. "No, Luther, she doesn't think I'm in danger. Nyla said that while it is uncommon for Cyrans and Avalonians to join, it's not unheard of. There have been no complications for the mother. She believes that given the right sustenance, I should have no difficulties." With a sigh, I dropped my hands away. "That being if we can avoid any more physically exertive abduction attempts."

Luther turned to face the window. Waiting patiently, I watched his shoulders rise and fall slowly, indicating deep breaths. He was thinking quietly. "You could have told me out there with the others, but you wanted to tell me privately." He turned to face me. "You do not want anyone to know."

"No, I don't. I want this to stay between us and the medics right now. I fear that if the Barbarian finds out that I carry another's child, he will change his game plan and no longer be trying to abduct me."

"He will kill you instead?" Luther asked. When I nodded, he pulled me into him. "I will need to let Hartwin know since he is the captain of your guard, but we will keep it quiet from everyone else until there is no hiding it any longer. Hopefully, by then, this war will be over." Kissing my forehead, Luther held me tight until the doors slid open.

"Prince Saboa, Princess Zira." Anberon closed the doors. "I have scanned all the residence. There was a listening device in your sitting room, office, and outer quarters which Hartwin found during his initial sweep the night of the attack. We have also found one in the throne room and one in the third floor's elite quarters. We believe the same person is responsible for placing all of them."

"Padget?" I asked, almost fearful of the answer. Anberon gave one stern nod then focused on Luther. "Why would she do this? What did she have to gain?" I queried in disbelief. She had seemed so loyal to her brother.

Luther rubbed my back. "I need to go deal with her. I have put it off all morning, but the evidence is piling against her. I need to hear her side of things." Tilting my chin up to him, Luther kissed me softly. "Go rest. I will call you down when your uncle arrives."

As Luther turned to leave, I reached out, capturing his hand. "If you need to talk or just be with someone after you've seen Padget, you know where I am." Rising up on my toes, I kissed him a little more passionately than he'd kissed me. "I won't ever betray you, Luther. I may not love you, but I've always admired, respected, and liked you."

Without waiting for a reply, I left the office. I didn't want to see the distrust in his eyes or undeserved admiration.

Chapter Fifteen

Two hours later, I was gripping the sheets on the bed in our room. Small whimpers leaked between my clenched teeth while Luther purged his frustrations at his sister's betrayal. When he entered the sitting room, Luther took me by the wrist and led me into the bedroom, shutting the doors. Thirty minutes later, his hands were still clamped around my wrists, pinning them to the mattress as Luther thrust his anger into me. The difference between his taking me with desire and with rage was that instead of moans, he roared ferociously.

Collapsing onto me finally, Luther shuddered violently, then both of us lay there panting. My dress was in ruins where Luther ripped it open down the back, and I think his uniform suffered the same fate. "Are you okay?" Luther asked while kissing my neck. Still breathless, I nodded. "Thank you for offering yourself up." Swallowing, trying to control my breathing, I almost moaned with relief when he rolled to the side. "Are you sure I was not too hard on you?"

"Not at all." I may not be able to walk right for the rest of the day, but the sex had been mind-blowing. Sitting up, I held the front of my tattered dress to me. "I'll need to eat again. Can you get someone to fetch me a snack while I wash and dress, please?"

While I went into the bathroom and the pre-poured bath, Luther moved to the sitting-room door. "Erhaird, the Princess needs to eat before we go down to see her uncle."

Throwing my dress to the floor against the wall along with the ruined undergarment, I slipped into the pool-sized tub and started washing. The tenderness of my bruised wrists made me cringe a little. Sliding into the tub behind me, Luther pulled me into his lap.

"Do you want to talk about it?" I asked as he took the sponge and started washing me gently.

"Her mother poisoned her mind; convinced her that if I produced no heirs, then her children would have a right to the throne. She confesses to helping in the abduction attempt, but only because they assured her you would not be harmed. She denies vehemently any knowledge of the attempt on my life."

"Do you believe her?"

His hands paused. "While I want to believe her, it wouldn't change what Padget has done."

Prying the sponge from Luther's clenched fist, I turned to wash him. His eyes focused on me intently as I sponged his entire body. "Padget isn't capable of hurting you, Luther. I believe she thought they would just take me home, but neither of us could take a new partner to have children because we are joined." Stilling my hands, I lifted my eyes to his. "Don't kill her, Luther. Naivety shouldn't be a death sentence."

Focused on my lips, Luther stroked my cheek. "She committed treason, Zira. There is only one punishment for that."

Closing my eyes, I remembered the Broadcaster's vidscreen depicting my parents kneeling, waiting for the death blow.

"Okay." Luther exhaled dynamically. "What would you do to punish her?"

My mouth was drowning in saliva that I struggled to swallow. "I'd charge Padget with conspiracy to commit treason and banish her. I'd send her to be enslaved in your father's palats as your mother's maid, perhaps." Luther's eyes went wide. "Then, I'd be looking into her mother because that gives us a lead to our on-planet dangers."

"Prince Saboa," Anberon's voice came from the bedroom. The elite knew not to enter the bathroom while I was in there. "The Avalonians have arrived, and we have food for the princess."

Placing me aside, Luther stepped out of the bath. "We will be right out," Luther responded.

Rising out of the water, I started drying as I moved into the wardrobe to find a new dress. "This one." Luther pulled out a dark red silk dress with black ribboning through it. It was an autumn dress with wrist-length black lace sleeves, but within the temperature-controlled palats, I could wear it in summer. Realizing that Luther was trying to hide the bruising on my wrists, I took it from him. Then, turning to find a black undergarment, I quickly dressed.

Leaving my hair out to let it dry somewhat, I quickly ate while Anberon briefed Luther on what they dug up on my uncle. Effectively, nothing more than I'd already told him. "Have you eaten enough?" Luther asked politely when he'd heard all there was to hear.

Taking another bite, I piled my hair up into a bun to try to keep cool. Fortunately, the palats climate controls were cold compared to outside. Unfortunately, it was set to Cyran temperature, which was still warmer than our hottest days in Avalonia.

In the outer quarters, our guard fell in around us. "I am sure I do not need to say it, Zira, but you are here as a spectator only. So, do not argue with me in there."

"And here I thought you wanted me as a bodyguard just in case my uncle turns out to be an assassin."

Luther turned with a look so fierce that I took two steps backward, backing into Jervaise. "You do not put yourself at risk again. If you recognize a threat to either of us, you will let my guard know and put yourself amongst your own guard to stay safe. Understood?"

Still pressed against Jervaise's chest, his hands holding my shoulders to stop me from falling or maybe running away, I nodded. Gritting his jaw, Luther then continued towards the elevator. I was still trembling in the same spot when he dropped out of sight.

Cyrans were scary. Their sheer size and strength dictated that your natural response should be fear. Add a bad temper to it, and they made a Quig seem almost as friendly as a house pet. "Princess?" Jervaise prompted from behind.

"Did I do something wrong?" I asked quietly, still shocked by Luther's rage.

"He's worried about you, Princess," Erhaird reassured. "Cyran women are built tougher than you, and even they would not have taken that knife for him."

There was that judging me by my size again. You would think after witnessing me taking out an assassin and dismembering several others, they'd consider me a little less frail.

Taking my elbow, Erhaird guided me forward gently. "Let us not keep the prince waiting. He is angry. You do not want to leave him alone with your uncle for too long."

We caught up to Luther just outside the throne room. My uncle and cousin were waiting in the alcove surrounded by Royal Guard. Not even bothering to look at them, Luther marched straight into the throne room. When I stopped to make sure they were visually okay, my uncle bowed his head at me. Returning the gesture, I followed Luther inside.

Taking my place slightly behind the throne, our guard fanned out around us. Commander Stark was the last to enter the room. He looked like he'd been traveling for days and was yet to bathe or sleep. "Commander, you are back. How did you go?" Luther inquired as Stark bent knee before his prince.

"It was successful, Prince Saboa. I will detail everything for you after we tend your guests." Stark came to stand by me. "Princess." He bowed his head respectfully.

"Commander Stark," I replied politely.

He'd known, of course. He'd caught us together once in Hartwin's bedroom at their estate. And after, when it was over, I'd broken into his room after he'd returned to the palats, just to sleep where I could smell him. Stark found me. He'd held me while I cried, then teleported me home and made me promise never to come to his house again. I never did. Not even for the annual soldier's revelry, which usually drew every single socialite on Praldia. I'd never even gone near the boundary or the place by the river that Hartwin made ours.

Peering at the Commander, I wondered if he'd known of the Prince's intentions or if he'd known I'd never stopped loving his son. Stark met my eyes for the briefest moment, and then, for the first time since we'd met, he averted his eyes from mine, taking a step back from me.

Waving his hand to indicate he was ready, Luther brought my attention back to the matter at hand. The guard by the door signaled to my uncle he could enter now. Ravid came forward, Vered slightly behind him. They both dropped to knee. "Prince Saboa, I am Ravid of Larmoyer. I come in peace and to offer an alliance. This is my son, Vered."

"I will hear your petition," Luther responded, folding his hands on his lap.

Ravid nodded. "May I greet our princess?" Luther nodded but tensed when Ravid stepped forward.

Placing a restraining hand on Luther's shoulder, I stepped forward to the edge of the step. Physical interaction was the norm for Avalonians.

Stepping forward, Ravid bowed to his waist, taking my hand and kissing it like he would his king. "Princess Zira, it is good to see you well. I was worried with the news that reached us of last week's events. We flew directly to offer our support and aid, whatever can be of use."

Waiting until he stood straight, I stepped forward and hugged him. "Thank you, Uncle. It gave me much relief to see you breathing."

Then, pulling back, I looked at Vered. "Cousin, you've grown to be handsome like our fathers."

Vered stepped forward, embracing me warmly. "When we heard you'd been stabbed, I was ready to storm the Barbarian's palats and try for that savage's head by myself," Vered announced loudly, forgetting protocol. Until Ravid slapped him up the back of his head. Vered ducked his head, blushing. "My apologies, Princess." He bowed, kissing my hand. "I'm glad you're safe."

Smiling, I patted Vered's hand and stepped back. Moving to my place by Luther, who was watching warily, I exhaled with relief.

"Very well, let's get on with this," Luther grumbled.

"It's straightforward, Prince Saboa. The Princess is the rightful heir. With the Barbarian's underhanded attack, we believe, you will be looking to put an end to things. We'd like to offer you our knowledge of his setup and the men of the rebellion to aid any attack you plan. We have loyalists inside the Avalonian palats feeding us intel daily, and we have the forces."

"If you have the forces, why have you not ended this war years ago?"

"Because we don't have her," Vered spoke, pointing at me. When his father indicated he should back up, Vered hung his head with a grumble and did so.

"Prince Saboa, we are people of certain... abilities. Our throne cannot sit empty, and the ruler must be recognized by the throne for the war to end. The throne has never recognized Abaddon, so to kill him is not enough. Others will just go to war to try for the throne. It is why Abaddon wants our princess. It has nothing to do with heirs and everything to do with his claim. The throne will recognize him if she stands with him. It is her blood that powers that throne."

Luther stood suddenly, looking at Ravid intently. "Her blood... her bloodline powers your throne?" Ravid nodded. "That is why the royal womb must produce the next heir; he must possess her blood."

Ravid nodded hesitantly. "The throne will accept a male heir, yes, but it is making do. If we are to see Avalonia come into its full power, then it must have the true heir sitting on the throne."

"True heir? As in not a half-breed son of mine?" Luther growled.

"As in, not a son, Prince Saboa." Ravid licked his lips at Luther's sudden surprise. "The throne has been waiting for the daughter to take control. It is the females who hold the true power and whose blood is purest. But, unfortunately, our people are sexist, so they have put the male heir on the throne and treated the princess abominably. It's time to change things, to give our people their true heir. Princess Zira needs to be the one to take the throne, and her daughter needs to inherit it from her."

"Mother to daughter succession?" Luther sat amazed.

"It will meet with some abhorrence. But if we can get the throne to recognize Zira before the elders can put her back in her place as an incubator, then we have a chance of forcing this change on them."

"If Zira is Queen of Avalonia, and I am the ruler here, I see a few problems."

Ravid licked his lips again. He'd thought it all through and tried his best to meet every argument with a solution that got Luther to see what truly needed to happen. "Once the throne recognizes her, the Queen can appoint a caretaker. It's what the elders will do to await a son to rule. That way, your companion can be by your side and delegate until your daughter is old enough to take on the role as princess."

Luther sat back, considering for several minutes. Then, taking out the blood-stained dice, Luther cast them on the side table. He studied them, nodding his head, collected them, and threw them again. He shook his head at whatever he saw. "What you propose makes perfect sense. I think I understand your explanation about the royal womb's true purpose, but I cannot act on this impulsively. Return to my wife's estate for the night. I will think about it, and tomorrow we shall see where we can work together."

"Thank you, Prince Saboa." Ravid dropped to a knee, Vered followed his father's lead. "Princess." They bowed their heads, then rose up and left the throne room.

Taking a deep breath of relief when I could no longer see them, I relaxed. Luther stayed sitting on his throne for several more minutes. Eventually, he stood, collecting his dice. "Stark, get washed up and report to my office. Erhaird, I want more information on what Ravid has claimed about the throne and its blood link. Go." Erhaird was running out of the room, Stark a step behind him as they ran ahead.

Luther looked me over once, then turned, walking for the doors without another word. As expected, I followed behind him, but the walk back to the residence was as silent as our coming. When we reached quarters, Luther walked towards his office but pointed to the inner quarters. Jervaise took my elbow, guiding me to the inner quarters without a word.

Sitting on the sofa, I stared at my hands for possibly half an hour before Jervaise couldn't stand it anymore. "Do you want to be queen, Princess?" I shook my head. "But you want your daughter to be queen one day?"

Looking up, I met his eyes. Suddenly, I realized just how intuitive the elite was. It made sense; they needed to foresee people's actions. That sixth sense made them better at their job. Jervaise focused his eyes on my lips like every other Cyran.

"Yes. I don't believe the males should hold the succession, but only on our planet. I don't wish to change it here. Outside of Avalonia, succession relies on physical strength and intelligence. Avalonia, it isn't your arms that will save you. It's this" –I tapped my head— "and this." Holding my arm out, ribbons of razor wire braided around my limb. Jervaise's eyes went wide.

Tucking my power away, I dropped my arm to my side. "I don't want my daughter to be treated like I was, or like my mother was, or her mother. If the female line is so important, they should be put on a pedestal, not wrapped in restraints then disposed of when they serve their purpose."

"I agree, Princess," Jervaise sympathized. "Our line of succession is father to son, but our queens are still adored and treated well even after they have produced the next generation. What happens in Avalonia disgusts me. It disgusts all of us since we found out. And now that we've gotten to know you better, none of us would stand for you being treated so poorly."

"Thank you, Elite Jervaise." Standing up, I sighed. "I'm going to have a rest before dinner. Just let me know when it comes."

"Yes, Princess."

Chapter Sixteen

"How does it work?"

Lazing in the bath with my elbows perched over the edge so I could watch the city lights in the distance, I looked over my shoulder at Luther. He'd never interrupted my night-time baths before. Usually, he was too busy ruling. "How does what work?"

"The throne recognizing you?" Stripping off, Luther slipped into the bath onto his knees to sit back on his ankles. For such huge men, they were pretty flexible.

Rolling to face him, I sat on the bottom of the bath. Of course, anyone who was not Avalonian or Cyran would drown trying to do the same. "I touch the chair, or more specifically the arm of the chair."

"What's to stop you walking into the empty throne room and doing just that?"

"Someone needs to be there to see it, Luther. The elders need to see the chair recognize me so that they recognize me, and I need to do it before they assign a caretaker."

"If Abaddon dies and you are not there to jump the throne, the elders will assign a caretaker before you can make your claim and any chance of you becoming queen goes out the window?" I met Luther's eyes with sadness. He sighed deeply. "I do not have much choice, do I?"

"You can choose to leave me here, to not have me claim the throne. But, even if you kill the Barbarian, my world will still be in civil war, and whoever takes the throne will still try to kill me. I could pop out a son tomorrow, but it would be eighteen years before he could take a throne. So, until my blood sits on that throne, we will be targeted by assassins."

"As I said, no choice." When Luther reached out his hand to me, I let him pull me through the water to him. "It is not just you getting hurt, Zira. You could be captured if we fail." His hand cupped my flat belly. "It is the life of our child at risk also. And, if this is a boy, this is the heir to my father's throne."

"Luther, I can fix this. I can bring peace to my home world. Ravid is right. I dare say he tried to convince my parents numerous times. Still, they feared what you do," I scowled, avoiding eye contact by studying his hard body beneath the water. "Now you're involved. It gives me the hope to think we can change my world for the better. To give my daughter a better and more fulfilling life so that she doesn't grow up thinking she's good for only her womb and the seed a man places within it."

With his hand at the side of my neck, Luther pressed his thumb beneath my jaw, forcing my head to tilt back so I would look up at him. "Any man who thought you were only good for putting on your back was never worthy of you, Zira."

"I'm pretty sure you've already admitted that your first response to me was exactly that!"

Luther laughed. "I am a man, Zira, not a priest. But, from the word go, I wanted you by my side. Maybe not in the throne room, but I respect your intelligence, and I had hoped that away from public view, we could see each other as equals. You balance me in a way that no other woman in all our systems could hope to do."

His eyes were focused on my lips, but I saw every bit of feeling behind his words. "Why can't I be your equal publicly?"

Moving my mouth closer to his, Luther breathed his words on my wet lips, tickling them. "Because even after we make you queen of your own world, you will still be classed as a child who is under my guardianship."

Smiling, I pressed my body to his. "Well, maybe I'll just go live on Avalonia where I am Queen, and you will merely be a Prince. That way, the scales will be tipped in my favor." Kissing along his jaw lightly, I hovered in front of his lips again, then ducked my mouth to his neck.

"Zira, I think you are learning quite quickly how to negotiate with your Prince." His hand moved my face back level with his. "But until you are an adult, I have seniority over you once we step out of quarters. I do not care what title you hold on any other world."

He kissed me deeply as his hands moved over me in the way I taught him. I tried to respond sarcastically, but all that came out was a gasped breath and a plea for more.

"Where are you going?" I asked, half-asleep, watching Luther dress.

"I need to make a decision tonight about your uncle's involvement. That means I need to look over the information available. Erhaird should have something for me by now."

Groaning, I sat up and pulled my robe into place.

"What are you doing?"

"I'm not sleeping here by myself. I'll get something to eat and watch the Elite play Kort until you come to bed."

When I stood up, Luther moved in front of me. "You need to rest, Zira. Surely you have not grown so used to me in such a short time that you cannot sleep without me?"

"I don't feel safe here, Luther."

"You are surrounded by two thousand guards—"

"They aren't in this room. This isn't my room. And I know that you have a traitor somewhere in your employ. So, how can I trust anyone but you?"

"The Elite would not betray me, Zira."

"This isn't about their loyalty, Luther. I'm well aware of what they forsake in the name of loyalty to you." I'd lost the man I loved to him. Luther's sudden glare told me he understood just what I was thinking. "The elite are not infallible! Did the last attack not prove that? Metas and Quigs make me a handicap to your Elite."

Luther's jaw was set like stone. "This is your home now. You need to learn to be here alone and to know you are safe in this room, if nowhere else in the entire palats."

Frustrated he wasn't hearing me, I pointed to the door. "Unless you plan to lock me in this room, I am going out there to get something to eat." When I tried to push past him, I got nowhere. Cyrans could be like stone walls when they are unyielding, and Luther wasn't giving way.

"You are going back to bed to sleep. Your eyes are beautifully liquid, so you are not in dire need of sustenance."

Damn his night vision. "Unless you are coming back to bed, neither am I. I'm not the only one who needs sleep, Luther. How can you make the right decision with little to no sleep?"

Luther laughed. "Cyrans can go days without sleep and food and still function rationally, Zira."

Beyond annoyed, I wasn't listening to any more of this. Turning, I lifted my robe, planting one foot on the platform for the bed, the next on the mattress, crossing towards the door using my natural speed.

"Zira!"

I was just reaching for the door handle when something heavy bowled into me from the side. Crashing to the floor, I got my hands between Luther's body and my own. As the breath rushed from my lungs, the symbol for sonic waves flash-burned on my spine and pushed out a sonic repulsion from my hands.

Luther hit the roof with a loud splintering resounding through the room. Rolling across the floor, I got out of the way before his body crashed back to the Crystalstar floor with a loud thud and crackle as roof rock fell around him. The bedroom door flew open just as Luther and I were making our feet.

When he rushed me, I made a leap for the bed. Luther adjusted direction, so I dived, tumbling across the bed as his weight hit with a huff behind me. Making my feet on the platform, I was just about to step to the floor when his hand ensnared my ankle and jerked backward. With a screech, I fell. Arms caught me halfway to the floor, pulling me up and turning me to face Hartwin. Thirteen other Elite stood wide-eyed behind him.

"I've heard the Avalonian women will play hard to get, but is this not taking it a bit far?" Jervaise cocked a brow as he picked up a handful of crumbled roof rock in his hand.

Still standing frozen in Hartwin's grip, my breathing strained, which had nothing to do with the physical exertion and everything to do with my body being pressed to Hartwin's.

Arriving beside me, Luther took my forearm in his tight grip, nodding to Hartwin to step back and join the others. "What the blackness was that!" he yelled, pointing to the cracked ceiling and floor.

Smiling smugly, I refused to answer. Glowering, Luther grabbed my jaw, forcing my eyes up so he could look into them. Scowling, Luther released me with a push towards the bed, causing me to sprawl across the mattress. "Someone get the Princess some food; she has used up her energy again."

Pivoting on his feet, Luther stormed towards the door, the elite opening a path for him. "The princess does not leave this room. A guard will be posted in the room with her and two in the sitting area." Luther stopped in front of Jervaise. "Get that cleaned up and find out if we can get it repaired without replacing the entire ceiling and floor." Looking back at me, Luther glared at me. "You will obey me,

Zira. I am your prince, your guardian, and your companion. If I tell you to do something, you will do it!"

"I will obey you as my prince in the throne room, but in our quarters, we are equals. If I choose to get something to eat and stay up later than you feel is appropriate, I will do so. Do not doubt for a second that for that simple freedom, I will fight you every night if I have to."

"Do not threaten me, Zira. You could have got badly hurt tonight."

Smiling menacingly, I simpered. "I'm not the one with blood on their face."

Swiping at the slow drizzle from his head wound, Luther assessed the green blood on his fingers. When he stepped towards me, Hartwin blocked his path, whispering something in his ear. Glaring at me, Luther nodded once, and Hartwin let him go.

Stopping no more than a meter from where I sat on the bed, legs still sprawled from where Luther unceremoniously shoved me, Luther glowered at me. "You want to act like an impetuous child, then I will treat you like one. Open that pretty mouth of yours one more time tonight, and I will put you over my knee, bare your ass to this room, and spank you like a child. Furthermore, I will insist our guards watch just to further your humiliation." Bending down close to my face, Luther glared, waiting for me to defy him.

When I simply returned his glare, Luther continued. "Now, you will eat, and then you will sleep, in this bed, alone. Do you have anything to say about that?"

While I did, I also didn't doubt his promise to humiliate and spank me. As such, I returned his glare but didn't respond. On my spine, the symbol for snow flash-burned. My ability to reduce the kinetic energy of atoms flared to life, and the room became freezing cold. Everyone's breath came out in a heavy fog, and several of the Elite looked at each other with surprise and concern.

Laughing, Luther stood straight. "Your opinion on the matter is noted, Princess. Good night." Without another word, he left the room, his guard following him out.

My Elite stayed looking to Hartwin for direction, but Hartwin was watching me. "He has gone, Princess. You can knock that out now."

Flicking my angry eyes to him, I glared as I righted myself. Registering the look I gave him, Hartwin dropped his shoulders with a heavy sigh that fogged. Angry, I went to stand by the window, wrapping my arms tight around me in the frigid temperature of the room. Fuming, I stood watching the city lights for a full minute before anyone moved behind me.

Moving into the wardrobe, Hartwin reappeared with a blanket, wrapping it around my shoulders. Taking it silently, I snuggled it tight around me. Then, with another sigh, Hartwin spoke to the others. "Very well, Jervaise, I know your shift is over, but the Prince gave you an order. Get to it." Jervaise left the room.

"I am not on shift, so I need two of you out in the sitting room and one of you in that chair," Hartwin pointed to a chair in the corner. "Preferably someone who can stand freezing temperatures."

"I will take the inside watch," Elite Chas stepped forward.

"Good. Go fetch your winter uniform and a few blankets for the others in case this permeates into the other room. Clovis, find the Princess and the others some food. I will stay until you all get back and settled."

"Utz and I will take the sitting room, Captain," Elite Tancred bowed.

Hartwin bowed his head, and the Elite left. "Shut the doors, so the Princess's mood stays isolated." The doors closed quietly, then Hartwin turned to watch me. "Looking for a fight, are we?"

"I wasn't, but I got it," I replied coldly.

"That you did." In the reflection of the window, Hartwin assessed the ceiling behind me. "You are in no condition to be getting physical, Zira."

Sighing, I glanced down and caressed my abdomen. "I'm not going to be dictated to about when I have to sleep, eat, and breathe."

Growling, Hartwin spun me to face him. "Luther cares about you, Zira. He cares about you a lot. Now that you carry his heir, he is going to be even more protective of you. So give him a break and just do what he wants."

"Do what he wants?" I snarled. "What do you think I've been doing? He wanted me as his companion. He wanted a son. I have done nothing but what he wants since I was dragged from my home a week ago."

"And now he is taking two planets to war for you," Hartwin replied quietly.

Gawping at him, I shook my head. "I never asked for any of this, Hart. I never wanted any of this. If he'd left me alone—"

"Then Abaddon would have taken you before you even came of age."

Swallowing the bitter pill Hartwin just shoved metaphorically down my throat, I scowled at him.

"Luther has been protecting you for years, Zira. So do not even pretend this is all new. For the time he has already invested in keeping you safe from that barbarian, the least you could do is open your legs and give him an heir."

Beyond insulted, I slapped his face, again and again, and continued until he grabbed my wrist and pinned me to the window by it and my good shoulder. "You are running on empty, Zira. Refuel and save all this hate for the man who deserves it. Which, just in case you have forgotten, is the man sitting on your brother's throne." Hartwin released me roughly.

Slumping to the floor, too exhausted to even cry, I clutched my stinging hand to my chest. It felt like I'd broken it on Hartwin's stubborn face. The doors slid open again, and Clovis carried a tray of food in, setting it on the end of the bed while Chas set his stuff down by the corner chair.

Taking in their assessing gazes of his standing over my obviously distraught form, Hartwin started walking to the door. "Chas, make sure she eats and sleeps. I will relieve you at shift change."

Hartwin and Clovis left, shutting the doors quietly behind them. Chas stood waiting for me to move for a full minute before he came and crouched beside me. "I have an aunt who is Avalonian," he informed me quietly. "My uncle encountered her in the Metasystem. She was a mercenary and kicked his ass. He tracked her down and kept fighting with her until she agreed to join with him. She thought he was quite insane, as did the rest of us. But, he adores everything about her, mostly her feistiness, and she is so passionate about her love for him..."

When I looked up confused, I noticed Chas's eyes were unfocused, as if he could see them in front of him. Blinking, Chas focused on my lips with a strange smile. "My parents died when I was ten. Aunt Mahalath was like a second mother to me, so I get the emotion behind you, Princess. In fact, out of all your Elite, I am the only one who has any personal experience with an Avalonian woman that did not involve lust or violence. The only time my aunt ever got hostile like this" –he indicated the cracked roof— "was if she felt like she was being disrespected."

Taking my arm, Chas helped me to stand. Amazed by his story, I didn't bother brushing him off as he set me on the bed. Retrieving the food tray, Chas considered the damage to both the ceiling and the floor. "Of course, I don't think Aunt Mahalath can throw a man three times her body weight twelve feet into the air with that much force." Shaking his head, humored, Chas carried the tray over and placed it on the bed beside me. "But, she can arm wrestle my uncle and win."

"She possesses abnormal strength?"

"Probably a good thing considering the trouble I got into the first year I lived there." He smiled. "But, after a couple of ass whoopings by her, I became a lot more respectful and well-behaved. In fact, it was her discipline which allowed me to go through the rigorous training to become a royal guard and then Elite." Chas sat on my other side and absently picked up ost slathered vetekex.

He took a bite, my stomach growled. While he told me more about his childhood, I started eating. How his cousins, who were half Avalonian, made him a better fighter. They'd fight unfairly as kids having combined strength and one or two random abilities. He even made me laugh once or twice before I'd finished everything on the tray, including a double serving of hälsodryck. It wasn't until he'd removed the tray to the floor, pulled back the sheet, and tucked me into bed that I realized that first bite of food had been his only bite.

"You manipulated me," I accused, half asleep.

Collecting the tray, Chas started for the door. "Did I mention I had a younger cousin? She was like a sister to me, and she was exactly like her mother. Stubborn as all blackness too. When she dug her heels in about something, it took some very gentle nudging to get her to move past it. She could manipulate the cold as well."

Opening the door, Chas waited. A second later, Utz removed the tray from his arms, and Chas closed the door again. Then, moving to his chair, Chas removed his winter jacket, and I realized that the room was back to average temperature.

"Was?"

Chas nodded sadly. "Was. She's with the stars now."

"I'm sorry." Feeling the weight of sleep approaching, I closed my eyes. "Is your experience what got you stuck on my guard?"

Chas settled into his seat. "I asked for the honor. You remind me of her, all that fiery passion when you're fighting for something you believe in. It was Kismet to be serving the Prince when you joined us."

"Fate," I yawned. "Fate has an awful sense of humor."

"Don't I know it," Chas replied quietly.

Chapter Seventeen

In the morning, I woke with Luther's weight and breath heavily at my back. Rolling quietly from the bed, I managed to get up without waking him. From the opposite corner, Hartwin lifted his eyes from his book to watch me. Now I was glad for having slept in my robe. When he bowed his head slightly to say good morning, I averted my eyes and stole myself to the bathroom.

Pressed the button to fill the bath, I watched as water poured into the empty tub from under the floor edge on each side. Once the basin was flooded, I threw in some fragrant salts and moved to the window.

The sun was still rising, glinting off the city's glass to the south, the city center still in shadow. In Praldia, the sun rose over the ocean, hitting the palats first, then slowly lighting the city from north and south until its rays rose above the palats and met in the center. For that reason, the city center was called Sistaljuset, the last light. The water cut off, letting me know the bath was full, but I stayed watching the sunrise. I wanted to see the rays of light meet in the center.

His footsteps disturbed my silence, causing me to curse under my breath. "The elite isn't permitted in here while I bathe." I kept my voice hushed, not wanting to disturb Luther.

"What I said last night..."

In the reflection of the window, I watched Hartwin move towards me. "Just get out," I sighed.

He touched my shoulder gently. "I never stopped being your friend, Zira."

Shrugging away from him, I glared at him over my shoulder. "You stopped being anything the day you left me by the river. We haven't spoken in two years, Hart, and now you want to be there for me?" Turning to face him, I kept my voice low. "I needed you two years ago. I needed you when my parents were executed live by the Broadcasters. But, instead, you abandoned me when I needed you most. Now, you are the captain of my guard, and I'm meant to trust you with my life. How am I meant to do that, Hart? How can I ever trust you again?"

"I have explained the circumstances."

"You explained them two years too late."

He pressed his palm to my cheek, pulling me close to him. "Zira, do not put this divide between us."

Stepped away, I put my back to him. "What did you think would happen? He'd take me as his companion; I'd give him his heirs and take you as my lover in his absences?" I shook my head. "No, Hart. Your father told me to leave and never come back. I left the dream of us, but what I should have done was leave Praldia and just disappear. Now get out; this is my time."

"Hart?" Luther's voice came from the door. "Leave her be. As a woman with child, her hormones are changing, making her emotionally unbalanced. For an Avalonian woman, that is like a grenade permanently armed. By lunch, she will have loved and hated us several times over."

Glaring at Luther over my shoulder, I hated him for making my feelings about my condition and not my heart. "You can leave with him."

Stepping aside to let Hartwin pass with a pat on the shoulder, Luther stepped into the bathroom fully. "I have to get ready for the day, and I also have needs to sate."

Facing Luther, I dropped my robe to the floor. He smiled, reaching for me, but I slapped his hand away, stepping into the tub. "You have a lover in the palats. Go and sate your needs with her." Sinking into the water, I started washing. Ignoring me, Luther slid in behind me. "Luther, I have the advantage in the water. Don't mess with me here."

He grabbed the back of my neck, not hard, just gripped it gently, but I knew a flick of his wrist could snap my neck. It was enough to make me freeze. Cautiously, Luther started massaging my neck with one hand. When I gave no further resistance, his other hand encircled my waist, pulling me onto his lap, where he started massaging my shoulders.

"You need to relax, Zira. I know you are stressed and upset by everything that has happened, but you will just make yourself ill harboring all this aggression. Not to mention, you are directing it at the ones who are on your side.

"I was unfair last night because I was worried about you. I'd just finished saying I wanted us to be equals in private, and I start treating you like a child." Luther's hands stopped moving. Then, picking me up, Luther shifted me to face him. "I have never had anything to lose before, Zira. If this all goes wrong, if I make one bad decision, I lose you and our child. They are high-stake risks for me to take lightly. So, give me the time and space to be sure of things."

Nodding, ashamed by my selfishness the night before, I slowly relaxed under the pressure of his fingers. "In return, I will try to be more understanding of how hard this all is for you. The joining, the assassination attempts, suddenly finding yourself with child." Running a strand of my hair through his wet fingers, Luther took a deep breath. "Being in close quarters with the man you love and cannot have."

"Luther—"

Luther put a finger across my lips. "I am not stupid, Zira. I heard what you said to Hartwin just now, and I heard what you did not say just as loudly. You waited for him. Until the day his father brought you before me, you waited for him to realize he loved you too. What you are missing is that it would not matter. You could never be together. Being his secret lover was the best you could ever hope for. You must know that?"

There was no way to confirm or deny it because while Luther was right, I hadn't known he would block our being together for his personal reasons. So, for a time, I believed there was a middle ground to be met. But now I knew the truth. It was always a hopeless dream. Closing my eyes as tears threatened to spill, I dropped my chin to my chest.

Hugging me to him, Luther held me tight. "I do love you, Zira, and I am free to do so. Maybe, one day, you will find yourself able to love me too."

Pushing away from Luther, I knelt in the middle of the bath with my back to him. Then, waiting to get my thoughts in order, I glanced over my shoulder. "You should go get yourself sorted, so you aren't distracted today."

Luther shook his head. "I dismissed my lover when you took me to bed without issue, Zira. She was free to find another and has done so. Admittedly, I did not expect you to be with the child so quickly; otherwise, I would have held onto her, so I had someone while you went through your closed period."

"Closed period?" I still didn't turn to look at him.

"Your mother told you nothing, did she?" Moving closer, Luther took me in his arms and hugged me from behind. "When a woman is with child for more than a month, she is no longer receptive to her companion's attention."

Unable to help it, I burst out laughing. When I turned to look at Luther, he was appeared put out by my outburst. "Luther, I am trying my damndest right now not to let you have me because I'm angry at you. But, trust me, I desire you quite strongly, probably more so than before I was with child."

"Really?" Luther gave me a calculating look. "So, if I did this?" He moved his hand, brushing my nipple.

"Luther," I gasped, "I'm angry, remember?"

Turning my face to his, Luther smiled, victory already evident on his features. "Then you should not have told me you want me." He kissed me fiercely.

"COMMANDER STARK, make arrangements for rooms to accommodate Medic Nyla, her companion, and son."

"We are moving them within the palats, Prince Saboa?"

"Within the residence," Luther answered without looking up from his breakfast. "The Princess will need Medic Nyla to be close by for several more months, and she will be teaching Medic Ellery how to care for the Princess during that time. Though, she may need to be here for a full year while the Princess recovers."

"But she is looking so much better already." Stark was obviously suspicious. I couldn't blame him. No one but the Elite, Ellery, and Padget lived in the Prince's residence.

"She can relapse at any moment, and Ellery agrees it would be highly beneficial to have Medic Nyla close." Swallowing another mouthful of his breakfast, Luther entirely ignored the glare I was giving them both for talking about me as if I wasn't here.

"Once that is done, fetch Ravid for me to talk to after lunch. I have a lot to deal with today, but I should catch up by lunchtime and be ready to continue planning our strategy."

"Yes, Prince Saboa." Dipping his head, Stark pivoted on his heel and left the room.

"Hartwin." Luther finally looked up, but his eyes were on me as he set his plate aside. "The Princess is confined to quarters until further notice."

Dropping my fork on my plate, I glared angrily at Luther.

"Consider it punishment for last night's temper tantrum, Zira. Argue with me about it, and I will extend it for the period of your illness."

Smiling peacefully as I stood from the table, I batted my lashes. "Do that, and I'll pull the plug in the bath just before I dissipate, and you can spend the next week trying to find me." Stepping away from the table, I walked to the bedroom and shutting the doors on Luther's quiet chuckle.

Moving to the windows overlooking the ocean, I sighed, running my hand over the fixed glass. If only the windows opened, so I could smell the sea, feel the breeze on my face, and get a lungful of fresh air. I missed walking around my estate each day. I missed visiting the schools and villages of the hard-working Praldians whose blood, sweat, and tears made the planet's wealth, even though they barely saw a cent of it. While I knew Luther was just trying to keep me safe, circumstances being what they were, I felt like I was hiding and losing who I was in the process.

Over an hour later, Jervaise slid the doors open, startling me. "Sorry, Princess, but the engineer is here to assess the damage to the room." Acknowledging him, I kept pacing. Jervaise stood watching me for a few seconds. "I will need to ask you to step into the sitting room with your guard while the engineer is in here, Princess."

Letting out a huff of breath, I resigned myself. It wasn't Jervaise's fault, after all. "Of course."

Moving into the sitting room, I found my full day shift of Elite spread around the room. Clovis jumped up off the lounge to give me a seat to myself, but I moved to the window and started pacing again like the caged animal I was.

The glint of sun off the turquoise ocean waters flashed in the corner of my eye with every about-face, mocking my confined status. The engineer was escorted into the room between Jervaise and Erhaird, successfully blocking the small Praldian's view of me. They shut the bedroom doors just as the engineer let out a curse not fit for a Princess's ears.

"Princess, you are making us tense," Hartwin finally announced, stepping into my path. "You should sit and read. You have always loved reading."

Glaring at him, I turned my eyes to the five Elite sitting in the room watching nervously. "Clovis, when you finish your shift today, what will you do?"

"Princess?"

"Will you go back to your room, shut the door, and stay there until your next shift? Would you do that every night?"

"Blackness, no, Princess. I would go stir crazy."

"How about the rest of you? How would you feel being locked up in a room, day in and day out for stars knows how long?" I looked at each of them in turn. None were willing to meet my gaze.

"We get you are upset, Princess," Hartwin sympathized. "Circumstances being what they are, there is nothing to be done. Please just sit down and relax a little? The second break should be here soon, so all I ask is that you sit until you have eaten again."

Leading the way back to the sofas, I sat serenely, taking up a broadcasting tablet that lay on the table. Swiping through the news headlines, I tapped on the ones that piqued my interest. There was a new mine opening in Simpia. A new school opened using the funds from the sale of my parent's city residence. The trend in fashion had shifted to follow my influence. The explosion of a Cyran supply ship was still under investigation. Still, it was suspected to be caused by faulty maintenance.

"He's covering it up?" I asked, looking to Hartwin.

Hartwin looked up from his own tablet. "Do you really expect us to advertise that there have been several assassination attempts on the Prince since he joined with you?"

"But people here at the palats must have seen what happened?"

"Well, of course. You saw the broadcast of another abduction attempt?" Hartwin reminded me of the broadcast that went live the day following the news of the supply ship's explosion. "We are quite happy for the public to know that Abaddon is a self-proclaimed mad king who is trying to abduct a woman he has been obsessed with for the past ten years. It puts the people behind us when we take action."

Frowning, I flicked to the people's impression polls. "There is already popularity rising for the Prince to take offensive action?"

Hartwin nodded. "You have tremendous support, Princess. The people here were thrilled with your joining, even with the rumors that it was not your choice. They do not want to see you harmed by a mad man."

Searching through the news cycles, I found an article about my stabbing. "I was stabbed when one of the abductors became desperate?" I raised a brow tossing the tablet back on the table. "And I was thrown to the ocean while trying to escape. That's why no one's seen me, because I was left quite ill? Everyone's going to think the ocean is polluted for an Avalonian to get sick in water."

Just as Hartwin opened his mouth to reply, a Royal Guard wearing the sleeve sash to indicate he was training to be Elite wheeled in the second break snacks on a trolley. All the staff was reinstated, but no civilians were permitted to the top floor until the staff review was completed. Apparently, only one other staff member raised a red flag so far. He was suspended until those flags were investigated.

Clovis took the trolley from the guard. Hartwin waited until the door closed again to answer me. "The public believes you were injured from the fall. That it took so long to recover you because you sunk to the floor of the ocean unconscious, Princess. A Praldian or Cyran would probably die from the fall alone and drown if they did survive. So, it is quite believable that even a race who can breathe underwater would be off-color after falling over fifteen hundred meters. And the fact is that you are ill, and your recovery will take some months."

Hartwin knew the truth, but no one else in this room or the palats did, so he was playing along. While Clovis placed plates around the eating table, Hartwin collected my elbow to help me stand, then walked me to the table.

"You've been seen since the incident, Princess. Your walks around the ring were slow. You look paler than usual and appeared exhausted as if every step took great effort. You may not have realized how sick you look, but it supported what we released to the Broadcasters."

Sitting at the table with the other guards, I felt insecure. "I didn't realize I looked as bad as I felt. I'd never spent that long gone in water before. I didn't know how exhausting it would be. I was too terrified to come back until it was quiet again," I admitted quietly to my lap, wringing my hands absently.

The guards paused, watching me before looking to Hartwin. If Jervaise or Erhaird, or maybe even Chas, were at the table, they would have just said what they were thinking, but the others were newer and a lot more reserved around me. Hartwin reached over, gently rubbing my upper arm three times, drawing my eyes to his, then he dropped his eyes to my lips instantly.

"None of us will ever understand what you have been through and how scary that was for you, Princess." He withdrew his hand. "We are just glad you are safe. We do not judge you for hiding."

"Actually," Dail confessed quietly, keeping his eyes on his plate, "I saw you on the edge of the cliff. You put up a hell of a fight, Princess. I saw the ship's teleport click in and thought they would get you. When I saw you jump" –he licked his lips and dared to look through his brows at me— "that was the gutsiest thing. I do not know many that would have chosen that out instead of being taken aboard the ship."

"I will risk death than chance the Barbarian ever getting hold of me again."

"I believe that is what scares Prince Saboa the most, Princess." Chovis locked his gaze on my lips. "He can rescue you from any who takes you, Princess. But, he cannot rescue you from death."

The other guards nodded in agreement then the room fell silent for a long minute. Picking up my spoon, I took a mouthful of soup. Everyone returned to eating. After a few more minutes of only eating, the general chitchat between the guards started again and saw us through the meal.

Chapter Eighteen

Stopping my pacing, I marched towards the door. "Princess," Hartwin warned. All of my six guards were in the sitting room with me despite the engineer leaving an hour ago. Lunch was eaten, and I'd become excessively claustrophobic as the minutes ticked by. For the last hour, I'd returned to pacing by the window, much to the guard's dismay, but I'd reached my endpoint.

"I can't stay closed up all day. So, I'm going for a walk."

"You are restricted to quarters," Hartwin reminded me forcefully.

"Fine," I snapped. Then, pulling the door to the outer quarters open, I stormed through.

"Princess!" Hartwin grumbled loudly as all the guards hurried to catch up with me.

Marching to Luther's office door under the watchful eyes of his elite, I threw open the doors, startling Ravid, who stood opposite Luther at his desk while they talked. Luther raised his head but merely watched me, waiting.

"I need to go for a walk."

"No." Luther looked back to the plans in front of him.

"I wasn't asking, Luther; I was telling you. I have walked the ring safely for most of this week. I won't stay penned up like an animal."

"This is not the time, Zira," Luther informed me patiently.

Ravid was studying me with his brows furrowed. "This isn't like you, Zira. You are usually so reserved and peaceable. Instead, you're acting like a..." Ravid's brows rose with surprise. "Oh!" His head turned back to Luther. "We should take a break while you deal with your restless companion, Prince Saboa."

Luther shook his head dismissively. "Do not be ridiculous. She will do what she is told."

"Luther," I growled, but my uncle stepped next to me, taking my hand and patting it.

"Prince Saboa, there are certain times in a woman's life when she needs more attention than normal. As a man who has seen my companion through those times twice over, I would highly advise giving your companion what she needs, lest she finds it elsewhere."

Glancing at Ravid speculatively, Luther turned to Stark and the two Elite in the room with him. "Leave!" Bowing their heads, they left the room quietly, closing the doors behind them. "What do you know of Zira's condition?"

Ravid smiled. "Only that she has one, Prince Saboa. Restlessness and neediness are the first indicators, along with excessive energy consumption. I would have thought you'd wait until things were more settled, but I understand why you might have thought it best."

"It wasn't intentional, Uncle," I murmured. "I didn't know what I was doing."

Ravid nodded. "Natural instinct. Either way, I will give you your time." Ravid turned back to Luther. "With your leave, I will collect my son and companion to settle them in our rooms. By that time, I think the Princess will be calm for a few more hours again."

"And what should I do to calm the princess?" Luther was irritated by their planning being interrupted, but I was probably more in the dark than both of them. I just wanted to go for a walk.

Ravid laughed. "The same you did to get her in this condition,

Prince Saboa. You will never be more welcome in your companion's bed than while she carries. This time usually bonds the royal womb and her companion, since he is typically chosen for her."

Luther pointed to me. "This is normal for Avalonians?"

Ravid nodded. "Usually, the men go without much sleep of a night so that the woman will rest most of the day and allow us to go about our day jobs. It is only fair we be sleep deprived before as the female will be afterward."

Luther's brows shot up to his hairline, his eyes flicking from Ravid to me. "I am guessing you were ignorant of this as you have been everything else?"

For some reason, the comment hurt, and I shrunk in on myself. My uncle squeezed my hand sympathetically. "It was wrong of her mother not to prepare her, Prince Saboa, but I think she was trying to undo her first decade of being raised for a single purpose. Living here in Praldia opened Zira's parents' eyes to a lot of new prospects for her." When I squeezed his hand as a thank you, Ravid bowed his head to Luther. "With your leave?"

Luther nodded, watching Ravid leave quietly. When the Elite guard went to step back into the room, Luther shook his head. Bowing, they closed the door to give us privacy. "You look confused, Zira."

"I am. I'm not sure what's going on. I just wanted to go for a walk."

Pushing away from the desk, Luther held out his arm to indicate I should come to him. Swallowing my confusion, I moved around the desk, letting Luther pull me onto his lap. Then, wrapping that outstretched arm around my waist, Luther caressed the cheek that wasn't pressed to his chest. "You are nothing like a Cyran woman, Zira."

Frowning, unsure if that was a compliment or complaint, I stayed quiet. Lifting my chin, Luther placed a tender kiss on my lips for a long moment. When he finally withdrew, Luther stood holding me close, making sure my feet were steady beneath me before releasing his hold. Taking my hand, Luther led me from the room. As the door slid open, all twelve Elite guards turned their eyes to us. Luther walked towards the outer residence without a word, and all the guards fell in around us.

We reached the area of the floor where the lift was, and for the first time, Luther stayed beside me. Four of our Elite went before us, two with, the rest after. Walking deeper into the residence on the ground floor, Luther meandered through the ground floor corridors around the kitchen and other staff work areas. Some of the Praldian staff quickly scooted back out of our way as we moved through, dropping their heads in reverence until we passed.

Exiting the building through a large metal framed glass door, we emerged into the pool area between the residence and royal guard compound. There was some construction happening in the pool courtyard over the past few days, but I hadn't known what it was.

Since the abduction attempt, a glass roof was installed and a wall of sliding glass doors at the garden end facing the grounds and the cliffs. "It is not finished yet. We are still waiting on an alarm to be installed and our normal high-level security access to the doors. But, once it is complete, you will be able to come down here to swim with only your Elite to guard you."

Gazing around the new indoor swimming complex, my heart swelled. "You did this for me?"

"I understand that you used to swim at home daily and go for long walks. This I can at least give you until you are free to wander around without risk again."

Letting go of my hand, Luther turned back to address the guard. Stepping away from him, I moved to the edge of the pool, magnetically drawn to the water.

"Two at each door, the rest can relax, but you will keep your backs to the pool. You are all aware of the Avalonian way. You will not embarrass the Princess."

By the time Luther joined me by the pool, I'd stepped out of my shoes, lifted my skirt to my knees, and stood ankle-deep on the top step. The cool water lapping around my ankles was thrilling after only having the bath since I'd been taken from my home. Touching my shoulder, Luther released the seam of my dress. Startled, I looked at him questioningly as he started to lift it over my head. His eyes were reassuring as he placed a kiss on my cheek. "They will not look, Zira. Arms."

Unsure, I glanced around the complex. All the guards faced the windows, chatting quietly by themselves. Swallowing my hesitancy, I lifted my arms, allowing him to remove my dress. Then, as Luther turned to place it on a bench nearby, I dove beneath the water, swimming the length of the pool beneath the surface.

A calm I'd missed moved through me as I swam. I knew then that I'd needed this more than a walk or even food. Swimming back to Luther's end, I completed four more laps before I came up for a rest. Luther was swimming laps at the surface.

Standing with my back to the wall, I watched him approach, admiring his stroke. It was graceful how his body seemed skewered down his center, hinging on a central rod to propel itself through the water with his natural Cyran strength. Pulling up just short of the wall, Luther breathed easily despite the speed he'd been moving through the water. When he looked at me questioningly, I smiled, watching as he pushed a hand back through his matted hair.

Stepped forward, Luther pinned me between his body and the wall, kissing me hard with need. His fingers gripped in the material of my drenched undergarment. Wrapping my arms around his neck, I grabbed the hair at the back of his head. Then, doing as my uncle suggested, Luther did me right there in the pool. Our men were just over fifty meters away and able to see everything if they decided to turn their heads. For once, the lack of privacy didn't bother me. Forgetting the men's presence, I lost myself to Luther's touch and kisses as he drove into me with a need that matched my own. Smothering my cries in the flesh of his shoulder, Luther gritted his teeth to hold in his own release, then he held me breathless in his arms.

"Thank you," I wheezed to his shoulder as he held me. "Thank you for giving me this."

"I would give you everything you desire, Zira. If it were within my power to give."

Surprised by his reply, I pulled back. Meeting my eyes emotionlessly, Luther hugged me tightly. My eyes fell on the back of an Elite guard at the far end of the pool. His shoulders were tighter than those of the men around him. Hartwin. Luther was referring to Hartwin. The one thing I wanted, the one thing I couldn't have.

I meant to bite my lip, but my teeth found Luther's shoulder instead as tears cascaded down my cheeks. Groaning, Luther held me tighter. Then, realizing what I'd done, I turned my face to the arch of his thick neck. "I'm sorry, Luther. You deserve better."

Luther's thumb found my cheek wiping the tears away. "You dare not pity me, Zira. I wanted you, I desired you, I fell in love with you knowing you did not feel the same. And when the power was mine to do so, I took you and gave you no choice in the matter. It is the alignment of the stars that your will would belong to another. I will never give up trying to change that alignment until it is me who shines in the light of your soul. I know I can be the dark end of a wormhole at times; last night was a perfect example, but I have my duty, and you have your place." Lifting my face, he met my eyes with a smile. "Would it be terribly bad to admit that I really enjoyed our fight last night?"

Not surprised, I huffed. "I should have known you'd think it foreplay."

"Well, I would not go that far, but it was definitely exciting to have my ass handed to me by a woman."

"I'm pretty sure you won, Luther," I answered with a roll of my eyes.

"But, it was a victory hard sought, Zira. That makes winning much more delicious. A Cyran woman may have got a good punch in, but it would have been over within a few seconds. I also held the advantage of you being unwell and not at your peak game, which makes me curious about how last night would have gone if you were at full health?"

Unimpressed as Luther turned my loss of temper and fight for freedom into a lover's spat, I glared at him. Ignoring me, Luther ran his fingers through my wet hair as he talked, then started massaging my scalp. Moaning, I leaned into him, closing my eyes, tired all of a sudden.

"You have been a constant amazement, Zira, from the moment we met, but I have a few tricks of my own, you know." The world became dark. In the darkness, I was only vaguely aware of being lifted from the water. "Hart, get a blanket."

Chapter Nineteen

"Princess," Jervaise's voice dragged me from the darkness. "Princess, you need to wake up and eat something."

Blinking my eyes open, I expected to find daylight, but other than the light from the sitting room, it was dark. "What time is it?" I moaned, sitting slowly. Outside the world was a dark grey indicating the sun had set maybe an hour ago.

"You slept through the afternoon, but I kept dinner for you. You need to wake up and eat now. Medic Nyla came to see you and told me to wake you if you slept longer than six hours."

Nodding absently, I put out my arm. Jumping his eyebrows in surprise, Jervaise studied me with a nervous look as he helped me from the bed. "He knocked me out?"

Jervaise blinked slowly. "We are taught pressure points when we become elite."

"Great," I growled. "So, every time I complain about being cooped up in the future, I can look forward to a long period of unconsciousness?"

"Princess," Jervaise sighed, leading me to the sitting room, "he knows you need to rest. He was just trying to give you what you need."

"And get me out of his hair at the same time."

Jervaise argued no more. I guess I now had a reputation of looking for a fight when I was upset about my current house arrest. All the Elite knew Luther was busy planning a war. People thought this war was about me. Frankly, if the Barbarian didn't bother about our joining and let us be, I doubt Luther would have embarked on this course of action. So, it wasn't really me he was going to war for. It was the personal insult of the assassination attempts.

"I'm just the trophy for whoever wins," my voice was quiet solemnity as we entered the sitting room. I hadn't meant to voice that last thought, but it slipped through my brain-to-mouth filter too quickly to catch.

On the opposite side of the room, Commander Stark turned his eyes to me from where he addressed his son quietly. Recognizing my mood, Hartwin sighed. "But at least someone who wants me is willing to fight for me."

It was said just as quietly, but I knew they'd both heard by the furrowed brows that creased both father and son's foreheads. Taking my arm back from Jervaise, I moved to the meals table, giving the other men in the room no more attention than they deserved. Slumping in the chair, I leaned my elbow on the table to hold my head up as I started eating.

Jervaise's eyebrows did that little jump thing again. "Are you ill, Princess? Should I call the Medic?"

Shaking my head, I took another bite reluctantly and forced myself to sit up properly. "No, I'm fine. Shouldn't the night shift be here by now?"

"They are being addressed by Prince Saboa regarding plans. Probably another half hour or so until the shift changes tonight, Princess."

"Fine. Commander Stark, Elite Hartwin."

"Princess?" Stark and Hartwin both turned to face me at my authoritative tone.

"Unless you are willing to speak so the rest of us can hear, you can go whisper in the outer quarters until shift change."

Stark bowed his head. "With respect, Princess, the Prince has ordered two elite in quarters with you minimum, and I need to keep the captain of your guard up to date."

"Share it with all or get out, Commander. My head feels like I've been head-butting a Crystalstar wall, so I do not have the patience for rudeness tonight." Returning my attention to my meal, I ignored them.

With a grimace, Stark moved to sit on the lounge. Hartwin went to the wall comms unit and hit a call button. "Request the medic's attendance on the Princess immediately." When he turned to join his father on the sofa, I could see the smirk on his face.

"That was unnecessary."

"You are unwell. It is my responsibility to make sure that you are given the best care possible, Princess."

"Is there any point arguing with you, Elite Hartwin?"

He grinned. "You would only be wasting energy, Princess." Both Jervaise and Stark smirked to their chests.

Acknowledged the truth of his comment, I sighed. "Apparently, that's always been the case."

The smile disappeared off Hartwin's face faster than I could blink, and Stark glared at me like I'd just urinated on his shoe. As the only person in the room who missed the undercurrent of my comment, Jervaise broke into a chuckle.

Stark's dark eyes focused on me. "Princess Zira, is it only your headache that ails you tonight? You seem quite aggressive of late."

So, he didn't know. "Commander Stark, you have always been kind worded and gentle towards me, but I remember a directive you gave me two years ago, one which proved to me that the future I sought was ruined partly by your interference—"

"Princess!" Hartwin stood, astounded I would be so brazen. He'd taken the entire blame, but I knew his father's words falling from his mouth when I heard them even then.

"As such, you can consider yourself a victim of your own directive."

Standing, Stark put a restraining hand on his son's shoulder. "What will you, Princess?"

Rising out of my chair, I met his gaze. "The inner quarters are my sanctuary. You aren't welcome here unless it is in the company of your Prince."

Stark's eyes flared. "You do not have that authority."

For once, his arrogance at meeting my eyes was his downfall. Holding his gaze, I created the psionic link that would give me power over him. He may control his own desires, but I'd fed his son's once. Throwing all that passion and desire his son and I felt for each other into his head, I then followed it up by giving him my grief for losing Hart and my hatred for where we stood now.

Legs crumpling beneath him, Stark landed hard on his knees before me as I moved towards him. When Jervaise made a grab for me to try and restrain me, I automatically threw out a ball of air to knock him away. Hartwin was yelling, at me, at someone else, but that was all background noise for the pain I was filtering to the kneeling Commander.

"I am your Princess. I will one day be your queen." Standing over him, I couldn't help but smile when a tear formed a rivulet down his tanned cheek. "Don't you dare think you are my equal. Now, get out of my inner sanctum before the Prince needs to have this room repaired as well."

With my point made, I broke the Psionic link. The Commander crumpled. Spinning on my heel, I discovered Luther and half the elite guard in the room behind me. "Taking your anger out on the wrong people again, Zira?" His eyes focused carefully on my lips.

"If you truly thought that, you would have tried to stop me."

"From what I heard, you were exerting your authority after it was challenged?" Luther looked past me. "Commander, are you unharmed?"

"I am, my Prince."

"Elite Jervaise?"

"Just winded... literally, Prince Saboa."

Luther nodded, returning his gaze to my lips. "Elite Hartwin, you called the Medics?"

"Yes, my Prince. The Princess was not feeling well."

Softening his glare just slightly, Luther brushed my cheek tenderly. "What is wrong?"

"Besides you knocking me unconscious?" Luther merely cocked a brow. Sighing, I softened my voice. "I had a bad headache when I woke."

"Had a headache?"

Smiling, I shrugged a shoulder coyly, aware that Stark was now nursing his own headache. "It seems to have gone now."

Twitching his lips as if resisting his own smile, Luther tilted his head. "Do your species always pick fights to improve their mood?"

"Don't yours?"

"Touché!" Turning on a pinhead, Luther marched out of the room, followed by what remained of the Elite. Most left when the situation was clearly handled.

Patting his son's shoulder with the hand that wasn't pressed to his head, Stark followed the others. When the room cleared, Hartwin, Jervaise, Nyla, and Ellery were all that remained.

Holding his shoulder with a grimace, Jervaise sat hard on the lounge, but there was a smirk pulling at the side of his mouth. "You pack a blackness of a punch, Princess." I was starting to get the impression the Cyran soldiers liked being beaten up by a woman.

Grabbing my elbow, Hartwin marched me towards the bedroom, anger radiating off him like a storm. "In a minute, Ellery. I need a word with the Princess about her behavior." Then, slamming the doors shut, he turned on me. "You bewitched my father? How? Why?"

Typical. No one really understood Avalonian powers, and maybe that was our doing on purpose. Because a reputation that incited fear was a type of power. "I didn't bewitch him. I couldn't if I wanted to. I know nothing of his desires, and he shields them like all elite guards."

"Then what did you do?"

Sighing, I sat wearily on the end of the bed. "There is one passion he has always held, Hart. You. His fatherly concern and need for you to be well and happy. He loves his son, and that gave me a way to hurt him. I showed him what he took from me."

"He took nothing, Zira. It was my choice to end things. You became too attached, wanted more than you could ever have."

"Your choice on the advice of your father, Hart. I was content with what we had. I just wanted it to be known that I dedicated myself to being your lover." The silence fell between us. "Did he tell you he told me to forget you, to go away and forget you ever existed? He told me you never loved me—"

"I already told you that, that I could never love you."

"—never wanted me, that you were just using me to release a man's need. That a Cyran soldier could never be attracted to someone so frail and emotional as myself. You left me feeling abandoned. He made me feel worthless."

Squatting in front of me, Hartwin took my hands in his. "You needed to move on. I needed to step away from a temptation. Zira, he was doing what was best for both of us."

"Was it?"

Hartwin sighed too heavily. "You are with the only man I will ever believe truly worthy of you, Zira. You are exactly where you should be." Standing, he left too quickly for me to believe he meant those words.

Once I was alone, Nyla came through the door with Ellery, concern evident on both their faces. "You have a headache?" Nyla asked. "Anything else? Nausea? Cramping?"

When she knelt before me, I fell into her arms, crying. Nyla held me to her shoulder, rubbing my back just as she did two years ago when I'd stumbled through the door heartbroken, the future I dreamed of crushed. She'd known; my parents, too. I'd told them about Hartwin only days earlier. Told them that I loved him and planned to be with him in whatever form that could happen, as long as I was his.

"Medic Ellery, I believe this is a matter of the soul and not the body," Nyla's voice was soft, soothing as she dismissed him. "I think I should nurse the Princess through this one alone."

"Has she always been this aggressive?"

Tilting her head to eye him, Nyla gritted her teeth. "No, but you have a powerful child, forced into a joining, not of her choosing. She feels threatened and trapped and now all those emotions, like with all women with child, is being amplified. Add to that," Nyla lowered her voice, "she loved someone, and Commander Stark is a constant reminder of what she lost. Every single day she must face that, it appears. If you know anything of an Avalonian—"

"They love for life," Ellery sighed miserably. "The Prince searched. There was no evidence of a lover."

"Well, no," Nyla spat scornfully. "The commander removed him years earlier."

A weird sound turned my tear-streaked face to Ellery. His face was red, eyes fierce with anger. "You withdrew from society. Stopped attending balls and only left the estate for your cause. Two years ago, you stopped existing as a woman and started subsisting only in name. You have been grieving all this time."

Blinking the slow blink that I learned from Hartwin, I admitted the truth without vocalizing it.

Ellery cursed. "Does the Prince know?" I blinked again. "Did he arrange it?"

Shaking my head, I hid my face to Nyla's shoulder again, but the sobs quietened. "No, he has been informed only since my coming here. He is my companion. He deserved the truth. Besides, he isn't stupid."

"No," Ellery confirmed, "stupid is one word not used to describe the Prince. I will leave you be, Princess."

Shaking my head, I pushed to standing. Nyla going with me. "I'm done. I'm hungry again and would like to know how long until my companion is ready for bed."

Bowing his head, Ellery left the room. It wasn't an order, but he took it as one.

Nyla insisted I lie down and let her examine me. "You are stressing yourself out, child. I didn't realize the boy... apologies, he's a man now. I didn't realize he was in a place that would affect you so profusely. Each day must be fresh heartache for you?"

Lying still while the monitor read my vitals, I didn't respond. What more could I say?

"Everything looks fine. The special hälsodryck I'm brewing for you should be ready by morning. It will allow you to exist on a normal food quantity and give you back your full energy."

"Thank you, Nyla." As she packed the monitor away, I sat up. "How long until we know for certain?"

"You will be a week along tomorrow by your calculations?" When I nodded, Nyla also did. "We should be able to scan tomorrow to confirm all suspicions."

When Ellery came back into the room, he left the door open behind him. "We have some food for you, Princess. Prince Saboa has advised he will be some time yet."

Reluctantly, I followed Nyla and Ellery back into the sitting room. "Medic Ellery, we will need to arrange a scan for tomorrow to confirm the Princess's illness," Nyla conferred quietly.

"I think we should be able to manage a distraction long enough to get her into the infirmary with only a select company to prevent suspicions being raised."

Happy with that response, Nyla gave my shoulder a squeeze, and they both proceeded to leave. Hartwin was gone along with Jervaise. Chas and Utz were sitting on the sofa, supposedly engaged in watching the media panels. Still, they were too engaged without the alertness of something special being broadcast.

"Am I in trouble?" I asked casually as I sat at the meals table to eat again.

"You are scary," Utz responded, not looking up from his tablet. "You reduced the Commander to tears. He failed to cry even when his companion died in childbirth."

"His tears were just his body's natural response to fighting me. They weren't from grief or excessive pain."

Utz looked up, brows lifting high, then he checked himself, returning his eyes to his tablet.

The loneliness of being a princess was nothing new to me, but I missed the comfort of my estate and staff, who treated me like family. Inhaling deeply, I sighed wearily. "My grudge with the Commander is years old. I had years of anger bottled up that was directed towards him. The rest of the Elite, except a few, are in no danger of that power. You are closed books for the most part. You can stop avoiding looking at me so adamantly."

"I'm not, Princess," Chas answered. "I was seriously interested in the Cyran news broadcast." Placing his tablet on the table, he focused his eyes on my mouth. "You should let us think you hurt the Commander. It is good for people to fear you. It would be good for King Saboa to fear you somewhat. He only respects who he fears."

"As it is, I'm surprised he allowed his son's joining with me," I responded kindly. "He can't really be happy with the idea of having a half-breed grandson take the throne someday?"

"Things aren't what they used to be, Princess. Worlds have merged. We have a high population of other species in Cyra now, and we have populated Praldia just as thoroughly. The Praldians will welcome a mix-breed king eagerly, even if the Cyrans are reluctant. And, if things go to plan, then Avalonia will also be ruled by a mixed king. It seems only fitting that if we subject two other planets to such a thing, that our own world should also suffer the same fate."

"You missed your calling as a diplomat, Elite Chas. That speech was delivered almost perfectly," I complimented. "The only weakness was the scowl that crossed Elite Utz's face every time you mentioned a mixed king."

"I meant no disrespect, Princess." Utz bowed his head.

"None was taken, Elite Utz. You will find it is more than a scowl that will greet that suggestion in Avalonia. The Praldians would have preferred a Cyran-Praldian King to one of a foreign planet that is already embroiled in civil war. Lady Ancelin may have been a much better preference in the Praldians' eyes."

Utz swallowed, eyes wide looking away, and Chas ducked his head too quickly. Placing the forkful of food that I was about to eat back on the table with a practiced restraint, I watched my Elite. "Lady Ancelin was the lover the prince put aside for me?" Neither man looked up. Instead, they both suddenly found something interesting being broadcast on their tablets. "Well, that explains her sudden fondness of me."

When I stood moving back to the bedroom, Chas stood. "Princess?"

"I'm fine, Elite Chas. I'm aware Cyrans are not monogamous."

"Princess, one of us is meant to stay with you at all times in case you suddenly fall ill again. Elite Utz or I will need to accompany you into your room."

"If the Prince has ordered it. But I wish to bathe right now. I will open the bedroom door when I have finished." Bowing, Chas allowed me to close the bedroom door. Moving to the bathroom, I pushed the spout with my toe to start the water pouring into the tub. Undressing, I then sank into the warm waters.

Ancelin made sense. She was a woman of worth, with easy access and physically appealing to the Cyran eye. The Elite were welcoming her advances all week, and Luther told me she had taken another lover.

Floating in the bath, a myriad of thoughts ran through my head. How would I feel if I were put aside like Ancelin? When Hartwin set me aside, it wasn't for another woman. The two were entirely different in the offense. I always knew Hartwin was not available to me as a companion without permission. Still, I'd hoped to declare myself his lover and thus take myself off the courting scene.

It was how Hartwin's mother and many other Cyran women won approval to be joined with an Elite by the King. After all, the Elite was the best, and any ruler would want the best of his people to breed. But Hartwin refused to acknowledge me and turned me away.

Ancelin would have held the hope for a joining since Luther was a prince and thus needed to reproduce. She would have anticipated being considered eventually. Ancelin had much more to hope for than me. Knowing how much it hurt me, I couldn't believe her wounds to be any less. How must it hurt her to now see me in the place she hoped to obtain? Yet, she didn't seem put out.

From the moment I arrived, Ancelin was friendly and welcoming and keen on friendship. But, did she think that as my friend, she may become his lover again since I was joined by politics and not love? No, if she took another already, she'd not hoped to return to Luther's bed. So, how could she be so amiable toward the woman who stole her lover? I couldn't understand it, not from an Avalonian's perspective, and certainly not from a Praldian's. They were the most jealous race I'd ever come across.

Rolling over, I folded my arms on the side of the bath, resting my chin upon them, so I could look out to the city lights. While I was highly emotional, I still could not comprehend jealousy. Trying a different tactic, I pretended Hartwin left me for another woman. Still, my anger remained focused on him, not the woman he'd chosen over me.

Okay, what if she'd targeted him? Tried to steal him from me and succeeded? How could she know I existed? He'd never proclaimed us. We'd always hidden our affair from everyone except our parents. Sighing heavily, I gave up. It was something I just couldn't comprehend.

I wanted to ask Luther if she knew and Ancelin if it hurt her.

Would the asking, and my knowing, be a fresh heartache of its own? Too many unknowns. Too many variables. Too many emotions.

Closing my eyes, I focused on nothing, blackness, until everything but the sound of my breathing vanished. Slowly, my heightened emotions began to seep away. The stress and worries that were plaguing me were washed from my soul. My breathing slowed and evened out as I balanced myself again.

When the emotions were settled, and I'd retrieved the calmness in my head, I left the solitude of my bath. Wrapping only my robe around me as I walked, I slid open the bedroom door just an inch and then climbed into bed, waiting until I was under the covers to remove my robe. Slipping into the room, Chas barely glanced over where I huddled beneath the covers, then he closed the door and found his chair. I tried to sleep, but I tossed and turned, unable to get comfortable. Hyperaware that Chas was there watching me, I couldn't settle. Eventually, my frustration spread to him.

"Lay on your stomach, Princess," Chas murmured beside the bed. He was just a silhouette in the darkness, hovering there. Frowning, I rolled to my stomach with my hands beneath my head. Tucking the sheet to cover my shoulders, Chas then straddled my hips, making me startle.

"Relax, Princess, I have no intention other than putting you at ease."

Unsure but confident Chas wouldn't do anything to gain his Prince's ire, I settled back onto the bed, somewhat hesitant. Large warm hands were heavy upon my lower back and started pressing up over the sheet. "This would work faster and better skin to skin, but I understand the Avalonian conservatism."

Relaxing beneath him, his movements halfway between a massage and just touching as his hands worked over my back. When he reached my shoulders, Chas slid his hands from the sheet to touch my skin, but by then, I didn't care.

He continued rubbing my arms towards my hands, pushing them away from my head. As he reached my wrists, Chas leaned his body forward, pressing against mine. His hands covered mine, and he laid his whole weight upon me.

Sighing with relief from the physical contact, I then remembered who it was on me. "Chas."

"Relax, Princess. I am fully clothed, and you are covered. The prince will not take issue. We do not get jealous like that. I will stay until you sleep, and then I shall remove myself to my chair."

Squeezing his hand where it held mine in a 'thank you', I was already drifting into sleep. Light split the darkness of the room as the doors opened. Lifting his head, Chas removed himself from me.

"Did something happen, Elite Chas?" Luther asked, stepping into the room. "Why are you holding the Princess down?"

"The Princess was restless, Prince Saboa. I was merely offering physical proximity to help her settle, and it was working. The Princess was nearly asleep." Moving back to his chair, Chas collected his boots. He bowed to Luther, who nodded his head, waiting for Chas to leave, and then Luther shut the door behind him.

Closing my eyes since I wouldn't be able to see him correctly in the darkness, I sighed. "I tried waiting up for you," I murmured.

Nothing but silence greeted me. Accepting that Luther must be in the bathroom or wardrobe undressing, I rolled over and sat up in the darkness. Luther's silhouette stood at the end of the bed silently. "Are you angry with me about today?" No answer. "I don't mean to be needy, Luther, or to cause you issue. I just react to my emotions."

Shifting forward, Luther touched the end of the bed. The sheet started sliding away from me. I didn't try to grab it, just let it slip over my legs until I sat there uncovered.

"Come here," he growled low.

Tucking my legs around, I came onto all fours and crawled towards him. When I reached the end of the bed, I reached out to touch him and found him naked. Placing a hand on each of his hips, I kissed him low and worked my way up his body until I knelt looking up at him.

Luther took my face in his palms. "You have always been frustrating, Zira. I would have been naïve to think that would stop just because I forced you to be mine. I knew Abaddon would fight this, I knew you would hate this, I accepted you may hate me."

Shifting his hold on me, Luther helped me to stand on the platform surrounding the bed until I found myself at eye level with him. "I prayed you may desire me, and you do. I hoped you may like me, and you do. I planned you would bear a child for me" –his hand covered my womb— "and you do."

When he fell silent, I kissed him tentatively, unsure if it was right for me to do. Pulling me tight against him, Luther forced me to kiss him harder. Opening himself to me, Luther showed me his desire for me. It was more than physical; it possibly never was until our first night together. Had so much changed in the matter of a week? As Luther lifted my thighs to embrace his waist, to engulf him within me, I knew it had.

Never had I considered the prince even desirable before; I'd only liked and respected him. Now, I not only desired him, his touch, and his presence all the time, I realized that I more than wanted him.

I didn't love him. But what I felt for Luther fell on the border of love. It was something more profound than 'like' that would hurt me to lose him. It may not last, like friendships that sour past their use-by date. But right now, losing him was more than being vulnerable to the Barbarian. Losing Luther would be losing the first man to want me for me and willing to do something about it. That, to me, was worth more than any throne.

Chapter Twenty

"We will be right to go in a minute, Prince Saboa." Hartwin approached us where we sat on the lounge to speak quietly.

Setting down the broadcasting panel he'd been flicking through, Luther took my hand as he stood. The royal guard who wasn't on duty were ordered to surprise drills; something regularly done to keep them on their toes. They were up against the Elite, who were assured the Prince planned to stay in quarters for the morning.

This effectively removed any chance of someone entering the infirmary for the next hour as well as emptying it. The medics would be watching the training games to assist if an injury occurred, which I was guaranteed it would.

Luther slipped one of his arms around my waist to whisper in my ear. "You are tense, Zira. Are you worried?"

"A little. What if they are wrong and I'm not?"

Nosing my jaw, Luther chuckled. "Oh, I am sure they are right, Zira. Your moods are just as fierce as any woman in your condition. It is only the quantity I think they are truly checking today." Turning my face to him, Luther kissed my lips softly.

As we pulled apart, Hartwin was watching us but looked away when his comms device beeped. We saw him check the screen, tuck it away and nod at us. Wrapping me into a hug, Luther kissed my forehead and teleported us to the infirmary.

It was one of the small buildings on the inner side of the ring opposite the Royal Guard compound next to the ballroom. We teleported directly into Medic Ellery's office, where Ellery and Nyla were waiting for us; Hartwin and Anberon stood behind us. Gazing up at Luther, I did not even attempt to hide my worry from him. Touching my cheek in comfort before stepping back, Luther turned to face the waiting Medics. "Let us be quick. It does not take long for a guard to try pushing his luck with an elite."

"This way, Princess." Going to his office door, Ellery stuck his head out before sliding it fully open and proceeding down the metal grey corridor. Holding my hand, Luther followed after the two medics, with our Elite captains a step behind.

We followed the Medics into a treatment room. It consisted of a bench for the patient to lay or sit and a wall full of shelves holding different equipment sections. Along the back wall was an extensive system that was already fired up, ready to go.

Nyla was waiting by the examination table, a tray of items on a trolley next to her. Gathering up my hand after I sat, Nyla imprisoned my middle finger and pricked it. My black blood bloomed across my chalk-white fingertip. Placing a microchip under my bleeding finger, Nyla pressed down, helping the electronic sponge to absorb my blood until it was saturated. Then releasing my hand, Nyla handed me a swab before giving Ellery the chip.

"Please lie down, Princess, and we'll start the next lot of tests while we wait for the computer to process your blood."

Lying back, I turned my head to watch as Ellery slid the chip into place and press a button to start the test. That's when Nyla put a monitor over my eyes, blinding me to the room. "I'm going to insert a probe which will give us an image and details of what's happening inside you now. It can be a little uncomfortable but is perfectly safe."

When Nyla went to lift my dress, I reacted automatically, gripping my skirt to hold it down. Luther's large hands took mine, lifting them away as he kissed my forehead. "You are safe, Zira. No one can see anything. Your dress will still cover you. If you bend your knees, it will make it less unpleasant."

"You've done this before?" I asked, surprised by how aware of the process he was. Bending my knees like he suggested, I gritted my teeth as Nyla slipped something small and cold where only a lover should go.

"Yes," he admitted quietly. "Former lovers have claimed to be with child before. But they were mistaken. Praldian facilities are not as advanced as Cyran. Normally, confirmation is not certain for several months. Cyran technology can confirm after the first week and pre-detect any possible dangers to the child's health from the mother's body, allowing us to remove those threats if possible. We can determine quantity and sex immediately."

"You can foresee the threat of missfall?" The device started buzzing. Only Luther's weight over me stopped me from jumping off the bench. Instead, I gripped his upper arms, somewhat disturbed by the sensation.

"Yes, Zira. It is why we have a low death rate. So just relax. It is nearly all over."

The buzzing stopped, and, after a slight tugging sensation, Nyla shifted my dress back into place, patting my outer thigh. "It's all done, child. You can sit up now." Removing the monitor from my eyes, she gifted me a proud smile. "You are with child. Multiple, as I suspected."

My hand went instinctively to my womb, still somewhat surprised I carried life inside me. Luther's hand covered mine. When I lifted my gaze, he was barely restraining a smile. For once, his eyes met mine. His desire to be a father floated between us, blooming across my chest like a warm breeze.

Ellery joined us, disturbing the moment. "Well, the blood work came back positive, and there does not seem to be any conflicts to worry about so far. The Princess is in good health, and so are your children." Looking between us, Ellery handed Luther his tablet. "Paternity is confirmed as yours, my Prince."

Nyla froze. My eyes bulged with indignation, but Luther turned to Hartwin and simply gave a slight nod. Hartwin met my eyes for a moment, then dropped his to the floor. Shame avalanched down upon me.

"Do I have sons?" Luther asked firmly. Finally, I saw the swab on his finger where Ellery took a sample to test paternity.

Ellery looked to Nyla, who wore her anger for me like a crown. "Congratulations, Prince Saboa, your companion carries the heirs to two thrones within her."

Ignoring the curt tone Nyla used, Ellery returned to his system to start deleting the test data. Nyla, in turn, gave us privacy by turning her attention to the portable tester she'd used, deleting its records.

"Let's return to quarters before the first injury arrives," Luther announced. When he put out his arm to help me down from the bench, I ignored it, sliding down from the Cyran height bench on my own, refusing to even look at Luther.

Sighing, Luther hugged me to him. "You can yell at me in private, Zira."

The teleportation channels buzzed, and we were back in the sitting room. Stepping back from Luther, I wrapped my gangly arms around me. I still couldn't look at him. Luther crossed his arms. "Zira?" I'm sure he was expecting another fight. "I needed to be certain, you understand?"

"Of course. You've been cheated in the past, and I've given you a reason to doubt. It was a logical expectation that you should make sure I carry the rightful heirs to your thrones. If you'll excuse me, I'd like a rest before lunch."

Luther looked skyward. "Hartwin, was she too reasonable just then?"

At the bedroom door, I turned to slide it shut. Anberon was trying to cover the smirk on his face, but Hartwin met my gaze.

"Excessively. I would avoid being near her and a large body of water for the rest of the day."

Raising a brow, Luther turned to face Hartwin. "She is angry? Her eyes are not bright." Luther glanced at me, then back to Hartwin.

"Not angry. She is ashamed. Much more dangerous if she feels you are the reason she is shamed."

"Would it not be you who should be cautious then, Hartwin? Since you are the one who brought her to shame?" Hartwin glared at Luther. Anberon shrunk back to try and make himself invisible during this conversation.

"Hardly. I tried to resign as Captain of her guard. I warned you of our past, and it was you who ordered me to comfort her in any way necessary. I believe even Zira can do the maths on that one."

Luther took a slow step towards Hartwin. "You claim I set you both in that position with intent?"

"No, Luther. I claim you and I are Cyran and do not suffer jealousy or shame for sating our needs where they are welcome. I also recognize that Zira is Avalonian and was raised to be ashamed at finding comfort in the arms of another once she was joined. I understand in her world such behavior would find a woman shunned by society, unlike in Cyra, where it is the norm."

Hartwin took a step closer to Luther, so close that we'd touch during inhalation if I stood between them. "The fault is not mine because I warned you. The fault is not hers because she did not intend it nor let it even cross her mind. She was distraught. She sought comfort from the only other person she knew. The fault is yours for not considering how her different cultural upbringing would make her feel when revealed to others outside of the situation as Anberon, Ellery, and Nyla are. Even worse, Nyla is one of her own people and should now shun her."

"I have known since it happened," Anberon chimed in. Hartwin glared at him. Anberon indicated Luther. "I am his Captain. I am as close to him as you are. If you think I have not noticed the subtle difference in the way you two talk now, you are wrong. Once the divide between you two was clear, it did not take much to see how you and the Princess interact. It is too subtle for most to see, but I would not be surprised if a few of the higher-ranked Elite is suspicious. I dare say Commander Stark is fully aware."

"Cyrans are not the problem!" Hartwin snapped. "Do you care?"

Anberon shrugged and shook his head. "She is not my cup of tea, but I can see her beauty, and I have observed her nature enough to understand Luther's attraction, and thus, yours. She is a woman. You are a man that, above all else, she must trust with her life. Taking you to her body is the biggest show of trust I can imagine the Princess ever showing."

Luther indicated silence. "I get what you are saying, Hartwin. It was the insinuation occurring in front of Nyla that has shamed her." With a bow of his head, Hartwin stepped back. Luther turned to face me. "I apologize, Zira. Do you think she will abide by your culture?"

A tear escaped my eye as I shook my head. "I don't know, Luther. We are much changed from our years in Praldia. We have adopted some Praldian customs, some Cyran, but at heart, we are still Avalonian. In my favor is that Nyla is aware of the truth of the situation."

"Nyla may put the fault at my feet for forcing your hand or at Hartwin's for his presence?" Luther asked.

"How does that change judgment?" Anberon asked, intrigued.

Staring at the pattern on the floor, I hugged myself tighter. "Because a woman is not shunned for being forced to betray her companion."

Anberon's jaw dropped. "She would accuse Hartwin of rape?" Anberon asked, astounded. When I shook my head, Anberon frowned. "Well, how does that work?"

Luther coughed, bringing his Captain's attention to him. "Anber, you are aware that Avalonians mate for life?"

"Of course! Everyone knows that."

"What Zira is suggesting is that Nyla is aware that Zira loved Hartwin and intended to devote herself to him some years back. I forced Zira to join with me. Therefore, I have forced Zira to betray me because, in her soul, she belongs to Hartwin."

Swiping another tear from my cheek, I stepped forward. "I don't; he refused me. I haven't belonged to him for years, Luther, and I don't see it that way." Striding to Luther, I caressed his cheek and gazed at him earnestly. "You are a good man. You have been good to me despite how our joining came about. Before we escaped to Praldia, I was raised to understand my companion would be picked for me and thus to accept I may not love the man I am joined with, but I would be his. I belong with you, Luther. I know that. Hartwin has told me he believes that. I want to love you too. It's just..."

"You love Hartwin," Anberon cut in.

Oh, that avalanche caused ice in my bloodstream. Stepping back from Luther, I folded my arms around me again. "I lost the man I loved two years ago," I confessed to no one. "I have been grieving him since, and I will continue to do so the rest of my days." I glanced up at Luther. "I'm not sure it's possible for an Avalonian to love again. It must have happened before when young companions are lost in the war? It's only been a week."

The room was uncomfortably silent. If I wasn't looking directly at Luther, I could have believed I was alone. But I was only too aware of Hartwin standing at my back. Shuffling my feet for a moment, I waited for Luther to say something. Still, when no one said anything, I hurried from the room, slamming the sliding doors shut behind me, so I didn't have to turn and see their faces. Hartwin's face.

I wanted to be angry that Hartwin's denial of his own feelings took from me the one chance I had to be joined with a man I loved. He'd stolen the possibility of growing to love whatever companion was chosen for me later when he'd slowly embedded himself in my soul. It saddened me that Luther deserved to be loved, and I wasn't sure I could ever give him that. Ashamed that others suspected what nearly occurred in Luther's absence. Most of all, I worried for my children's future.

My hands fell absently over my abdomen. It was true; it'd been confirmed. The door opened and closed. "Do you want Hartwin removed from your guard?"

"I don't know," I sighed. "Hart's right. He's the only other person I know aside from you, Luther. It's just hard wanting to touch him constantly, even to hold his hand, and knowing that would anger him. I have enough trouble restraining myself from having physical contact with you. You're my companion. It's the Avalonian way to need to be physical with those we care about."

Cuddling me from behind, Luther rested his hands over mine. "Then you touch me whenever you need to, Zira. If that little amount allows you to be more comfortable, then I want you to do it. Truthfully, I love it when you reach out for me." He kissed just behind my ear. "I crave your affection, and I want you to raise our children however you think is best, as long as they learn the staples for ruling. Of course, the boys will need to enter the guard." His hands were rubbing over mine, almost caressing our children.

"I want them raised the Cyran way," I revealed. "It's the freest of all the worlds. You're open-minded, emotionally and physically strong, but still kind people. Unfortunately, I can't say that of my people. While the Praldians are more unrestricted in physical appearance, they are jealous, suspicious, and somewhat greedy.

"Our children should be raised Cyran with an understanding and the values of the worlds they are to rule. Especially in Avalonia. Praldia has already started to change, but Avalonia has been isolated from all the other worlds. If it wasn't for their rich resource of water and the wealth it brings, I dare say Avalonia would never interact with the other worlds at all."

"Well, they are about to get shocked into modern times. Once you are queen, Cyrans will migrate there to support their future King and Queen."

Frowning, I turned to face Luther, wary of his words. "You've decided?"

Luther watched me for a moment. "You will claim the throne. You will be queen. You will instill a caretaker, and when you bear me a daughter, she will take the throne as Princess until you pass to the stars. Change is good for everyone, Zira. With Avalonia as a stepping-stone, perhaps one day, a granddaughter of ours will be the queen of Cyra or Praldia."

"Let's not get overzealous and radical, Luther. In Avalonia, it is the female blood that holds power, and therefore, it should be the female who holds the throne. Cyra relies on physical strength, and that has always been a male trait."

Luther kissed me then held me tight. "I do not, in any way, hold Hartwin against you, Zira. Not your past or what nearly happened here. If you choose to take him as your lover, I will not be angered or jealous. Anberon is right. You are to trust him with your life. Having him as your lover is the greatest sign of trust you could give. None of the Elite would blink at it, nor would they converse it."

"Luther—"

"Wait, hear me out." Luther squeezed me tighter. "Ravid has explained that an Avalonian woman is quite the opposite to a Cyran when it comes to desire and being with child. Apparently, your sex drive will only increase until you start to labor. From that point, your appetite will disappear for up to six months following birth.

"Apparently, I will not need a lover while you are with child. In fact, I may well be exhausted by your demands. But afterward, I may wish to take one until you show interest again. I think possibly, while I am busy daily with my duties, it may be a good thing to have someone who can take on that side of my duties."

Eyes wide at his suggestion, I started shaking my head. Luther caught my face in his hands. "I am not saying you must, Zira. I am saying that I am the throne of this world and the Prince and future King of Cyra. I have duties to both worlds which cannot be put aside to sate your needs. There will be times you need me, and I will need to turn you away, Zira. You can say no now, but in three months, maybe even six, if I turn you away and you fall to Hartwin, I will not be angered or jealous. In fact, by what Ravid has told me, I might be damn well relieved."

"Surely, if an Avalonian man can cope?"

"They do not cope." Luther smiled. "It is not spoken about or acknowledged, but it is quite often expected that a man's brother will assist him when it becomes too much. He explained that for the lesser powers, a companion may have no trouble coping. But the more powerful the woman, the more persistent her needs will be." Luther smirked. "You admitted yourself you are the most powerful female in centuries. I suspect, using just this past week as a foundation, that you will be insatiable by the end."

Gawping at Luther, I struggled to even consider taking a lover. "I... I can't even comprehend this."

Nodding understanding, Luther kissed me thoroughly. Our clothes were thrown to the corner within minutes. He was right about one thing. If my desires just the past few days were a baseline, the next few months were going to be quite interesting. I couldn't help but smile to myself as he touched me with well-practiced ability. If nothing else, I could definitely enjoy having the excuse to spend more time in his arms at the mercy of his pleasure.

"Luther?" I laughed breathlessly as I watched him redress from where I laid on the bed. Finally, he turned to look at me with a significant smile of his own. "Can I just declare I'm insatiable now and demand you come back to bed?"

He stopped dressing; pants pulled up but not closed, shirt hanging open. Looking at the light outside the window, Luther slid the shirt off as he stepped back to the bed. "You have until lunch, or the last of the guard leave the training field, whichever occurs first."

Chapter Twenty-One

The throne room was packed full for the sentencing. The Councilmen took up the seats on the left, their families and staff crowded into the back of the room, wanting to hear everything firsthand. It would seem the entire palats turned out. The Broadcasters were set up to the far-right, live streaming their second sentencing of treason in a month. In the petitioner's circle, Padget stood surrounded by the Royal Guard. Her beautified eyes painted her cheeks where her silent tears ruined her perfectly applied embellisher.

"Padget Fanchon, you have been found guilty of conspiracy to commit treason," Councilman Aldous announced. Of course, everyone expected outright treason, and the sudden hum of astonishment around the throne room mirrored the surprise on Padget's face. "Do you wish to say anything more before the throne passes sentence?"

The room would have been quiet except for the buzzing whispers of the Broadcasters narrating for the public. "I... I would address the Princess."

There were disagreeable mumbles throughout the throne room.

Swallowing, I stepped forward to stand beside Luther's throne. He didn't glance up at me, just nodded to his half-sister. "It was not personal, Princess. I never wished you harm or malice. I was assured neither of you would be hurt. I was deceived by my own family just as you were. I want to thank you for finding it in your heart, after what happened, to give me this last bit of kindness."

Luther kept his eyes focused forward, but I knew he'd told Padget that I petitioned him for a kinder sentence. Swallowing, I was unable to say anything I would have wanted in reply. Not here, not in front of the whole of Praldia as it were. Luther stood, instantly absorbing the focus allowing me to step back beside Commander Stark.

"Padget, you have been found guilty and have admitted to your part in the attempted abduction of the Princess. Therefore, you are sentenced to enslaved banishment. You will be escorted to Cyra. You will be enslaved to my mother, the Queen of Cyra, to be served as she best wishes. If you are ever found to have returned to Praldia, you will be put to death."

Shock echoed through the room. It was said enslavement in the mines of Praldia would be preferred over enslavement to either the King or Queen of Cyra. The last person enslaved to the queen by her husband was sold to a cruel Meta mercenary as a plaything. I'd made Luther extract a promise of kindness from his mother. He hadn't confirmed what arrangements he made with me, but I could only hope he ensured that other than hard labor, Padget would be well looked after.

Luther turned his back on the petitioner's circle. Around the room, everyone followed suit. All except the guards and Broadcasters. Commander Stark took my elbow, turning me to face our Elite. Padget was now shunned. My eyes locked with Hartwin's. For what occurred between the two of us, the people on my own planet may one day do the same to me if they ever found out. When a tear fell down my cheek, Hartwin blinked slowly.

There was movement behind us, the royal guard escorting the banished Padget from the room. When she was gone, Anberon nodded once to Luther. We turned back to the room. "Bring forward the next criminal."

A ruckus in the back of the room produced another Praldian woman. Much shorter than Padget, though similar in appearance. She held herself like a woman who'd been beautiful in her prime, but that beauty had fled her with age. Blinking, I had a moment to recognize the woman before Aldous started reading out her charges. "Blanche Fanchon, you are charged with treason..."

Placing my hand on Luther's shoulder, I bent to his ear. "I need to talk to you."

He patted my hand. "After the trials," he replied quietly.

"No, now, my Prince." Meeting my eyes at my insistence, Luther nodded, bringing the room to sudden silence when he stood.

Without explaining to anyone, Luther walked around the throne to meet me immediately in front of Hartwin and Anberon. "Make it quick, Zira."

"I know this woman." Luther's eyebrows jumped up, as did the Captains of our guard. "She was a friend of my mother's. A good friend. I never had anything to do with her. Still, there were plenty of times I arrived at the city residence, and my mother would hustle that woman out of my presence quickly."

"She did not want you to have anything to do with her?" Luther queried.

"I think so. I found it peculiar, but it didn't click until after my parent's execution. My Prince, this woman approached me after they were killed. Until you came for me, I only left the estate twice. Both times to visit a dying Praldian who worked with me to help the natives. She must have followed me and cornered me." I was speaking so fast that I don't know how Luther could understand me.

"What did she want from you?" Luther had his formal voice on now.

"She claimed my mother kept something for her. Some sort of ornate box. She wanted it returned to her. I looked through what stuff you didn't take, but I couldn't find anything fitting its description."

Luther raised a brow at me. "And she was keen to get it back?"

"She threatened my life when I told her I couldn't find it and therefore couldn't return it. Then, when I suggested you may have confiscated it, as you did many things from the city house, she told me that she most certainly would have known by now if you held her box."

"Did she ever approach you again?" Luther asked almost cheerily. I shook my head. Kissing my forehead, Luther stepped away, motioning to one of his Elite to come forward. After saying something quietly, the Elite disappeared into the crowded room as Luther returned to his throne.

Confused by Luther's reaction, I looked to Anberon and Hartwin. "We have had that box a long time, Princess. Before your parents were executed," Anberon enlightened me.

"It is what got your parents executed," Hartwin added just as quietly as he indicated I should return to my place.

As I stepped back to my place beside his throne, still confused, Luther nodded to Aldous, who picked back up. "Do you wish to say anything before the throne passes sentence?"

"He is not my throne," Blanche scowled.

The elite guardsman returned with a long metal ornate box, handing it to Luther. Blanche took one look at what he held and turned her feral blue eyes on me. "You lying fish! You had it all along, and you gave it to him!"

"This is the first time the Princess has seen this box," Luther stated quietly. "I have held it a long time now. An employee of the Sallees' brought it to me. It is what alerted me to their intended treason." Luther turned his focus to me. "Is this the box that this woman asked you to find, Princess Zira?"

"Yes, my Prince. She showed me an optic of it. She claimed the box belonged to her."

Blanche Fanchon was glaring at me.

"Is this your box, Blanche Fanchon?" Luther asked politely. Blanche just turned her eyes away in a sign of snobbery. "Councilman Aldous?" Aldous stepped forward. "Please take this box to the Broadcasters and let them see inside."

Collecting the box, Aldous took it to a small table in front of the Broadcasters, where he lifted the lid and laid out the contents for them to see. When I took a step to go see myself, Stark caught my elbow. "I have always tried to limit the hurt you have been exposed to, Princess. But, trust me now when I tell you, that box would break you."

My eyes drifted back to the Broadcasters. They were frowning, shaking their heads, some even hissing their disapproval of whatever it was that laid within the box.

"Blanche Fanchon, you are guilty of treason on two counts. You should have died alongside Eliora and Tobias Sallee for your part in their treason. I now believe you twisted their minds with your poison and led them to their deaths. Had we have caught you then, it might be that your daughter Padget would have escaped your manipulation. Sadly, that was not the case. I will ensure that you poison no other with your personal grudge. Blanche Fanchon, you are sentenced to death for your treasonous behavior."

Taking Blanche by the arm each, the two guards put their weight on her shoulders as they lifted her arms behind her, forcing her to kneel into position.

Commander Stark followed Luther. Blanche babbled curse after curse on Luther, who merely stood before her. Then, taking up the long-handled curved blade of an executioner, Stark swung. It was all over in a matter of seconds.

Silence filled the room as Luther muttered the Cyran execution words. "... I walk the path of justice. Your blood on my soles will show my righteous path. Be at peace, and cause no more harm."

The blood spilled around his boots, and the sight of it caused my breakfast to rise in my stomach. Stumbling backward, hands caught my upper arms. Hartwin's firm grasp stopping me. "Princess?"

"I think I'm going to be ill." My breath was shallow, eyes staring at my own feet, as the black blood of my brother pooled around my own soles.

Lightening cracked over my head, and then I was back in the sitting room of our residence. Running for the bathroom, I kneeled over the waste bowl and purged the contents of my stomach. Behind me, the bath started to pour, and then Hartwin began to rub my back.

A comms unit beeped. Glancing at it, Hartwin typed a quick response. "Just Luther checking to see what happened," Hartwin soothed.

"Stars, they'll think I'm weak," I grumbled, sitting up. Looking at the ceiling, I still couldn't get the memory to release me. Finally, giving up trying, I crawled across the floor and pitched forward into the bath.

"Zira, you are still dressed!" Hartwin scolded, sounding scandalized.

Floating until my dress grew waterlogged, then it dragged me beneath the surface. Closing my eyes, I surrendered to the darkness.

"Let me help, Luther." Hartwin's voice dragged me from the darkness.

"No. She was adamant. No one but her companion sees her uncovered," Luther snarled. Next came the tugging of Luther dragging wet material from my skin. "Just throw me her robe and get the medics."

"I'm fine," I breathed quietly.

"You were sick and passed out in the bath, Zira. That is not fine," Luther chastised.

"I'm Avalonian. I could lie at the bottom of that bath for hours and be fine. It was just too much, watching blood spill over a throne room floor again."

Stopping momentarily, Luther scowled and started pulling my robe around my wet naked frame. "I have to admit, I did not consider how that would affect you. However, you have to be able to stand through a sentencing, Zira. You are the Princess now. If the people see weakness..."

"As long as you are strong, Luther, it matters not. I have been your bleeding heart for eight years. The Praldian's love my compassion as they love your fierceness."

Picking me up, Luther carried me to the bed and settled me under the blanket. "You are to be the queen of your own people, Zira. You must be strong when needed."

Taking Luther's face in my palms, I stared into his eyes, even when his focus dropped to my lips. "Luther, do you not think that what that woman did to Padget was just a little too close to home for me?" Turning his face, Luther kissed the inside of my palm. "I am plenty strong. I am also plenty hungry. So, if we could have this lecture over food, I'd greatly appreciate it, and so would your sons."

The medics' arrival saved Luther from responding. "What happened?" Ellery was all business.

"I threw up and passed out." Then, sighing, I closed my eyes. "Now, I'm starving and exhausted."

The monitor covered my eyes. "When did this happen?"

"After I watched a woman beheaded in the throne room. My Elite got me back here in time to be sick, and then I fell into the bath. I'm not sure how long I was out."

"It took over an hour to finish up the sentencing of the four individuals caught for treason," Luther informed Ellery. "Hartwin pulled her out by then, but she was still unconscious when I returned."

"She's a child. She should not have been in the throne room," Nyla scolded.

"She is old enough to rule, and as my companion and the Princess, she needed to be present."

"And you know what she went through as a child," Nyla snarled. "You should have suspected it would affect her."

"Take care with your tone, Medic Nyla," Luther growled.

"Take more care with your companion, Prince Saboa." Nyla took a breath, toning her anger down a notch. "Avalonians do not easily carry multiple babes, Prince Saboa. It is a huge strain on the

Princess's system to provide enough energy as it is. Any excess stress can result in a missfall of one or all the children she carries."

The silence filled the room for a few moments before Ellery broke it. "What did you tell the Broadcasters?"

"That the Princess is still weakened after the last abduction attempt and needed to rest," Luther was still using his ruling voice. "It only added to the people's support of today's sentencing."

"From this data, I would say the Princess had an anxiety attack. Medic Nyla is right. The stress overtaxed the Princess's body. We'll need to keep a close eye on her for the next two days," Ellery determined, removing the monitor.

Carrying a tablet, Hartwin came back into the room and handed it to Luther. Flicking through a few screens, Luther nodded. "It could be worse."

"What could be worse?" When I reached for the tablet, Luther gripped it tighter, having no intention of handing it to me, but Nyla snatched it out of his hands and threw it back to Hartwin.

"Prince or no, if you let that child ever see that broadcast, you'll find out why an Avalonian's natal scale determines if you can be a medic."

"I had no intention..."

"Prince Saboa," Nyla cut him off. Glaring at her, Luther actually took a menacing step towards her. "I understand why the public deserved to see what was in that box. But did you at all consider removing certain items to avoid your companion ever seeking it out?"

"It was you!" I whispered. "You're the one who sent the Prince the box, which resulted in Eliora and Tobias being charged for treason."

It suddenly all made sense. Luther said an employee gave them the box. Nyla was the only one who knew where my parents hid their private documents. As Nyla shrunk away a step, I blinked back the tears. What could have made her turn on my parents? It had to be something terrible. Taking a deep breath and turned pleading eyes to Luther. "What does everyone fear me seeing?"

Luther's stern features never wavered. "Medic Nyla, while out of line, is right, Zira. I will not risk our children by exposing you to something that does not matter now. That box is poisonous, and you are the only person in this room, and now possibly on this planet, who is untainted by it. And I will keep it that way." Turning his attention to the sitting room, Luther lifted his chin a little. "Elite Anberon?"

"My Prince?"

"Contact the Broadcasters. I want the wave containing all images and information of the treasonous box deleted permanently. It is not even to be kept in the archive. The public knows. That is enough. After that, I want the box permanently sealed before being sent to Cyra and placed in the King's vault."

"Luther!" I couldn't suppress the pain in my voice.

"The princess is never to know exactly what her parents were involved in. Their charge of treason is heartache enough for her to bear. I do not wish the Princess, our children, or any other person to be subjected to Blanche Fanchon's toxic opinions ever again."

"May I quote your reasoning to the Broadcasters, my Prince?" Anberon's eyes flicked to me for only a second.

"You may. Make it a decree. If the Broadcasters wish, I will declare it personally." Bowing his head, Anberon left the room to do as he was asked. Caressing my cheek, Luther wiped away tears I didn't realize were falling. "I will save you any further pain from your parent's treason, Zira."

"Was it really that bad? Worse than planning your downfall?"

By the way that everyone suddenly became focused on inanimate objects around the room, I knew whatever my parents were involved in was much more than plotting the murder of the Prince.

Bowing my head in acceptance, I blew out a long breath. "Then I will accept your wisdom in this matter, my Prince, and never seek the truth of it."

Carrying a tray of food, Jervaise hesitated a moment as he assessed the room's mood, but then a smile bloomed across his face. "So, Princess, it seems executions are not your idea of a good time."

Chapter Twenty-Two

Lifting myself out of the water, I sat on the side of the pool. All six of my Elite stood with their backs to me; two at each door. The ceiling glass was frosted so that light may enter, but no one could see in. Wringing out my hair, I took a deep breath as my hand fell absently over my abdomen. How much things had changed in the matter of a few weeks. "Elite Hartwin, what time is it?"

Turning his chin to his shoulder, Hartwin kept his eyes averted. "Lunch will be served shortly, Princess."

Moving over to the bench, I collected the swim robe Luther commissioned Master Fabrice to make. It still looked like a dress, but it wrapped from hip to hip and was made of a quick-dry material that still felt and looked pleasant.

As I closed the robe, a knock sounded at the door connecting to the Royal Guard compound. The guard must have been waiting for their chance to train, which meant I was running later than usual. "I'm done. Let's go."

Pressing the code to the Royal Guard door, Elite Dail whispered something to whoever was waiting, possibly for them to hold back until we'd left. He and Tancred then jogged around the pool to meet the rest of my guard and me by the Prince's residence door. Once together, Hartwin unlocked the door, and we proceeded through the downstairs maze to the lift system.

"Wouldn't it be easier to just teleport me everywhere if security is such an issue?"

"Every individual's teleportation chip leaves a signature and a trace, Princess. We monitor every teleportation of both public channels and our own guards, and we track them. Teleporting you everywhere would not only be a waste of energy, but it would create an excessive amount of data for the monitors to file." Side-eyeing me, Hartwin brushed my arm gently and took my hand in his. "I know you are uneasy after everything that has happened, but you are safe with us."

Hartwin knew too easily what I was thinking. The only reason I didn't argue with him at that moment was his hand holding mine. With him touching me, I felt safe. My other hand was engulfed in warmth a moment later. Surprised, I looked down to see that Chas had my hand in his. He watched everywhere around us as we walked, just like everyone else. With Hartwin and Chas holding my hands, we arrived in the outer quarters. Detaching himself, Hartwin went to stick his head into Luther's office.

The doors stood open. With Luther, his Elite, Commander Stark, Ravid, and Vered all plotting war, they needed the air. "Hartwin?" Luther acknowledged him.

"My Prince, lunch is on its way up, and I believe the Princess could use your company before she rests for the afternoon." Waiting a moment longer, Hartwin returned to my side, took my hand, and led me to the inner quarters.

"Did you think he wouldn't stop for lunch today?" I asked Hartwin once safely inside and physically seated by Chas at the meals table.

"He wants to get things organized, so they have an idea of when it will all happen. Then, the Prince has to be in Fastlandet this afternoon."

Hartwin didn't need to say Luther would have worked through lunch if given the option. Luther was spending every free moment with my uncle and Commander Stark trying to organize and plan things. Currently, I got to see my companion when I woke in the morning for breakfast, lunch, dinner, and he made the time to see me after my bath to make sure I went to sleep.

Tancred wheeled in the lunch trolley. Despite the security team clearing his staff, Luther decided that the Elite would continue to bring the meals in, and that all non-elite were forbidden access to the fourth level.

Tancred touched my shoulder. "Anberon said the Prince will be in shortly."

Waiting until Tancred left, I set my gaze on Hartwin. "When did Cyrans get so touchy-feely?"

Chas smirked as he sat beside me, forcing Hartwin to take a chair further away from me. "That would be my fault, Princess. I have informed your Elite that Avalonians are comforted by physical contact more than words. Therefore, if they wish to put you at ease, they should include physical comfort with their words."

The look I gave Chas must have portrayed my concern. Flattening his eyebrows, he touched my hand delicately. "No, Princess. I did not encourage comforting you in the same manner as the Queen. Just as I am now, a simple touch of your hand, elbow, or shoulder."

Taking a breath, I blew it out and relaxed. I'd heard how the Queen of Cyra liked to be comforted by her guard. Across the table, Hartwin was struggling not to laugh.

Chas's eyes hardened on his plate. "Besides which, it allows for physical interaction between yourself and your captain, which will raise no suspicion with the Praldians if it is seen as normal for your guard."

The laughter in Hartwin's eyes died as he glared at Chas. Watching them in my peripheral vision, I stared at the bowl of food in front of me, trying not to respond.

"The Princess subconsciously reaches for you, Hart. Not in full.

But her hand will twitch, or she will clasp her hands together whenever you are standing near her. She does it around the Prince as well, but the last week has seen her hold back less."

"Does everyone think...?"

"That you are scared and the only people you truly trust are your companion and the captain of your guard? Yes, Princess. Everyone knows that. It makes your guard irate that you do not trust them as you should, but they hope, with time, that will improve."

There was more; you could see it in the set of Chas's shoulders, but Luther walked in, and we all let it go unsaid. I wondered if Chas thought Hartwin and I were lovers.

Sitting at the table, Luther opened his mouth, ready to say something, but then gave each of us a steady look. "Did something happen today?"

Clearing my throat, I wet my lips. "My elite have decided to try adapting some of the Avalonian ways when it comes to dealing with their Princess."

"The touching thing?" When I looked up at Luther, he continued to eat his meal. "Anberon told me. I think it was wise of Elite Chas to suggest it. Does it bother you, Zira?"

"No, I was just surprised by it."

Taking a scroll of seasoned dough from the center of the table, Luther returned to eating. When I put my fork down, Luther stood. "If you have finished eating, Zira, I am rather time-constrained currently."

Following Luther to our room, I started undressing while he closed the doors. "Your swim was longer than usual today." So, he noticed the times of my coming and going. "Is there something specific upsetting you?"

Breath hitching a little, I shook my head but couldn't hold back the tear that escaped down my cheek. "It's ridiculous. I just want to be touched and held. I feel so alone today." Blowing out a breath, Luther wrapped me in his arms. "I want more than you have time for."

Caressing my cheek, Luther considered me silently, then kissed me as we fell to the bed.

HOLDING ME TO HIS CHEST, Luther stroked my hair while I listened to his heart beating. When the door started to open, Luther tensed. "Wait!" he ordered as he quickly retrieved my robe and covered me with it. "Come!"

Keeping his eyes on the ground, Anberon handed Luther a document. "Sorry, Princess, but it is time to leave. Your Elite are waiting in the outer quarters, my Prince."

Taking the document, Luther skimmed it as I slipped my arms into the robe and sealed it. I didn't want him to go. I either needed to be in his arms, or I needed to get out. The confinement was driving me insane.

Handing the document back to Anberon, Luther nodded. "Let me get dressed, and I will be right out."

"Luther?"

"I know you need to be held right now, Zira. So I will ask Chas or Hartwin to come and lie with you."

"Actually, I was going to ask if you could knock me out." Studying me, he cocked his head to the side. Pursing my lips, I avoided looking at him. "I'm overly emotional and have nothing to distract me this afternoon. You won't be here, and we know what I'm like when I start to feel caged. So for my Elite's sake, I think it best if I spend the afternoon resting soundly."

Rubbing his hand along his jaw, Luther took a moment longer. Then, with a nod, Luther tucked me beneath the sheet and kissed me as his fingers wove into the hair of my scalp. "I will have them wake you for dinner."

"They can reverse it?"

Smiling in answer, Luther kissed me once more and applied pressure. A moment later, it was only darkness.

Blinking my eyes open, Jervaise sat beside me, smiling, his hands massaging my head. "Welcome back, Princess. Dinner is here." Pulling back, Jervaise handed me a glass of water. "You may want to drink this before standing."

Taking the glass, I drank quietly. When I finished, I handed the glass to Jervaise. "I think it's better to have it reversed than sleep it off."

"No headache this time?"

"Not so far."

Giving me a great smile, Jervaise held out his arm. Taking it, I let him help me to stand. "I think I might wash up before I eat tonight."

"As you wish, Princess. I will let the others know. Prince Saboa asked me to let you know he will not make dinner tonight."

Stopping in the bathroom doorway, I glared back at Jervaise. He threw up his hands. "Please don't wind the messenger, Princess." Then, with a chuckle, Jervaise stepped out of the room, closing the doors behind him.

When I stepped out to the inner quarters, I found three Elite waiting for me. Studying them all a moment, I huffed. "He's expecting me to have one of my tantrums, is he?" Erhaird, Jervaise, and Clovis just smirked as they rose and joined me at the dinner table. "Is he still in Fastlandet?"

"No, he is with your Uncle and the Commander going over their plan and looking for flaws," Erhaird answered. "The Prince has been back about two hours."

Accepting the answer, I ate my meal quietly. When I finished, I sat on the sofa browsing the media streams of Praldia and Cyra. A week after the executions, Praldians were still discussing the event like it was yesterday, filling up the broadcasting opinion windows with outrage at the contents of the box and Blanche Fanchon's plans. However, as soon as anyone mentioned the box, the words were deleted before they reached the panels.

After less than a minute of continuous treachery talk, the Broadcasters shut down the open-air channels and diverted the news to discussions about the new mine set to open in Dåligalandar.

Swiping through to find backstories explaining what exactly they were mining for, I couldn't find the information. Dåligalandar had been given up as barren of even Crystalstar before I came of age.

"Something wrong, Princess?" Erhaird lifted a brow but didn't take his eyes from his own panels.

"What are they mining in Dåligalandar?"

"That has not been released."

"But the Prince would need to have approved the mine?"

"Of course, Princess."

"So, he must know what's being mined."

"Of course."

"Do you know?"

Erhaird just looked at me over his panel.

"Of course, you do. Are you going to tell me?"

Erhaird returned his full attention to his panel.

"I'm his companion!"

"Then you should ask your companion," Erhaird murmured behind his panel and swiped to another story.

"The Queen's been busy," Clovis tried to distract me. "New fashion line, new embellisher line, new hairstyle to add to it."

Wiping my palm across my panel to bring up the menu screen, I chose the Cyran Skvaller feeds. My screen filled with captures and feeds of the Cyran queen exhibiting astonishing dresses and her face painted so heavily with embellisher, I nearly didn't recognize her.

The beautiful broad-shouldered Queen paraded around in revealing frou-frou dresses that only added more bulk to an already solid frame. They definitely required extra standing space for the area the dress took up around her. In addition, her usually long golden hair was cut so short that without her breasts nearly on show, she may have been mistaken for a Cyran soldier.

The screen slid through images and feeds of the general public. The young socialites imitating the Queen's new look filled the screen along with audio captures of high-pitched adoration for their beautiful Queen. Erhaird started laughing, and Clovis joined in. Appraising them, I wasn't sure what was so funny.

"All those silly girls cutting off their hair to look like the queen," Clovis's shoulders shook with laughter. "She must be throwing objects around her room like a madwoman."

"I am sorry, Princess, we should explain," Erhaird recovered and put his panel aside. "The Queen loved her hair; she never cut it, and she liked the females at court to keep their hair long also. She feels that the long hair softens a female's appearance."

"Secondly, it enables her to drag any woman who annoys her across the room by her hair should she choose," Clovis cut in. "If they all cut their hair, she will have to drag them by their throats, which prevents them screaming."

Eye's opening wide, I choked. "I sent Padget to live with a sadisten!"

Jumping off the lounge, Jervaise knelt beside mine. Taking my hand, he engulfed it in his. "You saved her life and gave the Prince a way to still look just. However, he did extract certain promises from his mother with regards to Padget's care."

"And one from his father. That one is the reason for the current hairstyle," Clovis chuckled.

"If the Queen were to break her promises with regards to Padget's care," Jervaise explained, "then King Saboa would extract a payment of brutnalöfte on his behalf."

Brutnalöfte was a law in Cyra. If you broke a promise you made, then the injured party could extract physical payment of deemed equal value. Some Cyran's lost their heads in brutnalöfte, literally. "The king cut the Queen's hair off?"

"The queen dragged Padget around by hers," Jervaise shrugged. "King Saboa felt the punishment fit the crime. He ordered the Queen's Elite to hold her down while the Royal Guard Barberare shaved her hair off. The king kept her golden locks and has them hanging in his private throne room just to further humiliate the

Queen." Sitting back on his haunches, Jervaise relinquished my hand.

"Of course, the general public is not aware this is the queen's punishment, and so—" Clovis waved his panel at me with a sly smile.

Suddenly understanding, I laughed also. It was a double blow for the Queen. Jervaise stood to return to the couch next to Clovis when I caught sight of a capture on Clovis's screen.

"What is that?" I grabbed up my panel in time to freeze one of the newest stories. It was a capture of myself. An old capture. "King Saboa is overjoyed to hear that Prince Saboa and his Avalonian Princess are already expecting an heir," Clovis laughed. "Where do they get this nonsense from?"

"Princess? You are looking very pale. Do you need to sit down? Have a glass of water, maybe?" Then, having stood too quickly, my head spun a little, and my legs started to tremble beneath me. Taking my elbow, Jervaise observed me.

Watching me intently, Clovis sat the panel down. "It is nothing to worry about, Princess. It is just a gossip broadcast. No one believes anything they put out there."

"They believed the Queen's new hairstyle." Swallowing hard, I started walking for the outer quarters. My Elite didn't try to stop me; they just followed. When I started towards the Prince's office, Anberon stood to intercept me.

"Anber, let her go," Jervaise stepped forward to ensure my path wasn't blocked and handed Anberon the panel murmuring something quietly. Anberon cursed but returned to his seat.

In Luther's office, the men stood by the wall looking at electronic captures of blueprints. No one even noticed my presence until Vered, who was leaning on the car window looking decidedly bored, moved.

"Zira." He smiled and wrapped me in a hug. Then, when his eyes met mine, he stepped back. "You're upset?"

"Zira, I explained –" Luther began.

"You haven't eaten," I replied to my cousin; I could tell by his eyes. "Anberon?"

Anberon stepped into the room. Holding out my hand for the panel, which he handed over, I stepped back a step. "Arrange dinner for the men. My uncle and cousin are not Cyran and still need to eat."

"Yes, Princess."

"Zira."

"Luther." Moving forward, I handed him the panel frozen with the old picture of me and the news headline.

Giving me an annoyed look, Luther took the panel and reviewed it. "Enjoy your dinner, and I will meet you back here to continue afterward," Luther dismissed the men. Commander Stark closed the doors on the way out.

Sighing, Luther put the panel on his desk. "What do you want me to do, Zira? It is gossip and speculation. Everyone knows that and will not believe it until we confirm it. It is an old photo of you. You have not even worn that dress since the opening of the Fattigby school last year." Blinking in surprise, I tilted my head. Luther smirked. "Yes, Zira, I paid that much attention. Plus, that dress was not flattering and did make you look in the early stages of pregnancy."

Frowning, I shifted on my feet, suddenly self-conscious. Sighing when I started fidgeting with my dress, Luther threw the panel onto his desk, looking back to the wall. "I need to work, Zira. We are running out of time."

"How?"

Luther appraised me sternly. "Remove your dress."

Swallowing hard, I did as he asked.

"And your undergarment."

Uncomfortable with this, I looked over my shoulder at the door.

Stepping closer, Luther caressed my cheek with his knuckles. "They will not come in until one of us open the door, Zira. Do as I ask."

Closing my eyes, I took a breath and let the slip fall to the floor with my dress.

"Two days ago, the dip between your hips could serve as a bowl.

This morning, I noticed your abdomen has risen to be even with your hip bones. I expect that I will be able to cup your womb in my palm next week. Within another month, with even your more conservative clothing, it will be obvious to everyone you are carrying."

Closing the distance between us, Luther slid his hand over mine, where I'd started caressing my growing abdomen. While I'd noticed the physical change, I hadn't thought about how long it would take others to discern it.

Smirking, Luther tickled up my arm and tugged me that last inch to have me pressed against him. "Since you have dismissed my strategists." Taking me in his arms, Luther kissed me heatedly as he lowered me to the floor. When he kissed me low over my abdomen, I gazed up at the wall above me and finally recognized the blueprint.

"It's the Avalonian castle," I breathed through the pleasure his mouth bloomed. Stopping his ministrations, Luther glanced up to the blueprint, then rose to hover over me as he readied to enter me. Gripping his shoulders, I frowned. "It's wrong."

"Tell me in a minute." Luther susurrated before latching onto my neck like a bloodsucker.

"Only a minute?"

Caressing my breast, Luther smirked as I arched into his hand. "How long do you think it takes a starving Avalonian to eat?"

"Oh, well, we have less than a minute, so I hope you're ready."

In answer, Luther shoved forward, taking no time to raise my heart rate. The force of his thrusts moved us along the floor until my head hit the wall. "Luther!" I cringed breathlessly, my hands going overhead to hold against the wall. Cursing, Luther supported my neck to prevent me from being injured as he pounded me into the oblivion of ecstasy.

Picking up speed and force, Luther roared as he spent himself, then stilled and shook as he breathed hard. Eventually, he smiled at me. "I am always ready for you, Zira." Then, lowering his body, he kissed me a lot slower this time.

Chapter Twenty-Three

By the time Luther sealed his uniform again, my companion was gone, and the prince returned. As I sat up, rolling my neck and cringing a bit, I decided sex on the floor with a Cyran was not the healthiest option. Picking up my slip, Luther handed it to me as he helped me to stand again. "Why is the blueprint wrong?"

Stopping momentarily to look over my already changing body, I cupped my womb.

"Zira?"

Blinking up at him, I realized he was back in planning mode and forced myself to pay attention while I stepped into the slip. "Oh, it's missing the throne room."

Wiping his hand through the display, Luther made it grow to be three-dimensional. "No, the throne room is here." Luther pointed to a large area.

"That's the public throne room, but it's not the '*throne*' room." Stepped into my dress, I slipped my arm into the sleeve before I pointed to an empty spot. "This is where the throne that matters is. This is where I need to be."

"Finish getting dressed." Then, moving to the doors, Luther threw them open angrily as I pulled my other sleeve into place. "Everyone in, now!"

Just as I touched the tab to seal my dress, Commander Stark and my Uncle stepped into the room. "Tell them," Luther ordered.

"This blank area in your map, it's not empty. This is the true throne room, the one the public never gets to see. It's where the blood throne sits and is where I need to get to if I'm to secure the throne."

My uncle stepped forward, confused momentarily. Studying where I was pointing, Ravid turned to Luther. "Your kind have methods of inquisition, one being the dragging of memories." Luther just glared at Ravid. "Use it on Zira," my uncle suggested.

Double blinking in surprise, I stepped back, not liking the sound of this. Taking my hand to stop me from fleeing, Luther raised his voice. "Anberon?"

"Yes, my Prince."

"Bring in the visualizer." Taking a firmer grip on my wrist, Luther ran his finger along my jaw until his thumb swept over my lips. "It will not hurt you, Zira. You merely have to remember being shown this room, and it will capture the experience for us." Hugging me to his chest, he kissed the corner of my mouth, then pinched my bottom lip between his. When he pulled back, he met my eyes. The trust he was showing in that action tugged at my soul. "Trust me, I would never harm you." What he gave, he asked for in return.

Nodding my head, I shifted Luther's grip on me to hold his hand. Dropping one more kiss on my lips, Luther led me to the desk and his chair as Anberon came in and set down a device. Connecting some leads to the wall unit, Anberon pressed a switch, and the top of the pad glowed green.

Turning to the wall unit, Luther touched a setting on the screen, and it went blank. Taking my hand, Luther placed it gently on the green light. When Anberon pressed another switch, my hand sunk into the coldest gel. I would have withdrawn my hand, but Luther held it in place. Picking up something similar to the medic's monitor but transparent, Anberon placed it over my eyes.

Instantly, the screen filled with the image of Luther as we coupled moments earlier. Luther coughed. "Concentrate, Zira. Show us the room with the blood throne."

Closing my eyes, I remembered the day I was taken to the actual throne when I was ten. My uncle, the king's voice, suddenly filled the room. "Before your coronation, Zimri, you will come here with the elders and your sister." The King opened the door to the blood throne room. When he turned to scowl at me, my mind instantly flashed to his severed head upon the blood-drenched public throne room floor. A sob escaped my throat.

A hand touched my shoulder and started massaging gently. "The blood throne, Zira," Luther encouraged gently.

Stepping into the gleaming silver room behind my brother, I looked around in awe. The sapphire blue waters of our ocean ran through a channel in the middle of the room, disappearing through a magnificent arched window level with the sea outside. On the other side stood a grand, dark grey stone throne. On this side, sitting in the corner by a window, sat one of the Elders.

"This is the blood throne." My uncle's baritone echoed through the room. "Only those of royal blood and the elders know this is the true throne. For the elders to recognize you as their king, you must first be recognized by this stone. It is the keeper of our people's magiks. The blood that runs in your veins is the blood of this planet."

Moving to the channel, our uncle walked across the water as if there was an invisible bridge. Turning, he waited for my brother and me. Glancing into the water, Zimri stiffened, his eyes getting very wide. Reaching back, he took my hand and pulled me close to him. Stepping together, we found our feet fell on solid ground.

Amazed, I laughed and glanced down, only to realize what Zimri had seen. Faces of dead Avalonians stared up at us from beneath the water. Freezing on the spot, my eyes widened in fear. Zimri pulled me tightly to him. "It's okay, Zira. They can't hurt you from their grave." Then, using his arm around me, Zimri moved us across the rest of the channel until we stood with our uncle in front of the throne.

Our king patted my head like he did his dogs. "There, child. Only those of the blood can cross that channel. If anyone not of the blood tries, the dead rise and steal them to the grave with them." Our uncle moved to the throne. "Zimri, you will be seated on the throne. Your right arm will be cut and placed thusly." The king sat on the throne and placed his right arm along the dark grey stone armrest.

"The royal womb will stand beside you, and her arm will be cut so that her blood blends with yours, and she will speak the words that make you the king." Our king smiled at the chair. "When I was brought here my first time, this stone was mid-grey. When my blood pooled and was absorbed into the stone, it became darker. I was the most powerful king in centuries. Your crowning may see this throne once again the black of our peoples' blood, Zimri."

"Not my blood." Zimri scowled, squeezing my hand. "Zira's blood, just as it was your sister's blood that darkened the throne and gave you your power."

Our uncle was out of the throne and Zimri's throat in his hand before I knew what had happened. Terrified of my uncle, I jumped away with a yelp and fell onto the throne. "The male rules this planet. The royal womb is here to breed the next king. That's all she is good for."

Smirking at our uncle, Zimri didn't even seem scared. "Are you that insecure about everyone realizing it was your sister's blood that made you king, or have the elders brainwashed you to believe this hogwash?"

Placing my hand on the arm of the throne to pull myself up, the room filled with the brightest light. A moment later, I was airborne, landing with a sickening crack and horrific pain. Huddling terrified against the wall on the other side of the channel, I cried.

As my vision cleared, Zimri was kneeling next to me. Checking my head, his fingers came away black with my blood. When I went to move, I cringed over the pain in my arm, choking down a scream.

"You!" My uncle shouted, crossing the deathly channel. "You are nothing. If it wasn't for the fact that the next king must come from your womb, you would be thrown away like the rubbish you are. You are never to touch that throne again. It's not for you. Even the day you crown your brother—"

"Enough!" Zimri stood glaring at my uncle. "She knows her place already. You've made sure of it from the day she was born. She is my sister and a Princess. You will not talk to her like this anymore. If you cannot be kind, then you don't talk to her at all!"

"I am your king!"

"For now!" Zimri stepped forward until he was chest to chest with our uncle. Zimri's hair—braided like our kings but midnight blue in color as opposed to the king's black—flicked like the tail of a cat. It was one of Zimri's talents that his hair became an extra limb. "In only two years, I will be the king, and you shall only be regent. You've seen my natal scale, uncle. Treat my sister poorly again, and I will make sure you regret it when I sit on that throne."

Glaring at my brother a moment, our king's eyes swirled with rage as they came to me. "Get up and seek Nyla, then get to your lessons." Then, with a look to the Elder who watched in silence, our uncle stormed out.

Helping me stand, Zimri glared over my shoulder. Following his glare, I observed the Elder standing, watching us, his piercing gaze focused on me. Swallowing hard, I held my aching arm and looked up at my brother. "I'm sorry." My head spun.

Lifting me into his arms, Zimri carried me through the cold grey corridor to the stairs that led to the castle proper. "You are more than they will ever know, Zira. When I am king, we will change the way the royal womb is treated. Your daughter will know she is worth something."

Stepping into the empty public throne room from the hidden staircase, Zimri carried me to Medic Nyla's rooms.

A clicking sound brought me back to the present. Blinking the deluge of tears from my eyes, I noticed the device was shut down, and my hand sat heavily on the black box.

"Zira," Luther's voice was too gentle as he touched my shoulder. When I shied away from his affection, Luther retreated. Ashamed of the way I was treated and of how badly I still missed my brother, I wasn't game enough to observe his face.

Swiping the monitor from my eyes, I threw it on the desk before wiping at the endless tears. "Did you get what you needed?"

"More than," Vered answered in a tone of voice that spoke for everyone. "Zimri would have been a great king."

Nodding, I stood a little unsteadily. Commander Stark slid the office doors open and gestured to the Elite outside. They must have closed the doors sometime during my recollection. "I'll go to bed now. Good night."

"That was most interesting," Luther grumbled as I walked out. Returning to the display, he started capturing stills from my memory and filing them with plans. "Did you know they treated the Princess so poorly?"

"My companion is her Medic. Of course, it wasn't like that for all of them, but the last king was fanatical. I think Zira's power scared him."

"The Elder did not seem happy about it either." Luther's eyes came to me; a look I couldn't recognize crossed his face. For a moment, I thought it may have been fear, but I'd never known a Cyran to fear anything.

"It's problematic if there is always an elder watching the room," Ravid worried. "He will try to stop Zira from getting to the throne. That's if she can slip past the Barbarian to get to it." Ravid looked at the capture of the hidden entrance. "But, if she can slip through and is fast enough to cross the channel before the Elder stops her, it may work in our favor. There is no waiting. There will be an Elder there to witness the throne recognize her."

"The channel is also a problem," Luther decided. He replayed the

King's explanation. "If only her blood can cross the channel, and Zira is the last of it, how can she appoint a caretaker?"

Stark stepped to the screen as Vered helped me to the door. "I found this the most interesting." Dragging a finger along the screen until a capture of the dead in the bottom of the channel appeared, he tapped it to play. It played a moment, then he stopped it. "There" –he pointed to a woman's face— "did you see that?"

Stopping, I watched as Luther took it back and played the snippet again, all of us focused on her face. Gasping, I was falling into nothingness before Stark stopped it again. "She blinked!"

Chapter Twenty-Four

My eyelids fluttered open as a body pressed against the back of mine. "Are you okay, Zira?"

I closed my eyes again. It was dark, probably very late, and Luther was just coming to bed. "Ask me again when the Barbarian is dead."

"Was it always like that, with your king?"

"No. When his companion was nearby, he treated me well. They didn't have any children, so she treated me as her own." Sighing, I pulled his arm around to hold me. "Let's not talk about it. It only upsets me and is in the past. Tell me about Dåligalandar?"

Luther stiffened and rolled away to lie on his back. "It is just another mining settlement."

Sitting up, I tried to see him where I knew he lay, but it was too dark. "That's not true, and you know it. Just the fact that you pulled away tells me there is much more to it. I was on the Native committee and had access to their records. I know they looked at mining there, Luther. I know what they found and the trouble the Dåligmark people caused." Placing my hand where I thought Luther's chest was, I found his thigh. He must have been sitting up.

Luther's hand fell over mine and pulled me into his chest, my head resting over his heart. "The mine is Cyran. It is my mine, Zira. While the Native council found nothing of value to them in Dåligalandar, they found something of value to us; they just did not know it to pursue it."

Pushing away from Luther's body to stare at the darkness where I knew his face would be, I frowned. "You're doing something I won't approve of. It's why you didn't want to tell me."

"I told you when we joined, Zira. I would not put blocks in your way as long as your cause does not interfere with my own plans."

"And my cause, my work to give the natives a better life, would go against what you are doing in Dåligalandar?" Luther's silence was its own answer. "Oh, Luther. When I come of age in seven years, you better hope whatever it is you are after in Dåligalandar is finished, or I will make your home life a living wormhole. Sooner, if I find out the details and can force a movement against you."

Luther laughed as he pressed my back to the bed. "Well, luckily, I have the power to gag you for seven years, Zira."

When I just glared at him, Luther kissed just in front of my ear. "I am not happy about some of the things I need to do, Zira, but I am the ruler here, and I am a Prince of Cyra. I must do at times what makes others unhappy."

As he kissed along my jaw, I placed my hand over his heart. While his face hovered over mine, his body moving to take mine, I used my free hand to trace a delicate finger along his jaw. "And I must do what I can to protect those who can't protect themselves, Luther, even if that makes you unhappy."

"You can try, Zira. I have missed your passionate pleas in open court." Luther laughed when I pinched him.

"Rövhål!"

"Now, now, Princess," Luther purred as he moved over me, "do not make me go get the gag already." Luther pressed into me, and I cried out the pleasure of it.

"There are five men in the room next door, Luther. A gag might be a good idea. With how good that felt just then, I don't think I can keep quiet tonight."

"Good, I like to hear you, Zira."

"But—"

"Zira, our guard are Cyran. What they hear us doing is just an everyday part of life. It affects them no more than watching you eat your dinner. And if it does" –Luther caught my nipple between his teeth— "the women in the palace are not complaining about the extra attention."

Raucous laughter came from the room next door before it was suddenly muffled. "What was that?"

"Your little outcry gave our guard the wrong impression. They think we have finished already." There was a wicked edge to his voice.

"Luther?"

"It has been a while since I have pleased a woman to sunrise."

When we emerged from the bedroom in the morning, I was exhausted and starving. Hartwin was serving up the meal as Luther and I sat down. Anberon was smirking in the corner, reading a panel. "Your Elite are eating breakfast, my Prince, but will be set to go when you are ready."

"Thank you, Anberon."

"Where are you today?" I took a mouthful and sighed with relief.

"Apagrind"

Frowning, not recognizing that name, I tried to recall it on the map. "I've never heard of that place."

Hartwin frowned. "That is because it is a place in Cyra, Princess. I am of the understanding from nightshift that you will need to sleep this morning?"

"I believe the night shift is right, Hart." Heat crept up my neck and face as I avoided looking at him. Luther had made me cry out his name and many other sounds in our pursuit of pleasure last night. "What's in Apagrind?"

Taking something out of his pocket, Luther put it on the table. Recognizing the amulet, I went to pick it up. As soon as my finger brushed it, pain lanced through my hand, and my power cycloned around me.

"Are you okay, Princess?" Anberon was kneeling beside me, moving my hair aside so he could see my face. Hartwin was examining the burn on the tip of my finger. "You could have just told her, my Prince."

On my back, a few feet from the table, I looked up in time to see Luther pocket the amulet, a frown set between his eyes. "I did not know it would do that to her."

Anberon made a sound of disgust. "She has got power. You knew it was not just going to sit there and let her touch it either."

"That's the amulet Commander Stark wore the day he came to take me. That's more than a protection amulet."

"Yes. If you had tried to use your power against Commander Stark, it would have turned your power on itself," Luther educated. Collecting his uniform jacket, Luther sealed it before Medic Ellery burst through the door and knelt on the opposite side of Hartwin, taking my hand to examine it.

Cursing at the pain, I glared at Luther. "I see you are overly concerned about what happened as well!"

"You missed my concern during your unconsciousness, Zira. Once your eyes started to open, I was sure you would be fine. Medic Ellery will see to the burn on your fingers and ensure no harm has come to you." Luther's tone indicated it was his heirs he was worried may have been harmed. "I need to get to Apagrind as it is nearly nightfall there and a treacherous territory to traverse even in the light of day. Anberon."

Stepping around us, Luther left the room. Anberon stroked my cheek. "He does care for you, Princess. You need not look so doubtful." Rising, he followed his prince from the room.

"Bring her down the infirmary, Hartwin. I will have Nyla meet us, and she can check the Princess's health while I tend to her hand."

"We cannot do that, Ellery. She needs two Elite with her at least. If I take someone else, they will know." Hartwin lifted me into his arms.

"Fine, put her to bed, and I will bring what equipment I can with me." Ellery left the room as Hartwin carried me back into the bedroom and laid me down.

"What's in Apagrind, Hart?"

"An Avalonian sorcerer who made that protection amulet." Hartwin sat down on the bed, finger combing my hair away from my face. "Luther is going to procure more amulets."

"An Avalonian makes weapons against his own people?"

"Protection for others against his people. Though, he is smart enough to make the amulets useless against himself. They are also exceedingly expensive. Luther and his father are the only beings who have been able to afford one so far."

"Luther can't afford one for everyone."

"No, but he wants at least two of your elite protected, Zira. As do you, Ravid and Vered have power, but we will have to rely on our speed and strength. After how quickly we have seen you move when in danger, Zira, Luther is just covering his bases."

"It is ridiculous that he does not include me on the plans, Hart. I'm walking into battle right beside him. I should know everything they do."

Hartwin didn't respond, merely stroked a finger down the side of my cheek. Ellery and Nyla came into the room pushing a trolley before they shut the door. On the top shelf was what Ellery needed to treat the burns on my hand. Nyla pulled a cover from the lower shelf and removed the machine she'd used to confirm my pregnancy only a week ago. An audible groan escaped my lips at the sight of it.

"I know you don't like it, Zira, but we need to make sure no damage was done." Nyla frowned, pulling back the sheet. Hartwin stood to move away.

"Hart." I grabbed his hand. "Please?"

Kneeling by my shoulder, Hartwin turned his body towards my face, leaned over me, and put his mouth to my ear as Nyla bent my legs and got the probe ready. "Remember the day I came to tell you I was Elite?"

Of all the moments to bring up, he chose our last day as lovers. Nyla pushed the probe inside, and I tensed.

"I was so proud of being one of the youngest to ever make Elite, and you are the first person I wanted to tell. Every step I took towards our meeting spot became heavier and harder to take. Reality sank in. I knew I had to end things with you then. By the time I reached you, I felt like I had dragged my heart through a razor grass field back home in Cyra."

Tears ran down my cheeks, Hartwin's cheek pressed to mine as if he might absorb my tears through his skin. The device started buzzing, and I jumped. Only Hartwin's weight kept me on the bed.

"I have never forgotten the way your smile vanished when you saw me walking towards you. You started pleading with me before I even opened my mouth. You begged just to be mine in whatever way that could happen, as long as I did not turn you away."

The device stopped, and Nyla removed it, straightening my skirt, but Hartwin stayed where he was. "I never saw you smile again. Not when I was assigned to watch your estate, not on any of the captures of you doing your charity work. Never again. Never how you used to. Maybe when this is over, Luther will remind you how to truly smile again."

Lifting away, Hartwin kept his face turned away, but I could see the tears in his eyes. Standing, he went into the bathroom before anyone else could talk to him.

"Everything is fine with your babies, Zira. Don't stress." Nyla patted my good hand as she pulled the sheet back up.

Taking her place beside me, Ellery started tending to my burns. "You look very tired, Princess."

"I am, Medic Ellery. As soon as you are done, I will be going back to sleep." I cringed at the discomfort as he applied a salve.

"Probably for the best, Princess, but remember you need to eat regularly."

"I will wake her at lunchtime, Ellery," Hartwin assured. He came back into the room without a shred of evidence that he'd just showed the most emotion I'd ever seen from a Cyran.

When Ellery and Nyla packed up their equipment and left, Hartwin tucked me in, assuring me he'd have me woken to eat a late lunch. Despite my usual unease of sleeping here, I fell into a deep exhaustive sleep.

Chapter Twenty-Five

Utz was sitting on the end of my bed when I woke up. "Is it lunchtime already?"

"Yes, Princess." He stood up as I sat up and threw the sheet back, ready to stand. The dagger in his hand caught my attention and froze me in place. "Normally, I would have just killed you in your sleep. A cowardly thing for a Cyran, but I like you, Princess, and I would have considered it mercy. However, you are the last of a royal bloodline. I could not very well substantiate saving the bloodline of my own people from pollution and destroy that of your own peoples. So it forced me to make other arrangements."

"With the Barbarian?" I cringed.

"No, actually. I know what he did to you, and he is also not pure-blooded. Others would align themselves with the royal womb to see peace and a child of pure blood seated on the throne."

"You know they will kill me as soon as they have their heirs, Elite Utz, and their method of getting the much-wanted heirs may make me wish for death sooner? And then there is the issue of me being joined already."

"Well, luckily for you, Princess, your people are not too

concerned with legitimacy. As for Prince Saboa, it will take him a few years to move on anyway. By which time, as you just stated, you will more than likely be dead, and he will be free to take a new wife of Cyran blood to breed with."

"You think your Prince and King will stand by and let me be raped and murdered at the whim of a purist?"

"I think King Saboa will force his son to obedience when the odds of war are weighed for its worth."

"Then you are wrong. Even if I wasn't with child, Luther would drag Cyra to war for me, but with his son in my womb, he will drag every world to war."

Smirking, Utz shook his head. "If you were with child, Prince Saboa would have announced it to his father."

"The King knows and agreed with us that it was best to keep it quiet for as long as possible. Anberon, Hartwin, and the medics all know. It's why Medic Nyla was moved into the palace in the first place. Luther got me pregnant the night I killed his would-be assassin in the throne room. Not exactly the thanks I was looking for, I assure you."

There was hesitation in Utz's face now. The dagger trembled in his hand a moment before he steeled his resolve and reached forward to grab my elbow. "I am sorry, Princess. It is too late. Arrangements have been made. In truth, what grows inside you is impure. Your people will know how to kill it without harming your womb of future children."

"I'm sorry too, Utz." As his hand closed on my elbow, the symbols for air and sharp flash-burned on my spine, and I snapped my wrist to wrap my razor ribbons around Utz's throat. Slicing at the air ribbon with his blade, my ribbon disintegrated. Shocked, I stared at him open-mouthed.

Taking two steps back, Utz touched the fresh wounds from the razor wire at his throat as he held up the blade. "A gift from the mercs waiting to take you to your new husband. Apparently, they had to rob a sacred temple in the far reaches of Avalonia to find a weapon that could counter your ability to ribbon."

Recovering from my surprise, I tucked my feet beneath me, ready to pounce. Utz shook his head. "You do not want to do that, Princess. If you fight me, I may accidentally kill you."

"If you think I'm going to let you hand me over for my children to be murdered while they still grow inside me, you are greatly mistaken."

Throwing out my sonic repulsion, Utz smashed through the bathroom wall. Leaping off the bed for the bedroom doors, I flung them open. Hartwin was unconscious on the sofa, and Chas was out to it at the table. "No!" Hesitating only a moment, I ran past them to the outer quarters only to find the remainder of my Elite in the same state.

"It was my turn to bring up the lunches." Utz's voice followed me into the outer quarters. As he stepped towards me, I turned to face him. "They will be out long enough for me to dispose of you and return to feign unconsciousness with them. They will never know who took you." He ran at me, dodging the ball of sonic repulsion I threw at him this time.

Moving quickly, I twisted out of the way as he made a grab for my waist. The teleportation channels buzzed around him. With them activated, ready to transport, all he had to do was get hold of me for a second. Having not eaten, I didn't have the energy to fight this out, or more if he got me out of the palats. This had to end now.

The symbol for sound flash-burned on my spine. The noise of running footsteps approaching the doors was overwhelming. "No!" Gritting his teeth, Utz turned to look towards the approaching doors. Air flash-burned, and my ribbon snapped out, wrapping around the wrist holding the bespelled blade. Blinking wide eyes at my ribbon, Utz turned his angry eyes on me.

"Never show your hand in a battle with an Avalonian, Utz, or you just may lose it." Sharp flash-burned. Utz roared his rage as I severed his hand from his body.

Using the ribbon to pull the dagger to me, I took it in my hand seconds before Utz rushed me again. His body slammed into mine, and I drove the blade into his chest. The breath rushed from my body as I hit the floor with his weight above mine.

Lying there, the transportation channels still buzzed with life, letting me know Utz wasn't dead yet. Gazing at my unconscious Elite, I knew I couldn't trust them now. I wasn't safe here, had never been safe here. Putting my hand over Utz's still-intact wrist where the teleportation chip was buried, I thought of a deserted piece of land I knew.

It didn't work. I was still stuck under his body. Crying out in frustration, I cursed the suns of every planet in our system. Groaning, Utz lifted his pale face to look at me. "I am sorry, Princess," he whispered as green Cyran blood started to dribble from his lips.

"Look at me!" I demanded. When Utz met my eyes, I used his need for forgiveness to create a psionic link. Giving him the address, I made him think of that place. Lightning cracked above our heads.

We were on the banks of a forgotten reserve overgrown with weeds and swamp damp. Trying to push Utz's body from me, I couldn't budge him, and he was dead weight now. Sonic repulsion flash-burned, and he went sailing into the air. Rolling to the side before his body crashed back to earth, I sucked in a large breath and cringed over the ache from having been slammed by a brick wall like Utz.

Kneeling there, I cried for several minutes. What would Luther think when he came home? The damage and Utz's blood would make it apparent there was a fight and that Utz was injured, with both of us now missing. Hartwin said they tracked every transportation so they'd find Utz. Still, this heat and the swamps, the bugs would ravage his corpse quickly.

Luther would most likely think I'd been taken, so I'd have to find a way to get word to him. But, first, I needed to find a safe place, somewhere out of Luther's reach. If Luther found me now, he'd just force me back to the palats surrounded by guards I couldn't trust now.

Drying my tears, I sucked in several calming breaths. I couldn't stay here. There was no telling what time Luther would get back, or when the Elite would wake and realize what occurred, or if the people Utz sold his loyalty for could find me. A safe place. That was my first priority. Then, I would need sustenance, or none of it was going to matter.

Gaining my feet, I stumbled through the long grasses and rolled Utz onto his back. Dead eyes stared up at me. Blinking away tears for a life wasted, I closed his eyes and put my hand to his head as I prayed for his transfer to the next life.

It was midday, and the heat of summer was unbearable out here in the marshes, but with only my robe on, it was more manageable than in clothing. Grabbing the dagger with both hands, I used my foot to brace and pulled it from his body. This was not a weapon I needed in the wrong hands. It would come with me, and I would hide it where no one could find it.

Ripping Utz's shirt free, I used the material to wrap the blade as I walked to the edge of the waterway. The reserve was on a minor river that started in the wetlands and flowed out to sea. Getting my bearings, I immersed myself in the water and sank well below the surface. I didn't dare dissipate this time. I'd need my clothing at the other end.

...To be Continued in Cyra.

Join the Beautiful and Deadly

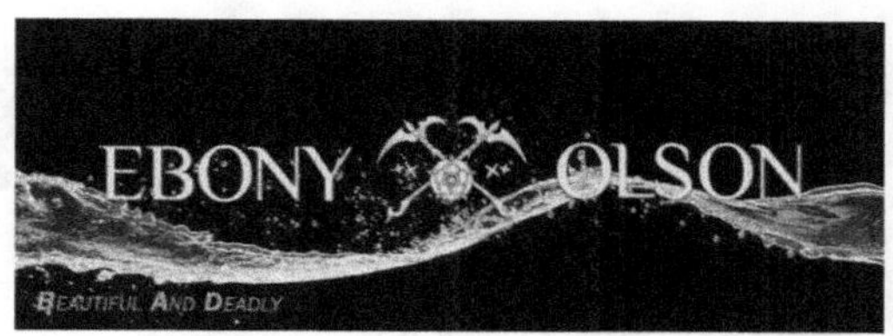

Join Ebony's Mischief List

Sign up to Ebony's mailing list for the following perks:

- latest news on new releases
- heads up on upcoming promotions
- exclusive content previews
- first chance at Giveaways
- get a free book

Go to https://ebonyolson.com for more information

Cyra Preview

Book 2: Chaos Star Trilogy

It was hours passed sunset when I dragged my body onto the jetty out front of the darkened cabin. Lying there exhausted for a moment, I fought the need to just close my eyes and sleep. I'd been attacked again, this time by an Elite Guard.

Flashes of Utz as he tried to kidnap me played in my head. How long had it been? Was Luther, my companion and guardian, home yet? Had he discovered the betrayal of one of his closest guards? It didn't matter. I couldn't go back to the palats. I couldn't trust those who were meant to protect me.

Trying to get up, I groaned with weakness and lethargy. I'd gone nearly the entire day without food or sustenance, something my body would have struggled with without two other lives needing to be sustained inside me. The thought of my unborn children drove me to my feet, and I stumbled down the well-maintained jetty to the familiar cabin door.

Searching my fingers above the door frame, I found the key and managed to still my shaking hands long enough to get the door open and lock it behind me. I scrounged around in the dark to find the lantern, blowing across the top to activate the light within. Sitting at the table, I continued to breathe on the lamp until the carbon from my lungs was sufficient enough to make the lamp burn bright enough to see the entire inside of the cabin.

It had been years since I'd been to the cabin. My need to keep my lovers secret from the general public, to keep my reputation untarnished in the eyes of the Praldian people and their archaic ideas about females and sex before taking a companion once made it a regular stop for me. This cabin belonged to the Cyran trader, who taught me much more than how a Cyran liked to tumble between the sheets.

Using the table to support me, I made my way to the food locker and opened it hoping the cabin was still in use. Luckily for me, it was only recently by the looks of the food inside. I didn't bother with preparing a proper meal. I merely grabbed and ate until I couldn't eat anymore. Then I pulled out a bottle of clear water and drank it dry.

Once I did all I could to see to the health of my offspring, I crawled over to the bed, removed my wet robe, and slipped into the sheets. I was asleep before my next exhalation.

"The Queen be thrown into a black hole!"

Blinking up into the Cyran face above me, I tried to raise myself to sit but couldn't. Whimpering, I fell back onto the bed.

"You're safe, Princess, do not try to move yet. Let me silence the alarm, and I will be back."

I should have known Ethelred would have his cabin alarmed. Moving to a power box, he flicked a switch and shut the door before pulling out a comms unit. "It's Ethelred, passkey lax faller. It is just a false alarm. Yes, a kattdjur got in through a hole in the wall. Thank you."

Putting the comms unit away, Ethelred returned beside the bed, bringing me a water bottle. He was the same large build as all Cyrans and kept his hair short like the Royal Guard he'd once been. Big and strong and so very intimidating if you didn't know his compassionate heart.

"So, Princess, what brings you to the wetlands?"

"I need somewhere safe to be. I couldn't think of a better place." Taking the water that Ethelred offered, his smile warmed me.

"Well, I would say make yourself at home, but by the looks of it..." He raised his eyebrows at my nakedness beneath the sheet before he picked up my robe. "I will hang this to dry for you." Ethelred looked at his comms. "It is late, but I know a market that's still open. I will get some food to see you through the night."

"Ethel," I hesitated. "I need Hälsodryck, or I will be unconscious by morning."

Pausing, Ethelred stared a moment longer than was polite. He shook his head. "Of all the times to get a woman pregnant, he chooses to do it on the eve of war. I know some people. I will see what I can do. Go back to sleep, Princess."

"Ethel, if this will put you in a bad spot?"

Ethelred smirked as much as a Cyran's mouth let them. "Prince Saboa got back to the palats hours ago. Everything has been in Chaos since, but no one knows why. As I have not been contacted by Commander Stark or the Prince yet. So, your being here is not an issue. But as soon as either of them calls me, I will be honor bound to reveal your location, Zira. You understand?"

With a nod, I closed my eyes again. "How long does that give me?"

"Depends how bad it is."

"One of my elite tried to sell me to a power-hungry Avalonian and planned to kill my unborn children."

Ethelred cursed so severely that I blushed for him. "Depending on how long it takes them to work it out, Zira. I'll give it between sunrise to lunch tomorrow at the latest. I will be back within the hour." The door shut and locked, and I drifted back to sleep.

I was only vaguely aware of Ethelred returning and lifting my head as he put a bottle to my lips. I sipped the Hälsodryck until the bottle was taken away. Then I was conscious enough to recognize a body slipping into the bed with me and folding me in large arms.

It wasn't until a comms unit beeped just before sunrise that I was able to fully wake. Movement behind me alerted my brain and forced me to open my blurry eyes to see the strong arm around me collect their comms from the bed, raise it up, and read the message.

With a sigh, Ethelred kissed the top of my shoulder. "They found the Elite's body at the mouth of the våtmarker channel just a short time ago. I have been called before the Prince after breakfast. Your robe should be dry by now."

Climbing out of bed, Ethelred placed my dry robe next to me before turning his back to dress.

"I didn't interrupt your evening did I?"

Ethelred laughed, his voice filling the cabin. "You are my Princess, you can interrupt the best sex of my life, and I would not begrudge you. But even before that," he turned to smile at me, "even as my friend. If you need me, I am there, Zira. Just like you were for me."

I blinked away tears, and Ethelred growled. "Now, do not start doing that, or I will have to take pity on you and pleasure you until you scream, and we both know how much trouble that will get me in with the Prince."

My belly flipped over at the memory of sex with Ethelred, and I sighed. "Don't start making those sorts of offers, Ethel. You know I can't, and right now, my desires are uncontrollable."

Ethelred's face became sympathetic before a devilish glint entered his eye. "For the first time ever, I envy my Prince. Imagine the burden of an insatiable, beautiful wife?"

"Most Cyran's would not find me so."

"But the Prince does, and I always have, Zira, since the day you soothed my loss."

The tease was gone from his voice now. Anything that prompted the memory of Ethelred's wife stirred his grief. It's how we met all those years past. I had just come of age, and he was a trader grieving the loss of his wife. I gave Ethelred a shoulder to cry on. He gave me some fantastic and invaluable experience on how to be with a Cyran male. Not to mention our mutual knowledge, which led to successful business arrangements.

"Do you regret your choice, Ethel?" I wouldn't have been game to ask it five years ago.

"Choosing Berdine over my career in the Royal Guard?" Ethelred started making breakfast. "I would have made Elite if I did not meet her and break my celibacy before the five-year stint. Still, six months with Berdine was worth an eternity of being seen as a failure."

"The Prince doesn't see you that way."

Ethelred smiled. "No, thanks to a certain lady, my business became very successful. At times, the Prince and his Commander see my training as a Royal Guard and my chosen profession as very valuable. Like when the Princess vanishes into vapor."

I cringed at the reminder of my predicament as he handed me the flask of Hälsodryck.

"I only managed to get the two flasks last night. The black market on this stuff is not exactly flourishing since you fund the free disbursement to pregnant women at every clinic. I lucked upon a dealer who just happened to pick up a couple of bottles while he was freeing a clinic of some more valuable product last night."

"I really don't need to know, Ethel." Taking the bottle, I skulled the remaining mouthfuls before replacing the lid.

"You said children."

"What?"

"Last night, you said the Elite tried to kill your unborn children. It is very unusual for an Avalonian to have multiples?"

I nodded as he took the empty flask from my hand and replaced it with a plate of food.

"The last flask is not going to last you long. Any idea where you will go since your Prince will be arriving here soon after breakfast?"

"No idea. The only place I've ever felt safe is the estate."

"Bad idea! Not only will the Prince be watching it, but also your enemies."

"I've nearly been taken three times from the palats. Each time gets closer to succeeding. I honestly don't know what to do."

"Can I make a suggestion?"

Meeting Ethelred's eyes, I nodded. If anyone knew where I would be safest, it was him.

"There is one place that no matter who your enemy is, not even the Elite would raise a hand against you while the King offers his protection."

I swallowed the ball of fear that suddenly collected in my throat. "I wouldn't even know how to get off-planet, let alone into the King's palats to beg for his protection."

Ethelred smiled as he sat down with his own plate of food. Of all the people who could smuggle someone off-planet and into the King's palats, Ethelred was probably the only person who could do it.

"Well, is it not lucky you crawled into my bed last night, Princess?"

Shaking my head, I smiled. "Let's reframe that when you inform our Prince how you found me."

Giving me the Cyran equivalent of a grin, Ethelred pointed to my plate. "Eat your food. You're going to need your strength."

Dark Romantasy / Paranormal Romance by Ebony Olson

Standalone Books

Of Shadow and Light

Boundary

Silver Rogue

Halos

The Grave Keeper: All Hallows

Angelis Series

Spectra

Angelis

Hierarch Series (Dark Romantasy)

Succumb

Numinous

Masked

Exodus

Burning Immortality

Orey Gelus Series

Gelus Hearts (Compilation of Orey Witches & Edge Gelus)

Vidal

Chaos Star Trilogy (Sci-fi Romance)

Praldia

Cyra

Avalonia

Anthologies

Booktober: A Halloween PNR Anthology

Romance Suspense by Ebony Olson

Hotel Series

Holly Claire Trilogy

Holly's Trilogy: Books 1-3 Hotel Series

(Compilation of Henderson, Cassidy, & Holmes)

Jess Butler Trilogy

Best Sunset: Books 4-6 Hotel Series

(Compilation of Best Man, Best Layover, & Best Knight)

Black Mark Series

Black Mark: The Complete Saga

(Omnibus of Resistance, Secret, & Heart)

Black Mark X

Standalone Books

Calypso

Rain: A Dark Past Romance

Protective Instinct (On KU as Hunter Enemy & Lover Enemy)

About the Author

Ebony lives in Sydney, Australia, with her husband, daughter, and six rescue cats. She loves to read fantasy, thrillers, and paranormal romance, spending most of her free time with her nose in a book or writing.

Having always possessed an over-active imagination Ebony spent her younger years regaling friends with fantastic stories, holding her audience captive with the passion and suspense of her characters plights. In adulthood, she shows no signs of stopping her imagination from spreading across as many pages as it can find.

Website: http://ebonyolson.com/
Ebony's Mischief & Mayhem Peeps

facebook.com/EbonyOlson.Author
instagram.com/ebony_olson
amazon.com/author/ebonyolson
bookbub.com/authors/Ebony_Olson
goodreads.com/Ebony_Olson
tiktok.com/@ebony_olson

www.ingramcontent.com/pod-product-compliance
Lightning Source LLC
Chambersburg PA
CBHW070003120726
47909CB00003B/783

* 9 7 8 0 6 4 5 1 5 7 9 6 3 *